alt.punk

Lavinia Ludlow

casperian
books

This is a work of fiction. All the characters and events portrayed in this book are either fictitious or are used fictitiously.

ALT.PUNK. Copyright © 2011 by Lavinia Ludlow. All rights reserved. No part of this book may be used or reproduced in any manner whatsoever without written permission except in the case of brief quotations embodied in critical articles or reviews. For information address Casperian Books, PO Box 161026, Sacramento, CA 95816-1026.

www.casperianbooks.com

Cover illustration by Nathan Holic.

ISBN-10: 1-934081-29-9
ISBN-13: 978-1-934081-29-7

For G.A.D.

Part I

Bred in a Studio

The act would be easier to stomach if Kree let me turn off the light, because then I'd never have to see his shimmering brown pubes, the same ones invading the shower, toilet, and my soap dish. He tells me to look at him when I do it, but I clench my eyes shut so tightly that they go numb. I wish I could super-glue them closed so they wouldn't pop open at random. What makes it worse is the sizable freckle that glares at me like a cyclops under his mushroom head. This is where he pees, after all, and that blasted freckle just won't relent; it taunts me as it bobs around in his bird's nest crotch.

What I'd give to be cramming chocolate into my mouth instead. I could be enjoying carb-induced euphoria, but right now, I'm in his bed and he's urging me to migrate south. As I part my lips, it takes all of my concentration and physical grace to keep from dry heaving. Maybe I *am* gay after all, because it can't be natural to hate it this much. Or maybe I hate it because in the ten years we've been together, he's always refused to kiss me after I do it.

Lately, I've been thinking a lot about the past ten years and how all I have to show for it is a dot-to-dot roadmap of failures sprinkled with headache pit stops: a couple of business degrees from a state school, a mediocre relationship, and a career in retail management. It feels like I'm eighteen all over again, looking down a one-way street. Back then, all I saw was a prison sentence in college and a string of mind-numbing jobs, but this time around I'm thirty, and all I see is life without parole in a resentful marriage with a parasitic family.

Earlier tonight at the restaurant, I tried explaining it to Kree, but he pulled his usual ostrich act and then changed the subject. "Whatcha mean, jellybean?" he said. "Hey, what DVD should we watch tonight?" Or maybe he wasn't paying attention to me because he was too busy packing Olive Garden breadsticks into his doughy face and smacking on them with his open mouth. His fuzz of sandstone hair was mashed against his scalp in a thousand directions because he'd spent the day passed out on the couch in a drunken coma. "How about *Black Sheep?*" he asked before shoving over a handful of sugar packets. "Here, put these in your purse."

"Why do you do that?" I asked. He's pocketed condiments for as long as I've known him, but for whatever reason, my confrontational side came out tonight. "Would it kill you to go to the grocery store and buy your own?"

"Aren't we struggling artists?" he asked. "Like, I'm the actor and you're the writer."

"If by struggling artists you mean to ask, 'Are we poor,' I'm normal, but you drag down my average, so yeah, I guess you could say that we, as a couple, are poor."

He hesitated before holding out the sugar again

"Maybe it's a midlife crisis," I said, trying to get back on the topic I was on before the mention of black sheep or sugar. "Either that, or I'm in crisis over the fact I'm going to have one very soon."

"You're not going through a midlife crisis," he said. "You're probably still at the end of the quarter-life one. Hey, my family's Fourth of July barbecue is tomorrow. You're coming, right?"

I shook my head, wondering when we'd finally get out of the public trough.

"Why not?"

"When you were visiting your parents last week, I called the house and your sister answered the phone screaming, 'It's your fat-ass girlfriend.'"

"I can't make them like you. Doesn't your family hate me, too?"

"At least they don't call you a 'fat ass' to your face. At what point can an ass be officially classified a bona fide 'fat ass'?"

"She didn't mean you're literally a fat ass," he said. "She just said that 'cause she hates you." His ability to comfort has always been shy of absolutely worthless. Years ago, after opening a letter addressed to me, he busted into my room to announce: "You didn't get into Davis' MBA program, but you shouldn't feel bad or anything. If you couldn't make it in as an undergraduate, there was probably no chance of getting in the second time around."

"I'm not going to your barbecue," I said.

"You have to come; the drive down there will be boring all by myself. And my mom and dad are getting a huge-ass sheet cake 'cause I told them how much you can pack away." He is also notorious for directly reminding me of my personal faults without even realizing it. Last month we were out to dinner with his acting buddies when he revealed: "Me and hazelnut are cool with having separate rooms. It gives her space to write and I need my own bed 'cause she has freakish night terrors that make her kick and whack in her sleep." For the record, I don't believe him when he says that I "kick and whack" in my sleep. I think he made it up just because he doesn't want to sleep with me.

Tonight he also reinforced the fact that he's a klutz. "I accidentally got bleach on your black slacks today, but no one'll notice," he said.

"The same way you said no one would notice how you dropped my master's thesis in gutter water on the way to my presentation?" I asked.

"Jeez, you never let anything go. You graduated, didn't you?"

While he milked Olive Garden's "unlimited breadsticks" for the next hour, I developed the urge to stab my fork through the imaginary bull's eye painted on his greasy, lemon-shaped head.

Now, back at our apartment, I involuntarily shiver when his cock pulsates against the walls of my mouth. I know something's definitely off when I think about how I'd rather suck on barbed wire than my own boyfriend.

Maybe it's the bitter disgust brought on by his asinine remarks throughout the years, maybe it's envisioning my future locked in a marriage with a sloth and his sloth offspring drooling all over my furniture while I spend the rest of my life paying off a mortgage I don't want in a house whose creamy white carpet and blanched tile will be engulfed by the scum-ridden, stampeding feet and atrocious body excretions of slobbering and unemployed parasites that I would have to, in social settings, formally refer to as "my immediate family," all while having to deal with the relentless scrutiny and judgment of my extended family, or maybe I bite down like a 'gator on a fresh piece of meat because Kree gives the back of my head an obnoxious shove to wedge himself into the depths of my throat. Maybe that's it.

"Jesus!" He knees me in the chin and squeals a few times. "What the hell?" He curls up like a fetus and sways back and forth against the mattress while saying, "This is not happening, this is not happening."

I regurgitate what he always preaches to me when I'm in any sort of crisis: "I think you're overreacting."

"You crippled it."

"Don't you think you're being melodramatic?" I pry his hands away from his crotch for a closer examination. "I didn't even draw blood. Stop being such a wuss."

"You crippled my best friend," he says.

Most people talk about a marriage of convenience. Kree was a relationship of convenience. He started tagging along with me on the college campus when I was about twenty, and after years of solitude throughout high school that led to relentless accusations about my enigmatic sexuality, I suppose he was the perfect opportunity to prove everybody wrong.

***

After all of this, I don't know why I agree to go to his barbecue in our hometown of Newark, California—a cesspool that not only spawned a specimen like Kree, but is also home to both sets of our parents—because the nauseating regret increases exponentially throughout the drive down and it peaks as we approach his parents' doorstep in the heart of the city's shantytown. I'd rather have my eyeballs sucked out by the flesh-eating, bacteria-coated beaks of vultures than make a trip here on a Friday when I could be in my room writing and vegging out with a couple of cans of frosting and a case of Diet Coke.

I claw at my neck as I swelter in the combination of dread and anxiety brought on by the muffled sounds of screaming toddlers on the other side of the front door. Maybe years from now, I'll accept the idea of having kids, but lately, I've been burdened with this weird phobia that I'll unintentionally torture mine the way my family tortured and continues to torture me, simply out of bitterness and/or resentment. It sounds like some schoolyard massacre waiting to happen, and I'm worried that a lot of innocent people could go down, all because Kree and I decide to breed.

The front door swings open. Kree's sister eyes me as she whispers something to my prospective mother-in-law, and they laugh in unison. I'm distracted listing off synonyms for the word "bitch" in my head, so I don't immediately notice their Doberman hurdling toward me till he's within slobbering distance. I do a one-eighty out the door, over the porch, and careen toward the sidewalk, screaming: "Fire! Fire!" (I've been advised never to scream "Help!" in an emergency because nobody cares, so the appropriate thing to do in a conundrum is to scream "Fire!")

"Fire!" I shout, and round the cul-de-sac toward my car where I scream it again before leaping over the hood to throw my body flat against the roof. Had it been the roof of a van and not a Camry, I might have had a chance, but the beast pounces and hungrily laps at my face with his grainy tongue, infesting me with its bacterial microbes.

"It's giving me worms! Help! Worms!" I scream, but none of the porch rubberneckers intervene.

Within the group, I hear Kree's sister comment: "She's so freakin' weird."

Kree's barbarian of a father summons the animal, but only after it slobbers on all of my orifices. He didn't have an opportunity to help me out earlier, since he was too busy bowled over his gelatinous beer belly in uncontainable laughter.

"Are you okay, hazelnut?" Kree asks.

I wince when the dog uses my stomach as a launch pad back toward the house.

***

Before the sun cooks my skin to charcoal, I ditch Kree's family inferno and drive a few miles to the superior (although no less sadistic) side of Newark to sterilize at Mom and Dad's inferno. Sacramento is known as a prime location in California since it's less than two hours away from the coast and two hours away from the snow, if one is into those sorts of things. It's also less than two hours away from Newark. Back when I was eighteen and headed for college, this seemed to be enough of an escape, but now that I'm thirty and fuel-efficient cars have become a reality, two hours may just as well be the distance across Mom's dinner table.

When I emerge from the bathroom, Mom turns the corner, already hurling criticism. "You're so antisocial," she says. "They're probably calling you a snob right now."

I'm tempted to mention that her two-hundred-dollar stylings are doing nothing for the wiry frizz veining out of her head. It looks like someone dipped weathered push-broom bristles in brown house paint and superglued them on her scalp. But I keep quiet.

"Hey, did you notice someone stomped on your car?" she asks. "There are footprints all over the hood."

I massage the irritation from my face thinking I could be in my room with diet root beer, three pounds of Skittles, and a gallon of ice cream. And there's something about Sacramento water which leaves a chlorinated scent on my skin; when I'm away from it, I never feel completely disinfected. Even after three scrub-downs, I still feel the dog's parasites undulating in my pores.

"We're meeting some friends for dinner," she says, "so if you're not going back to the Kellers', then you're coming with us. You can't sit here by yourself all night." She doesn't know me at all. "And burn those shoes. I refuse to show up with you wearing Vans." She hasn't figured out yet that I'd wear a black Hefty bag every day if I could.

***

Later, at the restaurant, I paint on a smile and attempt to converse with these people, but it's murder to put up a front and pretend to be interested in the lives of overachievers. If I wanted to do that, I'd crash a wedding reception; at least there'd be cake and people I'd never have to see again. As I stare into oblivion, Mom jabs me in the ribs. "Stop zoning out," she says. "You need to smile more."

I put on a smile, but after a few minutes, my cheeks droop in fatigue, and to compensate, I force the grin upwards into a flat-lined smile.

"Quit looking like that," Mom says.

"Like what?" I ask.

"Like you have a branch in your butt." I can't believe my mother just made an anal reference.

"What's your cell number?" one of Mom's friends asks. "I'll give you a call if I'm in the Sacramento area."

"I don't have a cell phone," I say.

"Why not?"

"She doesn't want to get brain cancer," Mom says.

"Is that the only reason?" he asks.

"Is cancer the only reason I don't smoke? Is murder the only reason I don't drive drunk?"

***

When Kree and I get home to Sacramento, I gun it for the shower in hopes of eliminating any hound microorganisms that may have lingered from this afternoon. With a pumice and spray bottle of disinfectant, I put to death every single- and multicelled bacteria that could be teeming in my pores. I stand under the beating stream of water till the surface of my skin burns red and numb, till the water goes cold.

And then I see *it*. The *it* that nullifies the forty-minute shower and bleach scrub-down: a brown pube straggling off the edge of my washcloth.

I shut off the water, pull on a rubber glove, pluck that auburn atrocity off my towel, and tote it at a safe distance from my body into the living room where Kree's stationed in front of the TV. He perks up when he sees me walking toward him, naked and dripping. "Whoa, are you ready to go or something?"

I hold the pube to his face. "This was on my washcloth," I say.

"It's a shower. Hair does end up all over," he says, nudging me to the side with his foot to clear a visual path to the TV.

"How'd it get on my towel? Were you jerking off?" I push it closer to his temple.

"Can you get that out of my face?" He tries to shove my arm out of the way, but I hold it in place.

"How hard is it to use your own towel?" We're confined to a two-bedroom, one-and-a-half-bath apartment, and even though I pay the rent without his assistance, it'd be worth the extra cash for a second bathroom just to confine his slobbering and jerking off to his own pube-ridden shower.

"I didn't use your towel," he says.

"Don't lie to me."

"Come on, let's go to bed." He gets up from the couch and lurches for me like a half-drunk hog, but I shove him back against the couch.

"Don't touch me."

He always does this. Right after I've scrubbed every parasite from my skin, he wants to immediately reinfect me. He whines and looks away glassy-eyed, trying to make me feel guilty.

The thing about him is, he's here and he's always been here, looking at me like he really wants me, and it works, so I get in his bed and let him gnaw on my boobs even though the fear of his parasites wriggling their way through my nipples, breeding, and turning my chest black with infection nullifies my ability to get anything out of it. Plus, he smells like a locker room and hasn't showered in a day, making visions of my horrifying, flesh-eating-bacteria-induced death flip like a slideshow in my head while he makes out with me.

While he ransacks the drawers for a condom, I lie in bed occupying myself with a box of powdered donuts. I'm on my back finishing off the last one when he slides his cold and clumsy finger in and out of me.

"Is that good?" he asks.

"Huh? Oh, yeah," I say.

After faking a moan, he gives me a friction burn when he rips out his finger and tries to pack in his naked boner. I squirm out from under him, kick him in the stomach, and shove him toward the other end of the bed, and as he teeters for balance on the edge of the mattress, I plant my foot into the arc of his spine. He thumps against the floor like a sweaty rump roast.

He should know by now that I refuse to be contaminated in the one place I can't easily sanitize. After kicking him out of my room, I spend the remainder of the night picking his repulsive little hairs off my sheets. The more I think about how irritating he is, the more I realize he's mostly harmless. He doesn't walk around with a chip on his shoulder, and he never overanalyzes life or becomes unnecessarily flustered; I don't even have to worry about doing anything to keep him devoted. He's like that outdated piece of furniture in our living room that we've had since college that I know I should replace or toss, but it's flown under the radar and I don't want to bother with the hassle anyway. Plus, he never criticizes me, intentionally at least, though I wonder if that's enough of a consolation to keep me going.

***

Kree and I end up in Newark a second day in a row because it's my birthday, though it's more of an obligation than it is a choice. Sitting in a room filled with members of my family is a lot like dousing myself in meat juice and jumping into a pit of lions with binge eating disorders. They can't officially call it a party without cracking on fat people, poor people, or people who aren't like them in general, and by that I mean waiflike, upper middle class, and moderately conservative.

We're having afternoon coffee in Mom's dining room, and so far the visit hasn't been too sadistic. Mom even catches me off-guard with a gesture of faith. "Pick where you want to go tonight for your birthday," she says.

"Rosicrucian Museum," I say. "Or the Winchester Mystery House."

"A restaurant," she says.

"Outback."

"Low class."

"Flames."

"The only thing worth eating there is their fudge cake, and that's the last thing you need. We're going to the Sonoma Chicken Coop where you're getting a plain salad with low-fat dressing on the side."

It's almost always been like this. I woke up one morning in high school to her smothering me with a pillow of frills like fad diets, fashion designs, and prestigious college aspirations. Shortly after, she wielded a rock-filled tube sock and heckled me about being gay since I didn't care what I looked like when I went to school. She'd switch off every other day: four days out of the week it was the pillow, and the tube sock filled in the remaining three. Her fears were probably a reaction to '90s pop culture and the decade's many notable controversies, from the White House sex scandal to California's legalization of medicinal cannabis, from the popularity of PlayStation to the prevalence of the illegal download. Maybe it was the overall summation of terror and pandemonium Generation Y was striking into Generation X and beyond, which I guess was pretty severe.

"Are we going to get a wedding announcement soon?" Auntie asks. Forget the rocks and socks; it's a spiked flail whenever Auntie is around.

I choke as anxiety rings my windpipe like a bully administering an Indian burn. I never thought I'd have to face a question like that, much less under circumstances like these: my boyfriend's an out-of-work, never-been-hired-for-money actor, which would ordinarily make him a homemaker, except we don't have kids and I do all the cleaning and bill-paying. On top of that, I hate his family, they hate me, my family hates him, and he's apathetic to it all. It just seems like a bad idea to connect all this resentment and hatred together with a marriage simply because it's the conventional "next step."

"Are you kidding?" Mom asks. "How can they get married? They have no money." I sometimes forget that Mom is the type of person who pokes an open wound with a blazing cattle brand and then asks if it hurts. Last Christmas at the dinner table, she turned to me and asked: "How many times did you have to take the SATs before you broke 1200? Oh, and then there was the GMAT disaster where your score kept dropping each time you took it." And she does it now with, "They can't afford to feed any kids. They'd end up leeching off of me."

And Kree, who's taken no note of the conversation as if he were deaf to the pitch of witch squealing, says, "I'm starving. When are we going to go eat?"

"Where's Avaline? I thought she was coming to dinner with us," Mom says.

Avaline's a chemically imbalanced acquaintance I met in the parking lot of Safeway, my workplace, four years ago. She sat in a handicap stall for an entire day crying over the fact that her favorite lip liner had been discontinued and no amount of money would bring it back. I played the role of a good Samaritan by nursing her back to stability in the break room, and since then, she shows up two or three times a week at the store or my apartment and calls on the odd days wondering what's up. Or down. One minute she's throwing a tantrum and the next she's hyperactively bumbling on about her plans with her ballet company. She's so absorbed in her own whirl of insanity that I never get a word in edgewise. For all the time we've spent together, she knows nothing about me, and if I mildly try to shift the topic of discussion onto something like the 360 degrees of abuse I get from my family and future in-laws, or the ignoramus that's been passed out in a Cup-o'-Noodles-and-beer coma on my living room couch every day for the last ten years, she'll revert it back to herself.

Why Mom cares so much about Avaline is beyond me. She's always asking how my elegant, stunning, stylish, slender, ballerina-model, and/or whatever other adjective or noun Avaline is in her mind, is doing. I think I even saw Mom hug her last year at Thanksgiving—and Mom doesn't hug, she just doesn't do that. "She got a date and decided to go on that instead," I say.

"Now there's a go-getter," Mom says. "That pretty girl knows exactly what she wants and how to get it."

"Something like that," I say. For the record, Avaline would choose to get laid over breathing, and she has on many occasions recited the details of her flavor-of-the-day lays and how some of them were into choking her during the act. She wasn't into it, but didn't want to spend the night alone, so she'd let them do it even though she blacked out a couple times and ended up in the hospital with a damaged windpipe, or broken eyeball vessel, or burns from whatever choked her, be it rope, towels, or fingers.

"Can we open your presents after we eat? I'm so hungry," Kree says.

I reach for a gift and slowly peel back the paper in spite of him. It's a refurbished Underwood typewriter.

"Happy birthday, hazelnut," he says.

I suddenly feel guilty about comparing him to old furniture. One thing about Kree is that his presents are always meaningful. Last year he gave me an old-fashioned bookstand and said I could display my writing in our TV room like people display books in museums.

"I got this for you, too. I told the guy at the store to suggest a good punk band."

I wheeze at the sight of the Fall Out Boy album, and—subsequently—the price tag. "You could have..." put these twenty dollars toward gas, food, or the rent he never covers. Come to think of it, these twenty dollars are my twenty dollars, because without an income, he's linked to all my debit and credit accounts because he has no money. It's my money that he spends on something out of his technological league like a Blackberry or Mac.

To add injury to insult, he says, "The guy at the store said it's hands down the best pop-punk album ever."

"You don't know me at all."

Everyone's ears operate on a particular frequency, and his ears operate on the Creed, Coldplay, and Hootie and the Blowfish (among other adult top 40 hits) frequency. I'd like to think that opposites attract, but he's oblivious to the difference between Rancid and the mass-marketed whining that disguises itself with punk's name.

I suppose anyone could disagree with my definition of punk. I suppose I could go to a library and read up on the complete history of over four decades' worth of punk. I know what punk means to me, though, and it's not Hot Topic pop bologna assembly-lined for the twenty-first-century thirteen-year-old MTV reality-show generation. It's raw and subversive, it's socially provocative, it's fueled by a whole lot of "anything goes." Drummers are irreplaceable and songs are two minutes or less because that's all it takes to get a point across. Then again, my increasing cynicism for the changing times may be attributed to the fact that I'm getting old. Or maybe I'm already old.

"This is from the family," Mom says. It's a gag gift of St. John's Wort.

"What's that for?" Kree asks.

But the worst isn't the question about marriage, pop-punk, or St. John's Wort; it's the birthday song. I've never known what to do or how to feel during those thirty seconds of agonizing embarrassment when I know everyone in a room filled by my family is meticulously pulling apart my flaws from physical and mental to social and political.

I don't make it to the end of the song because I hyperventilate out the candles and excuse myself to loosen my nonexistent shirt collar in the bathroom. My eyes tear from nausea, my heart's shattering my ribcage, and I can't figure out how to slow everything down.

Twenty minutes pass. Forty. An hour goes by before I'm able to lasso my pulse down. When I emerge back into the dining room, I head toward Kree because I need a good embrace, even if it's from the Pube King who's cutting me a piece of cake with his unwashed fingers. "I don't need any," I say.

"You have to eat your own birthday cake. It's hella good," he says, but I sit down and sip my cold coffee sans anything with calories, like sugar or cream.

"Don't give her that. She has to cut back," Mom says to him.

"How do you get so fat from just pecking at your food?" Auntie asks. "None of us ever see you eat."

"Closet eater," Mom says.

"You want to borrow my girdle?" Auntie asks. "I have Richard Simmons tapes if you want to borrow them."

"Is that the guy who wears glitter shirts?" Kree asks through a mouthful of frosting.

I'm grinding my teeth so rigidly, I'll probably hit gum soon. After hitting ninety-five pounds, candy wrappers were treated like drug paraphernalia and any evidence of sugar on my lips would have been better received if it had been cocaine. Fifteen pounds later, there is no way I am eating cake in front of these people.

***

At the end of the night, I make Kree drive us back to Sacramento. I sit on the passenger side scarfing down the leftover cake till my taste buds go numb.

"You're not fat," he says.

"That was the wrong answer," I say.

"If you were any thinner, you'd look anorexic."

"That was the wrong answer, too."

"Well, what is the right answer? That you do look anorexic?"

When we get home I stand in the kitchen ripping through a package of Oreos, a carton of ice cream, and a jar of maraschino cherries. After five spoonfuls of ice cream, I cram two Oreos into my mouth and pack in three cherries to feel the sugary syrup spray against my cheeks. I hose it all down with a case of diet root beer.

To counteract the sugar sweats, I move the furniture out of my room and vacuum up every dust maggot and loose fiber. I take down pictures so I can wash the walls with a Brillo pad and a bucket of disinfectant, and then spend the rest of the night immersed in a bath of bleach, inhaling the therapeutic fumes. It's the highlight of my day because, this time around, there aren't any stray pubes tarnishing the experience.

But there *it* is, tethering off the tub spout.

This is my life and what it's all built toward: pubes.

Something has to give.

Emotional Masturbation

It's a Monday night and I should have taken a different route home from work. While making my way over the American River Bridge, I find—not for the first time—my pseudo-friend Avaline sobbing against the railing. My guess is that no one in her bipolar support group would answer her calls at this hour, so she's strategically placed herself on my route home knowing that the slope leading to the bridge naturally slows a car and provides the driver an extended opportunity to get blinded by the reflection of her pale, stick-thin stork legs. It works. I pull over and put the car in park.

I lean out the passenger side window and say, "Quit trying to draw unnecessary attention that'll get you abducted, raped, and/or killed."

"He broke up with me," she says. "On Facebook. Then unfriended me, then blocked me."

I hold back on the temptation to say that the Internet was probably the only safe way he felt he could break up with her. "Get in the car, I'll take you home. Stop giving men so much power." She doesn't budge, probably because we both know she won't quit the act until I agree to let her crash at my place, but the thing about her is that she'll latch onto an offer of hospitality like a tick to skin, and she won't leave without some messy confrontation.

Since I don't want to spend the rest of the night parked on the street side, I get out of the car, pull her off the railing, buckle her into the passenger side, and bring her home like a stray animal. After three beers and two blocks of Ramen, she passes out facedown on the couch, drooling, snoring, and intermittently farting in her sleep.

She stays through the week, lounging around the apartment in her underwear, eating cereal from the box, and adding to the Couch of the Unemployed. She and Kree sleep till noon, watch daytime TV, order takeout, and drink till they're laughing at air. It's like the two of them adopt a symbiotic relationship based on cheap thrills: who can scarf a roll of Pillsbury cookie dough and chug the most beer in five minutes? Who can keep it all down without puking? And afterward, who's still functional enough to order a pizza?

On Friday night I come home from work to find her Boeing 747-sized dildos standing upright on my kitchen counter. "Why did I find Brad in the garbage?" she asks.

"Brad?" I ask.

"My pink rabbit vibrator."

"You named it?"

"I have to scream out someone's name when I'm—"

"Don't."

"I was telling Avaline that I had two penises in my dream last night," Kree says. "One for each hand. And when I went at myself, it was like milking a freakin' cow." He rolls off the edge of the couch and onto the floor in a drunken fit of giggles.

"Was one uncircumcised?" she asks.

"That would make sense, 'cause one was new."

Their inebriated and senseless laughter makes me want to go after them with something sharp.

***

Two hours later, Avaline's still drunk. She makes me drive her to the mall, hoping espresso will sober her up before her dance class. Over coffee and bagels, I ask if she'd go with me to see Flogging Molly play The Fillmore in October since Kree can't stand any music with such hyperactive buzz.

"Flogging? Sounds kinky," she says.

"No, they're a Celtic band. They drink Guinness on stage."

"If there's booze and kink involved, count me in. Hey, let's go to Black Angus for steak and mud pie later." I remind her that I don't eat at restaurants, nor do I eat steak. "Jesus Christ, you're not going to get Mad Cow from eating it once. You are the biggest spaz."

"Why don't we ask the CDC in Atlanta, Georgia, how many reported cases they're covering up for the government?"

"You take things way too seriously," she says as if it's insane to not want to wither horrifyingly into death. "You're like a depressing version of Daria."

"Fine, I'll go. Then check on me in a few years when I'm a foaming pile of brain-dead flesh decomposing in a hospital bed. I could already have it. It could be dormant, and you're making me eat more of it. You think I want to end up in a vegetative state: blind, deaf, and ingesting food through a needle in my arm while I wait for my brain to rot away so I can hurry up and die?"

"Wow, you need Xanax more than me. You'd be a lot prettier if you just smiled more."

"That's the same as telling someone she'd be a lot prettier if she lost twenty-five pounds."

"Hey, let's hit up Frederick's of Hollywood." With Avaline, if it doesn't involve food or booze, it involves sex.

"My mom says that's the low-class version of Victoria's Secret," I say.

"Notice you start a lot of your sentences out with 'my mom says'?"

I turn away to avoid having to come up with an explanation.

"You know foreplay is more than kissing, right?" she asks. "You can't expect him to want to bone you if you're lying there like a dead body."

I can only imagine what Kree's told her over the past week. "What's with everybody wanting it to last longer?" I ask. "If anything, I want him to bust a nut before I even have to come into the picture." It's impossible to even fathom the possibility of pleasure when Kree's hands are perpetual blocks of ice and his fingernails are chronically caked with dirt and he humps like I'm a faceless blowup doll. Meanwhile, I'm on my back mentally making a grocery/chores list and trying to ignore the revolting sounds of a doused-in-lube piston moving in and out of me.

"It'd feel a lot hotter for him if you got on the pill. Condoms are such a sensation killer."

"Yeah, 'cause hot intercourse takes precedence over a sexist death wish."

"Do you hear yourself talking sometimes? 'Cause I don't think you do."

"Just 'cause he doesn't want to keep his biohazardous bodily fluids to himself in a condom, I have to suffer the ick factor and the side effects of possible strokes and blood clots and heart attacks? He's lucky he gets to see me naked."

I kept Kree waiting for four years, and he'd still be waiting now if I hadn't grown sick of hearing him complain about how we were the only twenty-four-year-old virgins left in the free world except for maybe twenty-four-year-olds who've been in comas since they were teenagers. Intercourse itself only happened in the most controlled setting, and after he showed me notarized STD test results that proved he was free of every virus and infectious bacterium.

"And explain to me," I say, "how our squeamish society is grossed out by homeless people on the street, but they'll exchange bodily fluids with complete strangers."

"Things come out of you so fast that it's hard to know what you're trying to say," she says. "And it's always some spastic fact that only anal people would know about. By the way, are you into anal? 'Cause if you are, then you don't have to worry about going on the pill."

***

The bitterness from our conversation lingers and tightens the ligaments in my chest throughout the rest of the evening. I find it impossible to lie still against the mattress when Kree climbs aboard tonight. While on my back I mull over what is more demeaning: having him thrashing around down south or up north in my mouth. Neither offers more pros or cons, but whenever there's too much silence between us, he continues to indiscreetly mention how he likes my mouth better.

"What's wrong?" he asks.

"Tired," I say.

"You're always tired."

"Well, some of us are abused at work all day."

He resumes heaving, so I mention that Rise Against is coming to San Jose State in November.

"Rise against what?" he asks.

I don't even bother mentioning Flogging Molly. As it is, he's embarrassed himself before by pronouncing NOFX "No Fix," and for the longest time he thought Aimee Mann was, in fact, a man. "How was I supposed to know?" he said in his defense. "Guys have girl names all the time, like Kelly and Shawn."

They say fifty percent of people meet their significant others in college, and on a separate note, fifty percent of marriages end in divorce, which must mean the educational institutions which are supposed to advance society are actually guilty of twenty-five percent of all failed marriages, and more than likely, my own inevitable partnership.

***

Sunday night Kree knocks on my bedroom door to tell me that his mom has driven up to visit. "Wonderful," I say. It's been awhile since I've been treated like a gum wad on the pavement.

When I emerge, he's at the kitchen table gorging on her homemade beef stew while she's ransacking our fridge and kitchen cupboards. "Where's all your food?" she asks. "Did Safeway fire you?"

"You should have been a comedian," I say, then smirk, because I just upped the intensity of the passive-aggressiveness in our relationship.

"Diet soda, candy, and Cup o' Noodles? Are you guys on food stamps?"

I ignore the comment because I still have the self-control to tame my reaction.

"He's starving. Did Safeway run out of food?"

In my fictitious world, I laugh and turn to her, chuckling. "If your son hadn't chosen to waste money on a degree in Theater that's left him in debt and no further in credentials than when he was as a freshman picking his nose at orientation, he could be bringing home his own bacon." Although...I can't stand the blistering stench of pig fat cooking in its own tissue, so I don't know how I'd feel about him coming home with any bacon.

In reality, I've wasted way too much time plotting a response. "Is she okay?" she asks Kree.

"She's been loopy ever since we watched *The Stepford Wives*," he says.

I head back to my room where I down my daily dose of multivitamins, Echinacea, and a cod oil capsule. Couple the regime with a six-pack of Diet Coke and a bag of Twix and I momentarily forget about the psycho coddling her son in the kitchen.

***

When my alarm went off this Monday morning, it might as well have been the loudspeaker cattle call in the prison yard of Folsom. I thought about calling in sick to spend the day in a Benadryl blackout, but then I realized I'd have to witness another day of Kree's unemployment. He always says he's looking for acting gigs, and sometimes he has an audition to brag about, but I rarely arrive home at the end of the day to hear that he's landed any parts, and if he does, they're never paid. So he spends his time the same way he did in college: eating jars of peanut butter with his fingers, watching dysfunctional losers fist-fight on talk shows, and spending my money.

Because of it, Mom has tried setting me up with miscellaneous candidates, her motherly advice including these suggestions: "Find an egghead that works in high-tech; having kids with a tall and skinny guy will offset your genes. Clean up first and quit being so weird all the time."

I left Newark thinking that the parade of criticism would end, but now it's concentrated in a stampede of e-mails, phone calls, and slathered on thick at family get-togethers. If it's not *fat* this, *homely* that, then it's *when are you finally going to go to law school* this, *working in that scumbag retail industry makes you a scumbag yourself* that. Retail also happened out of convenience, of course, because it was a substitute to becoming a cubicle-confined bean counter. After college, I did a few rotational management programs with some mass merchandisers; the first corporation was soulless because it was a *discount* mass merchandiser, and the next was Target, whose office and sales floor politics sent me fleeing into the conveniently hiring arms of Safeway.

Retail wears on a person. Every day there's a customer scream-cursing at me for selling defective product, or a unionized worker crying in my office about something petty, like how another coworker called her a stupid cow. Even worse, no matter how hard I try to stand my ground, none of the employees take me seriously. It's a presidential election year and I don't know how I became a target for all the bottled-up angst the store's twenty-somethings have for Republicans, but almost daily my office door is covered in McCain fliers and bumper stickers swallowed in snot-rocket streams of all colors and textures. Some of the specimens are streaked with blood, as if someone was willing to suffer nasal tissue damage just to piss me off.

And around every corner there are walking health code violations that

I'm powerless to prevent. If it's not Deli Man snagging his fingers in the slicer and bleeding all over the sandwich counter, then it's Butcher Man seasoning the cuts with his chronic psoriasis, or it's Cake Decorator Woman licking the frosting off her fingers before she plants a saliva-spackled rose on some unsuspecting child's birthday cake. Sometimes it feels like an industry where I'm paid based on how much I can endure.

I'm not going to make it thirty-five more years in this industry. Hell, I'm not going to make it to thirty-five.

***

When I get home after a twelve-hour day, I find the kitchen counter covered in a sludge of crumbs, butter, and jelly. Kree left it a sty, assuming it'll scrub itself up. "Hey." He shuts off the TV and sprints toward me. "Let's practice lines at the park. I been stuck inside all day 'cause it's been too hot to go anywhere." He's pestered me over the last couple of days about practicing lines with him, but hearing him stammer with a bad British accent makes me want to jam needles through my eardrums. It's torture to hear his on-and-off-again accent and awkward inflections. I feel like screaming at him that—when his British accent falters—he doesn't even sound American, either, and that his acting is offensive, because he's somehow butchering his own native dialect while also butchering the British.

I shuffle the dirty dishes off the counter and into the sink without saying anything. My hope is that if I ignore him long enough, he'll slink back to his TV. "Is there something you want me to do but won't tell me to my face 'cause it's something you expect me to know even though I really don't?" he asks. There's an innocent ignorance in his voice. I think that's what makes it so frustrating.

"If anything, do less," I say.

"What does that mean?"

"It means that this is the opposite of the 'we're not going anywhere' problem. We're going everywhere all at once and I...don't want to."

"You want to go where?"

I slam the dishes in the sink and turn toward him, and from the corner of my eye I see *it* floating in a puddle of soapy dish water the same way I've found and will continue to find its next of kin on my washcloth and in my shower, the shower for which I've slaved away in retail all these years. "How does a pube end up roaming free in the kitchen?" I ask.

He moseys over to look at it. "That's not a pube. It's probably one of my chest hairs or something." He sweeps it off the counter and onto the floor in a moist streak. I force myself to hold my breath to prevent the onset of hyperventilation.

"You don't get it." I've said it to him so many times that I've worn the enamel off my teeth. "Life with you sucks."

"What do you mean by that?" He's noticeably hurt, maybe because I've never said anything like that to him before.

"It's not enough."

"This isn't you at all," he says. "That sounds so arrogant, hazelnut." I can feel the gloom in his voice, but it's hardly disarming.

"I'm not meant to put up with retail headaches or live with all your body hair. It's everywhere, and all I do is slave away at work for the sake of your pubes." I don't even know where this is coming from. This is one of those arguments that has manifested itself in my head throughout the day, and I'm letting it all out without warning. "And our parents live so close to us that they might as well tie us to the trees in their front yards while they sit on their porches laughing."

He hasn't blinked in a while; I can tell because his bottom eyelids are twitching. He opens his mouth a few times as if he wants to say something, but it never advances past an exhalation.

"I am thirty with nothing to own up to or call my own. I'm the same as I was at fourteen." I tear at the skin around my throat, hoping it'll loosen the strangulating grip around my windpipe.

"Well, you'll figure it out," he says. "And what does that have to do with us? Can't you just worry about it later? Like after we get married and have kids?"

"I'm pretty sure that's how most Dateline murder exposés start out," I say.

"Don't get mad, but..." he stalls. "I don't really get what you're trying to say."

"You're not listening. We're not speaking different languages here; nothing should be getting lost in translation." My kidneys hurt from all the diet soda, my mouth is infested with open sores from the acidity, and I'm feverish and achy from the pound of chocolate I scarfed down an hour ago. This is the last confrontation I want to have. "You're so lazy," I say. "You can't even help me clean."

"You get mad 'cause I don't do it good enough," he says as if I'm the one with unreasonable expectations.

"You are thirty," I say. "When are you going to get a job? Or a life? Let's start with that first."

"Just because you don't consider what I do a job, I'm not giving up my dreams for money." He's shouting, and he's never shouted at me. "What do you want from me?"

I gaze at him and hope he'll understand from the tone of my voice that I don't want to do this, but if I don't, it'll perpetuate my resentment for him. "This is it," I say.

I barely realize I've said it. I didn't wake up this morning and say to myself, "After work I'm cutting him loose," but it's happened.

***

We're both quiet in our rooms. I kill time by emptying my closet, vacuuming, and wiping down the walls with disinfectant. I wash clothes off their hangers and hand-wash the delicates in the kitchen sink. I usually wash them in the bathtub, but I'm afraid that if I see one of his pubes, I might get nostalgic and maybe knock on his bedroom door, apologize, take him back, and I would end up on my knees gagging on the same detritus as when all of this started.

I sit thoughtlessly watching the washer cycle and buzz against the dryer. At 3 a.m. I hear him open another can of beer in his room, which means he didn't pass out with the lights and TV on. I head to my room for the night and shut the door, and shortly thereafter, I hear him open his and head for the kitchen for more beer.

In the morning, I hear him hauling out his stereo, dresser, and clothes. I didn't think the split would happen so quickly, but this is apparently how he's interpreted my cleaning, so I drive back to Newark to escape the feeling of his room emptying.

Over coffee with Mom, I let the detail slip, hoping she'll put down her stoker for a few minutes and let me modestly adjust to a change I haven't known in ten years. "Wow, what happened?" she asks as if she cares. If anything, she's mentally licking her pencil lead and adding to her list of dateable prospects for me. I sip my coffee, hardly in the mood to discuss. "Are you okay?" she asks. For a second it makes me think that she's genuinely concerned. Then she says, "Stop slouching, your posture's terrible. You look like an eighty-year-old woman."

***

For some reason, maybe because Kree's no longer around to dilute the usual frustrations that occur in situations as simple as a shift call-out, my work irritancies have increased substantially as well.

"I can't come in today," Freak Stock Boy tells me over the phone. "I got a virus or something."

"On your hard drive?" I ask.

"No, you dumb fuck, the flu."

I fall quiet.

"Did you smear snot all over the hood of my car the other day?" I ask.

"Nope."

"I know it was you."

"There are other people in that store who can't stand your ass."

The line goes dead. My manager-subordinate relationship with him has become so severely reversed that I dread coming to work every day, knowing he'll be waiting with a new form of torturous domination. A few weeks ago, he was coming through the stockroom saloon doors as I was heading in and he plastered one into my face. While on my back mopping the blood from my nose, he stepped over me without even glancing down. All organizational behavior classes and articles on positive and negative reinforcement have failed to yield appreciable results, and I'm afraid that—very soon—I'm going to lose all workplace composure and end up hurling a Swingline at someone or something.

Maybe He's a Sadist

Otis, the frontman of a band called Riot Venom, jams a tape into the car's stereo, then plops a shoebox crammed with cassettes onto my lap. "You heard these guys before?" he asks. "From Autumn to Ashes."

I shuffle through the tapes with the tips of my fingers. Iron Maiden. Fugazi. Cure. Siouxsie & the Banshees. Sisters of Mercy. Smiths. Misfits. Pretenders. Dead Kennedys. Jawbreaker. Circle Jerks. Wasted Youth. Deftones. Velvet Revolver. Morrissey. Minor Threat. MewithoutYou. Misfits. Rancid. Black Flag. Thrice. Smashing Pumpkins. At the Drive-In. Blondie. Thursday. At the Gates. Sex Pistols. Damned. Replacements. Patti Smith. Velvet Underground. Hot Water Music. David Bowie. Clash. Misfits. Alkaline Trio. B-52's. Queen. Iggy Pop. Glassjaw. Tiger Army. AFI. Misfits.

"If you had to fuck to one album for the rest of your life," he asks, "what would you pick?"

Over the years, I've mastered the art of predictability—I've planned and expected and therefore assumed that my days, weeks, months, and maybe even years would never catch me off-guard. I expect unremitting persecution from my family. I expect to walk out of work every day having learned nothing new and having faced no meaningful challenges, just the piss-poor attitudes of subordinates, coworkers, or customers. Up until a week and a half ago, I expected that I would do loads of Kree's skid-marked tighty whities and scrub his saffron drops of piss and brown squirts of crap off the surface of my porcelain toilet for the rest of my life. And I assumed I would eventually go down for murder one after scrubbing it off for the last time.

So I didn't expect to be sitting here on the passenger side of a sputtering and backfiring El Camino with a box of tapes rattling on my lap. It just happened, and I didn't have much control over it, except maybe coming downtown with Avaline, which was a confusingly dark experience in itself. I never thought I'd end up soaked in garlic allergens while a stranger (and maybe potential criminal) searches for and fails to find an emergency room for me, somehow getting the two of us lost in downtown Sacramento's grid of one-way streets.

Come to think of it, the last week has consisted of a progression of situations I never predicted I'd have to deal with. I had to hitch rides to work the last couple of days because my car broke down. Before, I never had to worry about things like pumping gas—since Kree's always done it—and I still don't know how, but I figure I'll give it a try once some corporate engineer figures out how to eliminate gas-pump fires from the equation. Last night I was crouched on the ground at the very perimeter of my apartment complex parking lot wearing three layers of protective clothing, a chemical mask, and Kevlar gloves, sorting through over a week's worth of unopened mail. Kree was the designated mail opener who thoroughly checked for anthrax and letter bombs before bringing it inside, and now that he's gone, I have to bear the risk myself.

I'd been with him for over ten years. No one preceded him, but even so, I don't recall life outside of a relationship seeming so risky, and I never anticipated that the transition into single life would be so overwhelming. Earlier today, I jumped a ride to work with Avaline, which was supposed to be a quick fix to one of my problems but inevitably led to her hassling me the whole time about how I'm an antisocial workaholic since I'd planned to work on a Friday night.

Her interest-of-the-day is/was a booking agent for a trendy and provocative downtown club called The Empire. Every few days, it seems, she's hanging off the arm of a new jerk-off; the last was a porn star, and not a real porn star, but an Internet porn star, which was why I was hardly fervent about going out with her earlier tonight. "I had a rough week," I told her. "I want to stay in tonight."

It had come to my attention that Freak Stock Boy had been stealing vodka from the backroom, and although every cell in my body was popping the champagne cork as the cops hauled him off, I didn't derive as much satisfaction as I thought I would. On his way out, he'd threatened to blind me and put me in traffic, and I couldn't even think of an effective comeback.

"Getting horizontal with some guy will solve everything," Avaline said.

"I have an ecosystem down there in perfect balance," I said. "I don't need some diseased dick tracking in invasive species."

"Did your mom tell you that?"

"Herpes permanently resides in your spine."

"You are this gargantuan stick that's wedged into society's ass. Is that the view you want to have for the rest of your life?"

***

The inside of The Empire buzzed with disco lights and fog machines, and it was packed from wall to door with miscellaneous personalities decorated in spikes, face paint, and chains. No one looked over the age of seventeen. It was frigid, too, everyone clustering together for warmth, but somehow the air was still thick and clammy, as if everyone who'd melted during the day from the summer heat had come inside to aerate their sweat particles into the atmosphere. I didn't want to touch or breathe anything, and I didn't want anybody touching or breathing on me.

Avaline ditched me early to track down her date, so for the first twenty minutes, I stood alone on the sidelines, doing my best to swerve out of the way in case anybody came close to accidentally grazing me. It was impossible, though, when a band called Riot Venom took the stage, since their gut-wrenching sound brought out the animalistic side in all the midteen moshers. The frontman seemed to be in a significant amount of physical and emotional pain, headbanging and strangling himself with his microphone cord. He was wearing broken handcuffs, his face drowning in a mop of black hair, and his whole body seemed saturated in layers of sweat.

I remembered all the venues I used to frequent in high school: The Cactus Club in San Jose, The Gaslighter in Campbell, Slim's in San Francisco, and The Catalyst in Santa Cruz. And I recalled the energy and exhilaration I felt in places like that, alongside people like these, but the scene tonight seemed somehow foreign and phony.

After a half hour of avoiding the makeshift mosh pit, second-hand weed smoke, and overenthusiastic screamo, it came as a slight disappointment when I realized I'd outgrown the scene fifteen years ago. I went looking for Avaline, and when I caught up with her at the bar, I told her I was going to call a cab and go home.

"We have to relax that trunk out of your ass," she said, handing me a martini made at the slimy bar. "You're still wearing your work nametag."

I looked down and realized I'd mindlessly come to the show in my Safeway uniform—black slacks and white blouse accessorized with a nametag—which I ripped off and tossed, along with the drink. I headed for solitary sanctuary on a couch in the corner, staring at the grime and trash beneath my feet as I walked: the ticket stubs, the crumpled fliers, the band stickers, remnants of wristbands from past shows, black gum spots cemented to the surface, and random clutter in between—a penny, a paperclip, a bottle cap, a crumbled condom wrapper.

"I didn't know you were into this scene," someone said from beside me. The couch surged upward as he dropped against the opposite end.

He was adorned in ragged, cut-off gloves and a moth-eaten black suit, though it wasn't so much a suit as it was Dickies pants, a faded T-shirt, and a worn jacket that may or may not have been fashionable when it was new. Under his snarled grease-pit of jet-black hair were a fair complexion and a set of lambent olivine eyes that sat in the pits of grayish sockets. I shouldn't have looked, but now I couldn't stop staring, perhaps in the same way I wouldn't be able to stop staring at a dead body lying in the gutter.

"Hey, did you know it takes sperm weeks to grow up?" he asked. He pointed up at the club's plasma-screen TV, which was streaming some psychedelic seventies-ish music video that flashed clips of sperm, eggs, and heat-sensory silhouettes of intimate body parts, all to the beat of the music. I instantaneously remembered Kree's freckle.

"And thirty seconds to end up swimming down the drain," I said.

He laughed. "That's creative," he said, following it with a slurp that prevented the wetness on his lips dripping onto his chin.

"I bet if we showed this to kids in kindergarten, sex wouldn't be stigmatized the way that it is."

"What's that mean?" He slurped again.

"Like sex is a social taboo because we hide it from kids, and they end up finding out about it in some psychologically traumatizing manner anyway."

"I walked in on my parents," he said.

"Think I'd probably want to kill myself after that," I said.

He reached for his mouth to tear at the chapped skin dangling from his lips, flicking the bits off the ends of his fingertips before gouging in for more. There was something different about him, disturbingly interesting, and not just because of all the slurping and exfoliating.

"You were playing tonight, huh?" I asked. "Are those cuffs a fashion statement or did you just break out of Folsom?"

"Just something I do." He shrugged. "Are you really that color, or is it makeup?"

He slid over till he was hip to hip with me, and I flinched as if to warn him to keep his distance, but he just licked a finger and wrapped his sweaty, bacteria-laced hand around my wrist to rub his saliva into my skin.

"Don't do that," I said. I fleeced my bag for hand sanitizer, and after locating it, I slathered a thick layer all over the infected area. "The skin is a sponge and it absorbs everything that you put on it."

"Is that how acid works?"

I stood up and shouted at Avaline to take me home. I knew she wasn't anywhere near, but I thought he'd get the hint and leave me alone.

"I could take you home," he said.

Tempting, but I didn't feel like waking up in a ditch dismembered and missing organs, and I really didn't feel like becoming a human sacrifice nailed to a burning post or whatever these people did for fun. Instead, I went back to the bar where Avaline now had her skirt hiked so far up her hips that it looked like she was publicly screwing her date.

"I got some friends who wouldn't mind taking you outside," he said to me.

I should have retaliated by making a crack about his forehead zits, but all of Avaline's men are narcissistic STDs, and if I took the time to stand up to each one of them, she'd cycle through two hundred others by the time I finished standing up to the first.

"Do you like the double stuff?" he asked.

I turned away in disgust, not noticing the club waiter beside me carrying a serving platter of Bloody Marys. I blindly slammed into the tray, and the cold, red slop slinked down the front of my bleached and flawlessly pressed Safeway blouse. As I assessed the damage, a whiff of the pungent stench of garlic made searing flesh flash in mind.

"House garlic vodka," the bartender said.

There was a six-lane commute-hour highway of panic zipping through my head as I tried to come up with a solution that would neutralize the enzyme. I jaws-of-lifed my way through the crowd, trying to locate the bathroom while the would-be organ harvester nipped at my heels with handfuls of napkins. With the bathroom locked and a line of people crowding the hallway, I rushed back to Avaline.

"Hospital," I said. "I'm allergic to garlic." But she was too busy making out with Herpes King to realize that my skin was already feverish.

"You're really allergic to garlic?" the weirdo from the couch asked.

"My skin is going to fry off." When I was ten, I helped Mom chop garlic for her renowned teriyaki sauce, and soon thereafter, my fingertips bubbled up with pustules and I went without prints for months.

"I can take you," he said.

"I don't know you," I said.

"No, I'm Otis."

I hesitated. "Like *Milo and Otis?*" I asked.

"Yeah."

"Like Otis Spunkmeyer?"

"Like Otis Redding," he said. "My middle name's Declan after Elvis Costello."

"Demon?"

"No, Declan."

"Oh."

It was a tossup: stay and watch Avaline dry-hump for the next three hours and quite possibly get ditched at the end of the night anyway, or get into Otis' ancient El Camino. For the sake of my skin, I chose the El Camino. Of course, the problem now—as it has been from the start—is that neither of us knows where the hospital is.

"I'd want to fuck to the Misfits for the rest of my life," Otis says. "Did you know I painted this El Camino shell black so it'd look like a hearse?" On our third trip through the same intersection, he slows the car to ask: "Are you into J-horror? We could rent movies."

"Hospital," I say.

***

We never find a hospital, and with my keys in Avaline's car, I have no choice but to go to his "studio." It's the size of a utility closet. In all certainty it *is* a utility closet, because it doesn't have a kitchen and the bathroom is a notch in the wall with an entryway two feet in width. The architect should have just built the toilet against the wall like in a jail cell.

The disease and virus population undulating in these nesting grounds makes vomit well up in the back of my throat. The room is a black hole for junk, only nothing's sucked into oblivion: it simply accumulates. There are piles of Sierra Nevada bottles, makeup kits, and mirror fragments dusted with drug residue and a fine layer of grit. The floor drowns in Legos, Micro Machines, Masters of the Universe and Ninja Turtles action figures, *Rolling Stone* magazines, old-school Hulk and Archie comics, *Betty & Veronica* and *The Punisher,* cartons of razor blades, orange prescription bottles, boxes of black hair dye...

And his walls are no better: they have disappeared under waves of Polaroids that showcase black eyes, wounds, stitches, staples, oozing gashes, and torn flesh. The table is littered with a spread of paints, brushes, bowls of fecal-colored water, blood capsules, doll heads, and plastic body parts. There's an occult aura shivering between the walls, but it isn't a skull-collecting, incense-burning, freakish occult; this place is more of a punk wonderland.

"I'm practicing to be a makeup artist," he says. "This is what you'd look like if you had shrapnel in you." He brushes globules of red paint onto a rubber arm, then knocks everything off his desk in search of glue. "I'll use this for the wound ooze. Do you want me to do something to you? Or you could sleep if you're tired." He motions to a dingy bed cloaked in black sheets.

I politely bypass the DNA bath and stay in the doorway, knowing I could easily flee if it came down to it. "Is this what you do for work?" I ask.

"No. I take the wheels off cars and the tires off the wheels at Costco. Or I put the tires on the wheels and put the wheels on the cars. Or if people come in and want air in their tires, I put air in them. You can use the bathroom to wash off the garlic."

It only takes a few steps to get into the bathroom, but within those few steps, I accidentally crush Christmas light bulbs, a glass doll head, and all sorts of other unknown debris. The tub looks like it was doused in sewage and sprinkled with cat litter, and I'm almost certain it was. There are whiskey bottles lined up along the outside of the bathtub and all around my feet are empty orange prescription bottles.

Above the sink, he's written dates and event listings on the mirror like

Will Hunting might have done with math equations. On August 1st, apparently, Riot Venom plays Slim's. I sweep aside the clutter to read the rest of his calendar, when down go bottles of nail polish and prescriptions. While fishing the pills out of the miscellaneous floor junk, I notice from a bottle label that his name really is Otis. Otis D. Well.

"Were you named after anything?" he asks from the bedroom.

"You'll figure it out."

***

I get to work the next day with a migraine, a blazing fever, and a rash all over the left side of my body, all allergic reactions to the garlic. And I have no nametag. I spend the day incapacitated, staving off the thundering aches in my skull, and toward the end of my shift, a customer magnifies the agony by cussing me out for selling moldy vegetables. "I want to see the manager," she says.

"I told you, I am the manager." I don't understand why people don't take me seriously. Customers ignore me, coworkers don't respect me, and my boss laughs at my proposals about organizational change as he shuffles me out of his office. And I've always had this inkling that they band together to play practical jokes on me: once, I walked into my office and my desk was covered in smears of chocolate that, at first glance, looked like human crap. The only person with a key to my office is my boss.

"Do I look like someone who isn't serious?" I ask this customer. She's sporting a puff-paint-decorated shirt and her eyebrows come from pencils. She's the one who shouldn't be taken seriously.

"I want a real manager, not some kid," she says. She drops the vegetables with the force of a bowling arm, and they speed down the aisle in clumsy skips. "Now."

I am not picking those up. My professors didn't take me seriously; my family doesn't, either. "Lady, I assure you that I am a person to be taken seriously." This is one of those situations I wish would just disappear, because any addition to the ball of occupational stress may bring forth a very public and quite possibly violent meltdown.

"I want the goddamn manager."

We go back and forth a few more times, but I relent and head into the backroom where I ask Forklift Operator Guy to go out to the floor and stand in as the "real manager," just to get her off the property. I can't believe she listens to some guy in grease-stained overalls, but not me.

I scarf a family-sized bag of M&Ms in the darkest corner of the stockroom. When I emerge from the caverns of the back, I'm temporarily disoriented by the artificial lighting of the sales floor. I stumble toward the cash registers and see Otis in the liquor aisle with two six-packs of Sierra Nevada in hand. He sees me and waves with a slight swing of his wrist. "What time do you get off?" he asks.

"What time is it?"

"Eleven."

"Three hours ago."

"Why are you still here?"

"I...just am."

"Why?"

"Why what?"

"If you got off three hours ago, why would you still be here?"

"I'm salaried, so I can work as long as I want."

"But..." He seems confused. "I guess you really like it here."

I wonder if he can smell the chocolate on my breath.

I grab my things from my office and meet him outside. Though there's a bench against the wall of the storefront, he chooses instead to sit on the curb in front of the handicapped stalls, and though he only lives a few blocks away, he cracks open a bottle of beer right here in the open and guzzles it down like a runner would with Gatorade after conquering the Iron Man.

"Maybe we could get a Slurpee or something," I say, but he doesn't say anything. "Or we could..." do whatever people like him do. "Or go..." wherever people like him go.

He shrugs and takes a break from the beer to play around with the diseased gum on the bottom of his shoe. To keep from hurling, I force myself to imagine bridal-white tile doused in Clorox.

"Where do you..." I'm stuttering like I have a festering cold sore on my lip and it's making me drool. "...usually...date?" I can't believe I said it. I banned that word from my vocabulary a long time ago, along with phrases like "I'm happy for you" and "college sweetheart."

"It's never started out like that for me," he says.

"How does it?" One-night stands, drunken one-night stands, coked-up one-night stands, or doped-up one-night stands? If there's anything I learned about the scene back in the day, it's that girls will go naked for anyone in a band. They don't even have to be in a band, they could just look or have the attitude of being in a band.

Aside from his repetitive slurping, it's quiet. I'm burdened by our fizzling connection, plagued with the memory of how silence with Kree was always a one-way ticket to his freckle, but Otis scribbles an address on his Safeway receipt and holds it over.

It's an address in Roseville, a few towns over from Sacramento. "You want to hang out tomorrow?" he asks.

I have no religion, no belief system. I won't even devote myself to one brand of coffee, but the fact that tonight ends with a receipt and not a freckle is a victory.

***

It takes me a few minutes to suck up the courage to dart from my car to the diminishing overhang of shade outlining the building. The doors are open and there's a funeral in session up front. I want to double back outside and check the numbers on the building, but I see Otis sitting at the end of the last row. It's warm inside and everybody's fanning themselves with their service programs. I tiptoe around the back of the church and slide across the cool pew till I'm a few inches from Otis. "I don't do well with holy water, so maybe I could sit out whatever this is," I say. He tips his head in acknowledgement and keeps his eyes on the front. "Do you know this person?"

He shakes his head. "One time," he says, "this woman screamed 'cause she thought I was Death coming to get everyone, so the priests made me leave." For whatever reason, his lips tend to spew saliva after each syllable until he slurps up the excess. "When I was a pallbearer for my mom, I wanted to carry her out of the church, but my fuckin' uncles put her coffin on wheels so we couldn't carry her. So when we had my dad's funeral, they said I couldn't be there unless I promised not to make a fucking scene. And I wouldn't." He pauses and shrugs. "But Aunt Zee promised me and my brother that we can carry her all the way to the hearse by ourselves."

I have nothing functional I can think of saying in response.

"How many funerals have *you* been to?" he asks.

"One, but I didn't know the uncle at all and I only went because my family made me write the eulogy."

"Do you write for a job?"

"Self-realization or something," I say. "It's always been a stress diversion, like how people zone out in front of the TV after work."

"Like figuring out your shit?"

"Something like that."

"I think people figure out their shit when they jack off," he says. I launch into immature laughter that rings for a good minute in the hollows of the church and I have to focus on something unpleasant (biohazard needle disposal boxes) to stop. "'Cause you do it without knowing why it feels so damn good. But you keep doing it and make it perfect over your lifetime, and you get to know the two different peoples in you. I know I'm one person before I come and a different one right after."

I scratch uncomfortably at my neck, wondering how inappropriate it would be to go running down the center aisle screaming: "Fire! Fire!"

"When you're making yourself feel good, it means you're alive, and you being there feeling good is you being more alive. Do you know how to get yourself off? You don't have to tell me. I just feel sad for girls who don't know so they only fuck 'cause the guy wants it or to get a baby. What's it feel like when a guy's violating you?"

The collar I don't have is closing in on my throat; I can't even swallow. I wonder if this is what I've missed from the contemporary dating scene over the past ten years.

"I ask all girls 'cause I don't get how you could feel good when the guy is jizzing in you. It must feel so violating. For fuck's sake, that's where we piss." He sits back to analyze the details like he's decoding a derivative theorem. "I'd never make any girl suck me off. That's abuse. It'd be like someone hocking a loogie in your mouth and making you swallow it. But everybody does it, so nobody thinks it's sick."

My face hurts. It's been contorted for too long.

"I think girls are lying when they say they like giving head," he says. "The world makes them think they have to do it to make something of themselves. I wish it wasn't like that. But it's different for guys 'cause girls don't leave weird shit behind inside our dicks that we have to carry around with us. If I was a girl, I'd be a hardcore lesbian. I'd take cunt butter over jizz any day. Guys are fucking gross. All hairy and shit with dicks and ball sacks hanging out all the time. Girls have smooth skin with things we can grab onto and everything's tucked inside, you know?"

I reach for a Bible and flip through the rice-paper pages, hoping he'll stop and realize he's going on about sexual theory in the middle of someone's funeral.

"I hope you're not bored. Are you bored?" he asks. "Want to go back to my place and see what you'd look like if you were kebab on a fence?"

"Oh...kay."

***

In his hotbox of a studio, I lie in the folds of sheets that are probably soaked in every bodily biohazardous material that he or any of his past conquests could have emitted. I bet there are even mutant strains of diseases fused with other mutant strains, which created a super-mutant disease that makes flesh-eating bacteria look like the common cold. "I have a better time doing it when I get to do it on someone who's not my brother," he says, and a bead of spit flies onto my belly.

As he applies paint and gels on my stomach, his plump cheeks fluctuate in expression, and he furrows his forehead while biting onto his moist lip in concentration. I play with the strands of hair that frame his face in feathery clumps and I study the roundness of his face, the thick but sparsely populated black eyebrows. He's bulky in stature, but retains a softness in his mannerisms. "You have vampire teeth," I say.

"I filed them down to make them that way." He slurps again, licking his lips of the saliva that almost trickled onto my stomach.

***

Friday, August 1st, rolls around, and I invite Sean, an old high-school friend, to Riot Venom's show at Slim's. Of course, when I say high school, I'm talking generations ago. Sean and I stand against the bar watching the minnows fleeting around the venue in prepubescent clusters, so naïve and unmolded. We don't even drink because we don't want to let on that we're old enough to be legal; it's not so much being old that bothers us, it's more that we aren't running around with the same zeal anymore.

We used to swarm the local scene like this for new talent, hanging out at Rasputin, Streetlight Records, and The Campbell Gaslighter to ingest underground music in its purest form: raw, ambitious, so far removed from the droning of pop radio waves. Now we're lucky if we catch an old AFI track during our morning commute. These days, Oracle is working him into the ground with twelve-hour days, seven days a week, and I'm drowning in a sea of inventory counts, customer complaints, and profit-and-loss statements that mean nothing to me and will never enrich my life. We've become common, everything we've always been against.

I've been removed from the scene for so long that I forgot how refreshing it is to be in the presence of honest music unhampered by industry standards. Otis' sound isn't talentless screamo unnecessarily skinning the flesh off my face. The band harbors a peculiar melodic quality and emits an unusual energy that I can't pinpoint; maybe it's the torque of the guitar, maybe it's Otis' Viking voice and showmanship. As he maneuvers the stage, showers of sweat zip off the tips of his hair and, aside from his salivating problem and evident intoxication, he's violently appealing.

"What are they?" I ask Sean. "Not just hardcore. What about horror punk? No, more Goth and hard rock. Maybe metalcore."

"Why is everyone here fucking twelve?" he asks. He's irritated by the scene and vows to take bands like Social Distortion, Rancid, and Bad Religion to the grave in his cold, dead fingers.

"We used to kick ass like this," I say.

"We should be proud that we're nothing like this," he says.

"Neocon," someone says in passing.

We look toward the source and I instantly recognize the twiglike arms in the shadows of the hallway. The name on his termination papers is sharp in memory: Landon Well, Freak Stock Boy. I should have noticed he was on guitar tonight, but I didn't recognize him without a shirt on, and his starved body was so grotesquely unpleasant to see, I purposely refrained from staring in his direction. But now we're up close: tattoo sleeves, piercings in any and every bit of cartilage or skin, one blue and one brown eye, shag haircut, and a body so gaunt that it's like watching jointed breadsticks poking around like a human being. I toil over ditching Otis in exchange for never having to see Landon again.

"I'm going back to work," Sean says.

"It's 10 o'clock on a Friday and we're in San Fran," I say. "And we're supposed to go out with them after."

"I'm leaving."

***

We head for a bar outside of San Francisco, and while sandwiched between Otis and the drummer, Joey, in the backseat of Landon's questionably sturdy Mustang, I make the assumption that a coroner will be piecing together our body parts by the end of the night. For one thing, Landon is pushing ninety without his hands on the wheel because he's too busy guzzling rum and Coke, shoving chips in his mouth, and screaming to the Sex Pistols. "Last week I was picked up on a DUI for driving on the sidewalk," he says after nearly plummeting into the freeway's center divide.

"Where was I?" Otis asks.

"Passed out in the back."

I could be at home under the air conditioner eating a gallon of mint-chip ice cream and watching *Jackass* reruns, but we stop at a gas station in the middle of Murder Town, where Otis ventures off to take a leak in the bushes and Landon pumps three dollars worth of gas and then groans about how the needle on the gauge hasn't moved.

"Fuck, my cornhole itches like I didn't wipe the shit off," he says to me. "That reminds me, I have to be in court Monday for that DUI. That should be fun. So, what do you do for fun? Trade stocks?"

"I work a lot."

"Yeah, don't you have some labor union to oppress right now?" He spits at my feet then asks me how the spread of social conservatism is going.

"I—"

"Don't you and your Republican friends have oil to drill in some Alaskan refuge? Do you even have friends?"

I comb my thoughts for anything to burn him back with, but my mind is so tied up thinking about the diseases that must be eating away at the holes of his facial piercings that I can't think of anything.

"Check it out, I been working on a six-pack to fight off you righties," he says, lifting up his shirt to show off his emaciated torso covered in thickets of russet hair.

"That's not a six-pack," I say, "that's...free world famine." If I looked past the fur I could probably make out the outline of his organs.

"I'm a hundred and seventeen pounds of pure Republican ass-kicking."

"How do you only weigh seven pounds more than me?" I ask.

"Maybe you're fat." It knocks the wind out of me. "Check it out," he says. "I'm going to make a shitload pioneering the green condom. I got the perfect slogan, 'Feed it to poochie after the coochie.'"

"I just wrote 'Bush' with my piss," Otis says, still zipping his pants as he emerges from the bushes. "And I wanted to write 'sucks' but it was too hard to pinch off once I got going so I just pissed all over his name."

"You should have pissed on Johnny Ramone too," Landon says.

"I did that yesterday."

"Then piss on that one." Landon points at me. "What do you listen to, anyway?"

I'd take the piss any day over a question about music, since my experience hanging out with punk aficionados in high school, Sean being one of them, has led me to believe that I'm damned if I don't listen to the right music and double-damned if I listen to the wrong music.

"Any Misfits?" Landon asks. "Iron Maiden? Descendants? Smiths? What about Velvet Underground? Pogues?" I turn to Otis, hoping he'll rescue me, but he's busy picking something out of his teeth. "I bet you listen to pussies like Jimmy Eat World, huh?"

My former boyfriend of ten years couldn't recount a single one of my top five bands, but my nemesis, who knows nothing about me outside of my Safeway nametag, can look at me and come up with an intimately secretive detail like that at the drop of an insult. How humiliating. I turn to Otis and reach for his hand, which rests against the hood of the Mustang. I curl my fingers around his and squeeze. He looks down at them and smiles.

"What about Morrissey?" Landon continues to probe.

I turn back to him, distracted with Otis, and ask: "The Doors?"

"You wouldn't know good music if it bit you on the cunt, cunt."

Otis laughs. "You said 'cunt' twice in a row," he says, seemingly more interested in the gratuitous use of the word than its intent. It's unsettling.

Part II

Maybe I'm a Masochist

It's August 2nd and I'm a day late for my midquarterly physical because I was too busy taking it last night from an ex-employee who tragically and coincidentally happens to be the brother of the most fascinating enigma I've come across since moisturizing hand sanitizer. I should have seen my doctor earlier. Over the last few days I've scratched the rash from the garlic into a garden of blisters and this morning it looked like smallpox and elephantiasis bred under my skin. "I've also been opening my own mail lately, so I could have anthrax," I say. "Have you seen all those lawyer commercials about mesothelioma? And Sacramento is the mosquito capital of California so it could be West Nile and dengue fever, but I stand by my initial hunch of it being tuberculosis. Once I start coughing blood, that's it. Nail me into a coffin."

"It's hay fever," my doctor says.

"I have this scaly patch on my shoulder." My fear of skin cancer has reached such unimaginable proportions that I don't go out in the sun unless absolutely necessary, and if I do, it's never in direct light unless I'm wearing three layers of clothes and have SPF 45 slathered on the exposed regions. A Sac summer can topple 110 degrees of dry heat, but the sweltering discomfort I've dealt with under all those layers of wool and goo has paid off: I don't have cancer. Yet.

"Looks like eczema."

"Have you heard about drug-resistant Ebola?"

"We've done the Ebola thing for years and you've dodged it this long."

"I hear people get tumors that spread through their whole body."

"Doing a scan could lead to cancer you didn't have in the first place." He always has this way of talking me out of things. I used to coat my skin in Off! to deter potential AIDS and hepatitis-infected mosquitoes, but he told me that the insecticide in Off! causes muscular paralysis, seizures, and (consequently) death, which turned me off not only repellents but other things containing pesticides as well, like produce. I'd really like to ask about a potential outbreak of diseases and bacteria like smallpox, bubonic plague, and cholera, pertinent information that probably goes undisclosed by the Centers for Disease Control, and my own chances of contracting something with antibiotic resistance and immunity to modern medicine.

"My eyes are bloodshot and yellow. Do you—"

"Sweetheart," he says. "I'll give you a mild antibiotic for the blisters and you should keep the bandages clean, but other than the allergic reaction, you are young, beautiful, and perfectly healthy. Enjoy yourself."

But he can't see every little cell in me. One might have cancer, hepatitis, tuberculosis, typhus, or be on the verge of turning flesh-eating. My eyes may be crawling with bacterial conjunctivitis and my lungs coated with anthrax, but he's sending me away empty-handed.

I down a fistful of Echinacea in the car. It seems to take the edge off.

***

Shortly after leaving the doctor's office, the UC Davis Medical Center calls me because Avaline attempted "suicide" by driving her car into the American River. I still haven't figured out why someone like her is associated with someone like me, and vice versa. We have no commonalities and the opposite qualities repel, but she keeps popping up at work or on a bridge and I don't know how to remove myself from her emergency contact listing, so the hospital and police station continually call me whenever she needs claiming. Or identifying.

When I get to her hospital room, I have to squirm through walls of balloons, flowers, stuffed animals, and candy that have been showered on her by friends, boyfriends, ex-boyfriends, one-night stands, and quickies. "Did you honestly think it'd work?" I ask, then tear through a box of chocolates courtesy of one of her visitors.

"It's really hard," she says, gazing at the ceiling in a miasma of hospital drugs.

Maybe I hang out with her because she makes me feel better about myself. "Were you seriously trying or was this another...you know," I say.

She glares at me like *I'm* the psycho in the hospital bed. Last week she ran into a police station screaming about how a drunk tried to mug her. When I got to the station, the shoulder of her sweater was torn down the side, but she later told me it didn't really happen, she tore her own sweater because she just needed the comfort of unbiased strangers. Telemarketers and door-to-door salespeople loathe her. She'll snivel on and on to Jehovah's Witnesses for hours about petty things like how the stylist accidentally colored her hair "winter sandstone" instead of "summer sandstone." They usually end up gunning for the door or hanging up. There's probably a national Do-Not-Call-Avaline list circulating the continent.

"Think this'll scar? I have a shoot next week." She points to a cut under her chin before replacing the bandage. "Damn, I didn't think I'd get so mangled this time."

What a psycho. A psycho crammed into the body of a ballerina and catalog model. She's 5'8", 102 pounds, models for department store magazines, owns and dances in her own ballet company...Avaline's just another rich Daddy's girl from Danville with no real job, no real social pressures. She just lives to burn other people's money and fret over re-streaking her hair. Maybe *she* hangs out with *me* because I make her feel better about herself.

On the way out of the hospital we take a wrong turn and end up in the nursery gawking at the newborns. We watch them as they sleep, nestled into their blankets in naïve bliss. I press my face to the glass and say, "Welcome to the world of unaffordable medicine and escalating taxes."

"I am never having a kid," Avaline says. "I hear it tears your vag up and makes it all saggy and loose. I don't want to have to settle on fisting for the rest of my life just to feel something. Speaking of fisting, anything ever happen with that guy from the other night?"

I'm kind of surprised she asks, much more surprised that she remembers details outside of her quest for easy sex. "I'm kind of worried he might be bisexual," I say. "I don't think I can handle that. I mean, what if he comes to me one day wanting a three-way? It'd be like an inferno of bacteria."

"I was with a bisexual once." She sighs in warm recollection. "But he always turned on gay porn while we had ass sex, so I kept wondering if he was thinking of me as a dude. Plus, he called me 'man-daddy' in the heat of the moment a few times. So I set up boundaries. No bisexuals, drug addicts, or anyone in a band. They'll never want you more than anal, drugs, or music."

***

I slaved for an eighteen-hour day at work from Saturday afternoon into Sunday morning: first the company-required ten, and then an additional eight of labor relations crap, sifting through employee-filed grievances, reading such highlights as "there's no more sugar packets in the break room" and "a fifteen-minute break is not long enough for me to go to the bathroom all the way," with the words "all the way" underlined multiple times.

When Mom calls around 8 a.m., she immediately jumps into:

"When's the last time you disinfected your apartment?"

"Have you been working out or sitting around your apartment like a beached whale?"

"Find a good-looking yuppie, and don't screw it up."

"If you keep lying around like a mole, you'll end up looking like the Michelin Man."

"Did you hear about that woman they found dead in her apartment? No one knew she was dead until the neighbors complained about the stench. She'd been dead for four days, and when they went into her apartment, all they found was toilet paper. She had Costco packs of toilet paper stacked from floor to ceiling."

We squabble yet again over why I've repeatedly turned down dates with her prospects, and it goes something like this:

"Why do you want to be a mole all the time? They're such ugly creatures."

"I really don't care what I am."

"You need to get out and meet some husband material."

"I need an ice cream sandwich."

"You need that like you need another loser boyfriend. You're going to end up dying miserable and alone."

"That sounds awesome."

"Excuse me?"

"Oh, stop acting so surprised."

"You're going to end up like that hermit, Aunt Alison, living in a secluded cabin somewhere in Nevada."

"Thanks, Mom. That's really...motivational."

She goes into the details of my future death, how there won't be any reason to have a funeral because I'll have had no one in my life to hold one, much less claim my carcass at the morgue. She's still elaborating upon the last part, when someone knocks on the door. Through the peephole I see Otis' mouth slobbering microorganisms all over the glass like a dog sniffing out a scent.

"Let's go stand near a stoplight and hold up a sign that says 'Listen to Lou Reed,'" he shouts through the door. "Last week, me and Landon was out there with one that said, 'Stop female genital mutilation.'"

With the phone still against my ear, I unlock the door and crack it open a few inches. His foamy eyes shift downward and stay fixated on a paint roller stewing in a pan of disinfectant at the foot of the doorway. "Are you painting?" he asks, softly now.

"The walls are dirty," I say.

"Oh. So do you want to go for a ride or something?"

I hesitate because I don't know his definition of "ride," but I hang up the phone and step out because I'd rather take my chances with him than submissively take more of Mom's unsolicited advice.

***

He drives us a half hour out of Sac and then off the highway onto a dirt road. A few dust paths later, he parks in front of a "house" (or, in layman's terms, a crumbling shanty built with slabs of waffle tin) wherein his "friend" (or, in layman's terms, drug dealer) answers the open doorway. He's rail thin, has a full head of disheveled blond pube hair, his neck is inked with spinach-green tattoos, his goatee's a trap for cigarette ash, he doesn't have front teeth, and the ones in back are questionable. He eyes me with a squint of distrust.

"She's cool," Otis says to him. The dealer nods and extends his hand toward me for a shake. I involuntarily jerk back and wince.

"Weird, man, weird," the dealer says.

After the exchange, Otis drives farther down the dirt path and pulls up to the edge of a meadow. I can feel the sun's radioactive rays burning cancer into my skin, so I shift to the far end of the car for safety in the shade. He reaches under my seat for a half-empty bottle of whiskey and I look away, wishing I didn't have to hear a handful of pills tinker against his teeth that he washes down with the booze. "Did you know Maria Shriver opened a part in the history museum downtown for historical and influential women?" He squeezes out the big words as if his mouth were constipated. "We should go see it. And did you ever want to see *The Vagina Monologues*?" he asks, then slurps the excess dribble off his lips.

I zip up my sweatshirt to shield my neck from the sunlight, then bury my hands under my thighs for protection. I can sense him observing my actions like he's a breath away from asking me what the hell my problem is...no different than the employees on the loading docks—or my family at barbeques.

"You know, I used to see you in the Safeway parking lot when I'd come see Landon," he says. "I wanted to talk to you all the time."

I don't remember ever seeing him in the parking lot, but to be honest, I don't remember paying attention. There was never any reason to pay attention. "Why didn't you?" I ask.

"You were always running to your car and holding a newspaper over your head. I couldn't get to you in time."

"I don't want to get skin cancer."

"It looked like you had a lot to say." He slurps again. "And it looked like you were always going someplace important."

"Probably not."

"What would you be if you could be anything?"

"Six inches taller with a better skeletal design."

"That's trivial shit," he says. "The important shit's the shit you can change. I'd be a makeup artist for the movies at the Sac Horror Film Fest."

"You wouldn't do music?"

"I'd do that too. And I'd say 'Fuck you, Costco,' just like Landon did to Safeway. It doesn't make sense to me to waste a good life. You're damned anyway, so you might as well feel good. You hear people say, 'You could die tomorrow,' but you could kill yourself tomorrow too."

There's such a zealous animation in his voice, almost as though he isn't a social misfit but more of a dreamer. "How old are you?" I ask.

"Thirty-two."

I remember people like him and I don't know what's worse, the fact that he didn't grow out of it at fifteen, or that I did. "You know, when you're up there performing, it hits people and they see themselves differently," I say. "You back the most phenomenal set of words with the perfect instrumentation, and in that moment, your song is divine."

"What album would you want to die to?" he asks.

I stop to appreciate the look of interest in his expression. "Aimee Mann. *Lost In Space.*"

"What song?" he asks.

"*Invisible Ink.*"

"Maybe you can let me come over and read what you write."

I laugh. "Where were you in high school?"

"I never went. I got sick a lot so it was easier not to go. I take all these meds for it, but sometimes I can't feel me anymore, so I stop. But then shit starts again and I have to schedule work around my freak-outs, and it's such a pain in the ass for everyone. My therapist says—"

"Are you going to start every sentence with 'my therapist says'?" I ask.

"This guy's pretty badass. He knows lots of shit that makes me think about stuff."

"People like him cut up brains to alter behavior," I say.

"But this guy doesn't cut my brains up," he says.

"He might as well, he's got you on all those soma drugs."

"I do a lot of drugs."

"No, I'm talking antidepressants."

"You mean my medicines?"

"Yeah. And you might as well jump into a bunch of mass orgies while you're at it. Unless that's already your thing."

"What?" he asks.

"Have you ever questioned why you're taking those pills and what they do?"

"I don't know. I've always been on them and they seem to work."

"Benadryl and Dramamine work too, but that's because they knock you out and you sleep through everything. Do you want to sleep through the rest of your life?"

"No. I don't know. What?"

"It's all a ploy to shut down innovation and free will in the masses. I'm not talking to you right now, I'm talking to a bigwig pharmaceutical product."

"But they have to be good or else they wouldn't feed them to people. Right?"

"Only if you want to be controlled by the government."
"The government's trying to control me?"
"Seems they already do."

***

He wants to head home, but I don't know what's more horrifying: risking bodily infection at his place or voluntarily letting him contaminate mine. He's just so icky (there's no other way to put it); whether he's picking at his lips, teeth, ears, nose, or the corners of his eyes, he can't keep his hands off his face, and then he'll touch something and turn it into a petri dish of his microbial offspring. As a kid he was probably that creepy weirdo who spent recess eating mud and walking around with head lice and stomach worms.

As we stand at the door of my apartment I finger each key on my ring, wishing there were more keys, more time, because I haven't scripted out all the warnings I need to prep him with. I want to tell him not to touch anything or sit anywhere because it looks like he's been backpacking cross-country for months. I want to ask that he take off his shoes before coming in, but then again, maybe he shouldn't, because his sweaty/diseased feet will leave grubby footprints all over my carpet. It all seems like such a headache, so I'm tempted to tell him that I'll get a chair so he can sit in the hallway and talk to me through the protection of the door.

"Are we locked out?" he asks, inching closer till I can feel him leaning over my shoulder. I open the door and head in, and not only does he not take his shoes off, but he pulls an Enemy You album out of my CD collection and uses the edge to grind his pills against the surface of my coffee table.

"I got a lot if you want some." He's talking but I only hear the sound of his slurping. I only see his muddy shoes and sweaty hands, and he's using my favorite Enemy You EP to cut lines of whatever the hell is on the surface of my Ethan Allen. I grow faint, focusing on a stationary target to regain my balance. "Come here." He coaxes me with sticky hands to sit perpendicular over his lap. "You're shaking."

He runs his fingers over the rigid scales on the back of my hands. They're scalier than normal and my nails are crusting away from cuticle to tip—almost as if my cleaner concoction has dissolved them—but he says nothing. He worms his fingers under my shirt and feels up the moguls of blisters on my back, making my flesh tingle like a combination of Pop Rocks and gunpowder are igniting under my skin. As he runs his hand down my waist, he glides his tongue up the side of my throat. "Hazel?" he says. "I used to jack off to girls like you."

I shift the weight of my head, wondering if I heard right.

"Now I only jack it to you."

I'm offended, yet somehow flattered, because nobody's ever said anything like that to me before. I lean against him, putting my head in the cradled space between his shoulder and neck, and I don't stop him when I feel his hand creeping back under my shirt.

***

We spend the remainder of the day playing old-school video games on Atari and Nintendo; we rent *The Audition, Creepshow,* and almost every Tim Burton film ever made and watch them while gorging on Twinkies, washing them down with vodka-soaked watermelon.

I'm drunk, and I know I'm drunk because I can make out with him and not fixate on the thought of him injecting biohazardous saliva in my throat, or the thousands of herpes germs possibly colonizing in my lip tissue. The more I lose myself in his interpretations of Rise Against lyrics or hear him going on about all the familiar venues he's played up and down the coast of California, the less I find myself worrying about herpes or, even worse, another freckle. We spend the night counting each other's teeth with our tongues and kissing until our lips become bulbous extensions of our chins: red, rare, and swollen.

We pass out together in bed, and apparently, I do kick and whack in my sleep, and (allegedly) I scratch. He wakes me up in the middle of the night, laughing about how I kneed him in the stomach, how I head-butted him in the forehead and then elbowed him in the cheek when he tried spooning me. He gives me the summary behind a smile, like maybe he's entertained.

Of course, Otis is hardly the poster child for a good night's sleep. In the middle of the night I wake up to a massive thud, as if a whale has dropped from the sky onto my apartment floor. He scrambles back onto the mattress, then falls back into a cadence of snores with his face smashed into the pillow and his mouth ajar like a fish on ice. After his third face-plant into the floor, we get up and push the bed up against the wall, but the next time he just steamrolls over me and flies forehead first into the dresser. And he sweats profusely. I wake up drenched in his sweat and stuck to the sheets. Even at a distance, I can still feel my side of the sheets soaked and chilled from his emissions.

In the morning, we lounge in bed eating popsicles and listening to Aimee Mann. I let him take Polaroids of my blistered skin so he can try to recreate the horror with his makeup kits. In the afternoon, when the heat's the worst, we sit in a cool bath of Epsom salt while we read each other's scrapbooks of lyrics and compilations, critiquing or commenting on the ones which stand out for better or worse.

"This story you wrote, *Winter Persimmon*," he says. "What's it about?"

"Surviving."

"What's a persimmon?"

"A bright orange fruit that grows in late fall. It's neat, because after everything's barren and dead and the tree loses all its leaves, it'll still have fruit on its branches."

"Sounds cool." He shuffles through the pages not noticing that he's dripping water over them and making the ink bleed.

"When did it unravel for you? Was it your parents?" I ask.

"Before. It just happens. Like getting sick."

Most of his theories are juvenile, but somehow they make sense, and it's been a long time since anything's made sense to me. So it doesn't matter anymore if he works in a grease-ridden jumpsuit, eats cheese from a can, shops at the dollar store, tastes like a whiskey-guzzling grandpa, and suffers from a salivating problem accompanied by a runny nose that leaves his upper lip encrusted with layer upon layer of snot trails.

While he goes on about Bad Religion's blunder of a psychedelic experiment, I think about all the overzealous educational messages chiseled into us as kids about *safe sex* this, and *you're going to end up an unwed mother in welfare statistics* that. Simultaneously, one side of my brain is showing a slideshow of diseased genitalia to the other side that's uninterested, because it's too busy listening to him hyperactively describe how Greg Graffin must have been on super 'shrooms when he decided to take the band on that tangent.

I like listening to him. I don't have to zone out or pretend to care because I want to hear everything he thinks. It feels like I've been sleeping through interactions with everybody else forever and now I'm sitting upright and attentive.

***

It's Tuesday night and I purposely take the bridge route home thinking I'll find Avaline there. No surprise, she is, and after picking her up, I regurgitate how awkward the sex was, and how our first attempt consisted of Otis stuttering the whole time.

"Um...do you have a condom?" he asked. "I just don't want to...if I leave, you know, my...in your. I mean, I don't mind your slime, I really like it, but I didn't know if you wanted my...to get all up inside your..." Yeah, I got it. "So, do you mind?"

"Mind what?" I asked.

"If I leave my...jizz in you?"

"When you put it that way, yeah, I kind of do."

"I'm sorry," he said, reaching toward the floor for his pants. "I didn't even kiss you."

"That's okay."

"Sometimes I can't get my firing squad going 'cause I feel so guilty."

And our second crack was just as disastrous: he rocked inside of me in two-inch intervals, every once in a while smiling at me like we were strangers waiting to get off an elevator. "And toward the end he asked if he could come in me," I say to Avaline. "What was I supposed to say? 'There's the sink, knock yourself out.' I think he ended up faking it. I didn't find any...you know."

"Who goes on a treasure hunt for that?" she asks. "And aren't you *the* spokeswoman for Clorox? I mean, did that just go away or did you finally get on knock-out pills or something?"

"It's different with him."

"Do you zip yourselves up in hazmat suits and then go at it?"

"It's just different. He likes that I'm pale and he laughs at my sleep-whacking." He points out the natural highlights streaked in my hair and he likes to poke what he refers to as an "old-fashioned beauty mark" on my chin, things that Mom has always referred to as "genetic abnormalities." He doesn't ask why I have so many different kinds of hand sanitizer, some with aloe for when I have cuts on my hands, others with lotion for when the dry fissures in my knuckles get bad. "He's different."

"Yeah, it always seems that way at the beginning, and then you find out they're just like the rest of those assholes who leave you at the restaurant table or fake a headache and never call you back."

"You know, I hate it when people tell me what to do, but for a while there, it sounded so good coming from him."

"Oh God, you're not a closet submissive, are you? Fantasizing about being bound and ball-gagged in the dishwasher while someone in a groundhog suit pours sour milk and oven cleaner all over you? A word of advice: don't screw a computer geek. Last night, this guy screamed out weird shit like, 'Yeah, harder, hack into me, break through my firewall. You're a nasty little hacker, aren't you? Download me, now!'"

***

Anxiety puts me back on my doctor's examination table. In a white-picket-fence world, I would have waited till Otis showed me his health records that proved he was free of all STDs.

I shiver as my doctor swabs anywhere a virus or disease could be breeding. He lectures me about protecting myself, and I try to come off as guilty and regretful, but underneath it all I know I'd do it again. Even if it was just as awkward, unsuccessful, and left me just as guilt-ridden, I'd fuck Otis till he grated my flesh away and left a gaping hole between my legs.

DIY Regression

Throughout the week, Otis casually nudged me about heading to his semi-hometown of Roseville to meet the great-aunt who's raised both him and Landon since the ages of fifteen and eleven, respectively. Every time he appeared to be formulating the suggestion, I changed the subject long before he could realize he'd been interrupted. For one thing, Landon still lives there, and that's not simply a fifty-fifty *Lady or the Tiger* chance of being mauled, but a guarantee, and second, I've gotten it from too many families already (my own, Kree's...), and I didn't think I could handle it from yet another source.

Eventually, though, I folded. "Did you hear Flogging Molly's playing The Fillmore in October?" he asked, and after that, there was no way I could turn him down.

I agreed to Saturday morning brunch, but throughout the drive, I couldn't help involuntarily picturing a haggard woman with green skin cackling something under her breath about coming to get me and my little dog. As we pull up to her house (and a front yard that looks like a dump of decaying garbage with weeds crowning the mounds), I think she's probably more of a shopping cart lady than a witch. I'm surprised, in fact, that the house's windows haven't been boarded up and spray-painted "Condemned."

Otis romps through the wasteland as if this is completely normal, but I fall behind as I dodge tetanus-laced shopping carts and dumpster tires teeming with unidentifiable critters that I can only hope are roaches, because at least then I'd know I'm not in some nuclear wilderness crawling with new breeds of mutated parasites. Otis waits in the doorway of the house, holding open the screen door that doesn't have a screen because it's disintegrated over the years, so really, he's holding open a rusted metal frame that he could remove altogether. I thank him anyway and step inside, escaping the horrors of the yard only to be sucker-punched by the reek of mildew and clammy cat.

When the hall opens to the dining room, I stand in the heart of what my mind has previously only conjured up in nightmares. The ground is a compost of fast-food wrappers, car parts, and even strings of Christmas lights. The spaces between the bigger clusters of junk are filled with thickets of dust, dirt, and unidentifiable organic matter (probably dead bug carcasses and cat dander). What was, at one point, kitchen linoleum is now a dirt floor of rocks and black dust. Landon sits at the table, shirtless, and says, "Get that Republican out of this house." He's slouched over a plate of food and so inconceivably emaciated that the sight of him reminds me of a scene from one of those "just pennies a day to feed and clothe the less fortunate" ads.

Above the fireplace mantle, I see a hodgepodge of stolen street signs tacked in a vertical listing:
Zelda Way
Landon Lane
Evelyn Lane
Otis Avenue
Below the signs, there's a four-and-a-half-foot-tall, ninety-something-year-old, osteoporosis-raped, shriveled prune of a lady who comes at me and latches on to my body in such a frenzy that it feels less like a friendly embrace and more like Kree's family's Doberman. She's wearing a lacey dress that looks like it was made from once white (now stained yellow) table doilies, and I don't want to imagine what those stains are—it's horrible to think that they could somehow be piss. Has no one around here heard of Clorox Stain Fighter & Color Booster bleach?

"Otis finally found himself a sweetheart," she says, looking up at me through trifocals thicker than double-paned Plexiglas.

I go board-stiff, hoping she'll realize my discomfort and let go! for the good of everything sane, let go! but she won't. I dry-heave over the crown of her head and the act makes me do a face-plant into the top of her straggly gray hair shimmering with scalp grease. When I yank away, her hair sticks to my lips, so I convulse a few feet backwards, till I realize I'm stepping into boxes upon boxes of aged kitty litter and the contents are squishing out from under my feet. The only thing I can think of doing to prevent a horror-induced meltdown of epic proportions is to hold my breath and press my hands against my face till my eyes throb with psychedelic blooms behind their lids. "Nice to meet you, Mrs. Fitzgerald," I squeak.

"Call me Auntie Zee, deary," she says.

Otis pulls out a chair at the table for me, and I sit because I'm so dizzily nauseous that if I tried to flee the way I came, I'd puke myself into a coma.

I have a clear view of the kitchen from the table. The sink is loaded with moldy dishes, unwashed Tupperware, and stale casserole plates, and piled beside the stove are moldy garden vegetables still dusted with the dirt from which they were yanked. To top off the botulism fest, two fleabag cats wolf down mystery meat inches from where Aunt Zee is cooking.

As if this place couldn't be any more like a hillbilly slasher film, Landon hoists his bunion-infested feet on the table to clip the inch-long talons shooting out from the ends of his toes. Each nail that flicks against a solid surface sounds like a wrecking ball plummeting through the front of my skull. I shut my eyes for a minute and try to imagine towels soaking in bleach and scalded dishes steaming in dishwasher racks.

When Aunt Zee asks someone to get a few oranges from the yard, Otis volunteers, and I want to plead with him not leave me alone in the middle of this death trap, but he does, and I can already feel Landon's claws dragging through my skin.

"So, how's the national debt going?" Landon asks. "Cut a few more social programs and it's bound to pay off."

"What does that have to do with me?" I ask.

"You know, I can't get a job now with a fuckin' record, you cunt wipe."

Aunt Zee waltzes back in to serve me two jet-black circles next to toast topped with egg yolks so undercooked, they're staring at me like they've just been dropped from their shells, and juice in a Mason jar coated in raw egg residue that she failed to wash off her hands.

"What is this?" I ask.

"Black pudding sausage," she says.

If that's sausage, then Spam must be filet mignon.

"Oddie said you don't like beef, so I used pork," she says.

I should have been more specific: hoof-and-mouth disease has turned me off everything with hooves. And mouths.

I cringe as Landon pops the yolk of his salmonella toast, and the pressure of the membrane makes its innards spurt like a month-old pustule. The puke in my throat's under so much pressure that it's pooling up in my brain cavity.

"You're a walking nervous breakdown. You know, they say OCD's a rich suburban pussy disease."

"I don't have OCD," I say. "OCD would mean I only eat the red Skittles or I wash my hands fifty times in a row."

"You were always lathering up in the break room like you were going in for surgery, and everyone knew you drove home to piss and shit. We all wondered why you didn't just wear a face mask like Michael Jackson." He loads a forkful of dribbling yolk into his face and intentionally lets a yellow streak of slime snake down his chin. "And what's this about getting an AIDS test every time you get a mosquito bite?"

That's not OCD; that's reactive medicine. That's common sense. If everyone could afford it, they would insist their healthcare provider do so after anything penetrated their protective layer.

"I have to piss," he says, getting up from the table and heading toward the yard.

"Oh, yeah," Otis says from the doorway. "We don't have a crapper that works. So if you have to go, I can take to you to the gas station." The two of them stare me down like they're waiting for a nod of understanding.

"What time do you kids want to go to mass today?" Aunt Zee asks.

"Are you Catholic?" I ask. "I don't think I can handle that. There are holy water germ baths evaporating Legionnaires' disease into the air, and you can only imagine how many people touch those wafers before they end up in your mouth. 'Here, have some herpes and/or hepatitis while you sip Christ's blood.' Why don't we all just take a trip to Safeway and eat from the bulk candy bins? Or roll around in hospital bedding? Mmm, staph infection. Look, I'm sure your God as well as the World Health Organization will forgive you for not partaking, knowing that you're actively trying to prevent a twenty-first-century plague." I stare them down hoping for a nod of understanding.

"She's a keeper," Landon says, heading out toward the corner of the yard.

I scratch at the exterior of my throat, wondering why it's so hard to breathe. Otis pulls out a bottle of cough syrup from his jacket pocket like a wino would a flask, and says, "It's got codeine in it."

Before I can comment on how the prescription bottle has Aunt Zee's name on it, I see Landon hosing down the corner of the yard. His gaunt and revoltingly emaciated body makes its way around the garden like a walking corpse; he hocks a loogie, scratches his balls, then drinks from the hose. His comment reverberates in my ears like the squeak of cold car brakes.

Rich, suburban pussy.

As Otis wolfs down his food, I think that maybe this is the status quo for them; maybe they're normal and I'm descended from a clan of freaks. All I really know is that in suburbia, misery flows like filtered water.

***

I escape the Roseville horror, and in the car home, I lie back and let my head dangle over the edge of the front seat. I shut my eyes and listen to Otis fiddle with the cassettes on his lap.

"How come you didn't eat your food?" he asks.

"I'm not a breakfast person," I say.

"What do you want to do now?"

I want rest. I'm tired of the chronic sores on the backs of my hands from all the bleach and rubbing alcohol. I'm tired of having raw cracks in the corners of my mouth that never heal because of all the Listerine. I'm tired of looking at Otis and involuntarily pinpointing all his nooks and crannies that I want to scrub with steel wool and Formula 409.

"Where do you want to go?" he asks.

My clothes are dusted with Aunt Zee's house grime and my skin is coated with her dried piss. The last thing I want to do is go home to my immaculately hygienic apartment where I'd do nothing but contaminate it and have to face the perils of cleaning it, just so I could go to work and come home and do it again.

"Hazel? Where should we go?"

I'm filthy and it's exhausting and disheartening to keep doing this. "Anywhere but here."

He swerves toward the Madison Avenue exit, heads east, and cloverleafs back onto the freeway, this time driving west, back toward Roseville. He hums a few versus of Morrissey, and then laughs about how I-80 leads all the way across the country, from the edge of California to Maryland.

He drives. I doze. We stop at random places to pick up sodas when we're thirsty and candy when we're hungry. When the afternoon heat gets too intense, we pull over and lie beneath the shell of his El Camino camper, staring up at the water-logged ceiling and talking about all the places he can't wait to see when the band hits the road in September. I hear about the history of Riot Venom, how they played a downtown Sac venue called The Warehouse at the beginning of the year and an indie label scout signed them that same night.

When I'm not listening to him, he's listening to me go on about the best live shows I've ever been to, the most memorable of which took place in the basement of a Campbell city building where a bunch of local bands, some formed that night, played on a makeshift stage, and nobody gave a damn about the constant distortion or the horrible acoustics because we were all too stoked about the fact that we were under fifteen and witnessing a real rock show. It isn't fair to compare him to Kree, but I can't help it; Otis understands that intimate connection between music and himself, and when he knows more about music than I do, he challenges me to understand what I don't.

He's a thirty-two-year-old guiltless weirdo who still has action figures in his bed, still wakes up in the middle of the night crying from nightmares he can't remember but willingly admits scared the shit out of him, and he still describes the world with the creative imagination of a child. Earlier today, he felt up the vertebrae in my back and said, "You're so skinny I can feel your stegosaurus."

We drive into the evening, through Nevada and into the heart of Utah. There's a dragging exhaustion in our bodies that turns into delirium, but neither of us want to stop because there's always something else we want to ask or say. I use a penlight to read lyrics that I find on the floor of his car, lines he scribbled on random receipts or show stubs. Though they may have been composed in one of his more shitfaced moments, he can still recall exactly what he meant to convey at the time.

I need a good scrub-down, a toothbrush, and a bottle of bleach, but after a while, I just give up. I drink club soda and that musty feeling in my mouth washes away. I scrub my face at rest stops and it somewhat alleviates the feeling of greasy road grime. We only turn around when we realize that if we don't, we won't make it back to Sacramento in time for work on Monday. He drops me off at my apartment Sunday night and I'm so exhausted that I pass out on the couch in my clothes.

***

I work a few days without any contact with Otis, but I barely notice since the usual work crises keep me tied up. Temp Deli Man, who is standing in for regular Deli Man, catches his fingertips in the slicer and I spend most of my time on the phone arguing with my boss and subsequently headquarters over how much cheaper and less painful it would be if they'd just give me the budget to replace the old slicer with a new high-tech slicer. But no, they'd rather pay out the worker's comp claims and urgent care bills than purchase an improved slicer, which would cost them a percentage of what they're paying out now (plus two Deli People and whoever else was de-fingered in the past would still have all their fingerprints).

"I think you need to pick your battles with this slicer thing," my boss says. "You just got new registers up front and metal toilet paper holders in the cans."

It would go against humanity to not hate this guy, and not just because he's a human padlock. Last Halloween he came into the store dressed as Clark Kent/Superman, and he went up to all the girls from behind, tapped them on the shoulder, and when they turned around, he shouted, "Boom!" as he tore open his white dress shirt and heaved his beefy spandex-covered chest in their faces—an act which, to this day, he refers to as "the Superman experience." Example: "I haven't given the backroom girls the Superman experience yet!"

"You really want to waste a favor over a slicer?" he asks. Not hating this guy, in my mind, is the same as doing jack shit during genocide.

"When it's turning my deli into a *Titus Andronicus* scene..." I say. "Then yeah, I kind of do."

"First you wanted hand sanitizer in the break room, now this. God, Hazel, you're such a tight-ass."

"What!"

"Don't go crying 'sexual harassment' to Legal. I didn't say you have a tight ass. I said you are a tight-ass."

I am the only female manager in his district. I think it pisses him off. Plus, we started in the company as coworkers, went through our management training program together, did our final project together, and then he sold me out during our presentation by saying it would have been more innovative had I not stagnated it with my "play-it-safe" mentality. In a nutshell, our everyday demeanor toward each other has always had fewer boundaries than it should.

"What do I need to do to get this slicer?" I ask.

"Start hanging out with us. Stop being so antisocial." Funny how that's Mom's keyword. "Come out tonight with the rest of the managers. We're going to this bar where they have go-go dancers dancing in cages fifteen feet up in the air."

"This crosses the line of professionalism."

"Tight-ass."

***

Wednesday afternoon I finish a thirteen-hour shift and head for Otis' studio to check up on him. However, when I get inside his complex, there's a stench polluting the hall that makes me think twice about rubbing up against the source. I know it's him, because he's the only thing in the building that could accurately reproduce the smell of dead bodies doused in decomposing sewage. His door's locked, but the wood is so warped that I get inside without much struggle. The lack of air conditioning coupled with the triple-digit summer heat has hot-boxed the pungent odors together and cooked them into a mist I can taste on my tongue.

After breaking through the miscellaneous junk holding the bathroom door shut, I'm slugged with a whiff of toxic bacteria. The air's weighed down with the stink of barnyard shit, hobo piss, and jockstrap sweat. There are broken compact mirrors sprinkled with drug deposits, beer cans littering the floor, and empty liquor bottles lined up against the wall. As if this cesspit couldn't be more festive, there's both dry and fresh puke painting the walls, puddled on the floor, and backed up in the sink.

He's in the bathtub, inert and stony pale. When I slap him for consciousness, I get cold puke on my hand, so to avoid having to touch him, I tap him on the forehead with an empty beer can. When that fails, I haul his 175 pounds of dead weight out of the tub and toward the door, my left arm clenched around his chest and my right clawing at the carpet like a lifeguard towing in a drownee. Actually, he's probably more like 180 pounds with the Southern Comfort and Jack packed into his bladder. Possibly 177 now, because he's unconsciously pissing.

I'm tempted to dump him on the curb of an ER and change my address and phone number, but I call Landon instead.

A short while later, the two of us sit in the ER waiting room pretending to be occupied with our own thoughts. After an hour, he nudges me and says, "I told him he can't have any of my liver 'cause I've already fucked the hell out of it."

"This is ridiculous," I say.

I know I just met Otis a few weeks ago, but he seemed to (for lack of a better phrase) have his shit together better than this, and the recent sucking on cough syrup and binge drinking is making me rethink my initial impression.

"We can't afford the ER, so even if he's puking organs, call me first," Landon says. "And stop giving him your shit to read. I have to decode it for him like a fucking *CliffsNotes*."

"He doesn't understand a lot of things, huh?" I say.

"You can't even pump your own goddamn gas."

"That's different."

"Yeah, 'cause it's common sense. You know how to change a flat?"

"My mom says why go through the trouble when you can just call AAA?"

"You are a prime example of how money reverses Darwinism," he says. "Have you ever had to identify a body?"

"Now you're just being ridiculous."

"Ever been forced to visit a loan shark? Or better yet, been threatened by one?"

"You know what—"

"Name one song by The Misfits."

"*Totalimmortal.*"

"That's AFI, dumb fuck."

"Can you stop calling me that?"

"What year did The Descendents release their first album, dumb fuck?"

"Who?"

"Name a classical guitarist, dumb fuck."

"Clapton."

"Try again, dumb fuck."

Maybe I'm sheltered in a different way. After all, I only recently found out a pacifist is not someone who sucks a pacifier and dominos is an actual game as opposed to just a bunch of tiles stacked in snaking rows and knocked over.

"Fuck, he deserves more than cheap symbolism," Landon says.

***

Friday, August 15th, is an epic date for Riot Venom. They won a Bay Area radio station poll that landed them a spot to play Warped Tour in Mountain View, as a featured local band. They're on a side stage, a toe-jam-reeking building code violation decomposing in the corner of the grounds behind the smoke of a burger tent, although for them, getting into Warped Tour for free overshadows the low billing. After their set, Otis and I pile into the portable "dressing room" where a few of his friends and bandmates pass around meth on a CD case like a basket of bread. Otis, on the other hand, chops up heroin and dives nose-first into the small pile. He tries bringing remnants to my nose but I slap his hand away. It's not just the drugs, but also his dirt, dead skin, sweat, grime, and disease-ridden finger. If I had to break it down, I'd say my problem resides sixty percent with his finger and forty percent the drugs. Maybe it's eighty and twenty. Or maybe it's all about the finger.

"It makes shit fun," he says.

"One, that was probably shat out of some human mule's ass, and two, this is like playing with fire. No, it's like pumping gas in Death Valley wearing a sweater that wasn't washed with fabric softener, while talking on your cell phone and smoking and repeatedly going in and out of your car. You're going to go down in a blanket of flames."

The room rustles like everyone's confused but no one has the patience to mine through a wall of booze and drugs to formulate a response.

"How can heroin catch me on fire?" Otis asks.

I head outside to catch my breath.

"You need to mellow the fuck out or get the fuck out," Landon says from the doorway. "Besides," he stutters with a cigarette balancing between his teeth, "anything he does goes through me. That shit's so diluted, he hasn't had that much Carnation since he was a baby."

***

Since they'd already seen Warped in SF at the beginning of summer, we ditch the rest of the festival for the opening night of the state fair, a place that affords a much cheaper assortment of concessions. As Landon says: "Kids not only have to pay an arm and a leg to get in, but they have to shell out twelve bucks for shit beer and six for a hot dog the size of Cheney's dick. Fuck Warped Tour. You can get drunk for half price here."

In all my years of living in Sac, though, the state fair's never been something I've braved because the thought of carnies—with their back tits, beer bellies, and body hair heaving over the food they're serving up—is more than I can stomach. But when we get inside, the atmosphere is much more civilized than the run-of-the-mill traveling carnival I imagined. There are stands selling vegan snacks, organic farmers selling produce, and though there is a side of the CalExpo property devoted to farm animals, there are also art displays and architectural models and California vendors sampling eco-friendly jams and cheeses.

Otis and I migrate through the expansive carnival sampling onion rings, fried Oreos, fried candy bars, fried artichoke hearts, fried Coke, and whatever else someone could think of battering and frying. We inject warm Twinkie cream into each other's mouths and slather it over our teeth before rinsing it all down with lukewarm beer. I've never been much of a drinker, but it's different this time around because everyone else is doing it and it's easier to endure Otis' booze-laced kiss if I taste the same.

And like so many brown pubes spoiling the victorious shine of my white countertops and porcelain toilet, I see it. I see him: Kree with his brown hair poking out of his head every which way, sucking a Slurpee through a straw wedged in the corner of his mouth, a half smile peeking out of the straw-less side. Everything about the sight of him infuriates me, from his reddened lips stained with cherry Slurpee dye to his untied Converse dragging what were once white laces but are now blackened grime magnets that probably leave dark trails behind because he's the type to walk obliviously onto white carpet with dirty shoes.

When he notices me, he charges in our direction. I worm my hand out of Otis' sweaty grip and meet Kree halfway, hoping to keep this former world separate from my new one. However, it's hard to formulate a greeting when the booze buzz puts normal function on the back burner. Kree's always spoken quickly, but listening to him behind a wall of sugar and alcohol makes him sound like a fast-forwarded episode of *Alvin and the Chipmunks*. While he squeals that it's good to see me outside of the apartment, I realize how unusual he looks. His skin's cleared up, his eyes seem vibrantly blue, and the tire around his waist has flattened. I get the unruly temptation to ask him who he's torturing with his pubes, chest hair, and skid marks now. "Why are you here?" I ask instead.

"Smash Mouth's playing."

"Oh."

"What are you doing? It's like you're drunk or something." He emphasizes the word "drunk" like he wants to broadcast to Mom, a hundred miles away, that I'm under the influence. "Who's that?" He motions toward Otis.

"Some guy."

"What's his name?"

"Otis."

"Like the cookies?" he laughs.

"Yeah."

"Like Otis and Milo?"

"It's *Milo and Otis*." I think we've spent way too much time together.

"No, Otis and Milo."

"Oh, cut the chit-chatting crap. What do you want? You want to make me feel bad? Go ahead, tell my mom so I won't have to."

There's something about Kree and everything associated with him—Newark and college and the jobs I've worked throughout the years—that brings out this seething hate in me. I just got done watching my boyfriend, or whatever Otis is, play Warped Tour, and I'm eating public food that actually tastes pretty good and drinking beer on tap and I haven't thought about the shackles of Safeway or Mom all night, and at first sight of Kree, all that aggression is back with a vengeance because I'd put it down for a moment and forgot how to gracefully contain it.

"You're my biggest mistake," I say.

His eyes relax into soft crescents like he realizes he shouldn't have wasted his time. "I'm not going to tell your mom," he says. "I'm happy for you. You deserve to be with someone." He smiles before reaching for my shoulder to squeeze. "Just don't go changing everything about yourself."

Oh, here it comes, let the shooting star fly overhead as he delivers the public service message about staying true to myself.

"Come here."

I admit smelling bad since Otis christened me with his sweat, spit, and whatever other bodily fluids I can't think of at the moment.

"I don't care." He coaxes me against him and even though the fireworks snap above us in the sky, he doesn't move, not even to glance up. "So what have you been up to?"

"Work," I say. "It's refreshing to make money that isn't sucked into your black hole."

"Oh." He laughs. "Buy anything cool?"

"No." But I should have, and I regret not doing it because then I could burn him back with some remark about getting to buy something I've always wanted but could never afford because he was too busy spending my money on useless crap like a massaging chair that he used to get drunk and pass out in. I bet Otis would never choose a massaging chair over my kicking and whacking.

"You still write?"

"Something like that."

"You should just quit Safeway and figure out a way to live off of it."

I press my face against the vibrations resonating from his chest and deny that I want him to ask me to go home with him. The thing about him is that he's familiar and I know exactly what to expect from him day in, day out, and there's nothing about him that's truly a menace, except maybe the pubes.

"Yuck, you hella smell." He lets go and stares at his arms like I've left garbage water on them.

I shove him against a concession stand and weave through the swarms of patrons and mobile snack vendors looking for Otis. He's lying on a random patch of grass on his back, flailing his arms and legs back and forth trying to make a grass angel. The other members of the band and their respective girlfriends are scattered beside him, aiming popcorn at his open mouth.

When I get to him, I lean over his chest to watch the firework embers reflect in his eyes. When the fireworks stop, I turn over to gaze at the octopus-shaped smoke clouds dissipating downwind and the images are replaced with a close-up of Landon's girlfriend Evie as she pounces and horizontally pins my hips between hers and Otis' stomach. She's Edie Sedgwick-thin with shoulder-length black hair, and the only features of her body that are truly fleshy are her wide-smiling lips and free-rolling chest.

"Are you really that pale or is that foundation?" she asks, dropping her face toward mine till we're close enough that I can see the crust in her eyebrow piercings ripple when she wrinkles her temple. My eyes unintentionally do a quick dot-to-dot exploration of the piercings in her face: she has two juxtaposed through her left eyebrow, a ring through her nose, one through the side of her lip, countless others through her ear lobes and cartilage, and I'm pretty sure the protrusions poking through her shirt at the very peaks of her braless chest are piercings. I don't want to visualize what might be dangling between her thighs, thighs that work their way upward to straddle my stomach.

"Do you want to come to my piercing party?" she asks. Before I can ask what that is, not that it isn't self-explanatory, she crams her tongue so far in my mouth that it high-fives my tonsils on the way to my stomach. I feel the cracks in the corners of my mouth stretch to capacity and split painfully as she maneuvers her lips in between mine, my tongue held hostage by hers as it meanders around in my face. The ring in her lip and the barbell in her tongue clank against my teeth and I taste metal. I spasm and almost hurl upward against gravity into her mouth, but I refrain, pushing a palm against her throat and one into her chest to shuck her mouth-vacuum off my face. She's winded when she pulls back, smiling and licking her lips of leftover Twinkie cream. "I always kiss the new one."

Regardless of what that means, I hurl her tiny frame off my body and dump my bag's contents onto the grass, searching for my travel-sized bottle of Listerine, hoping it isn't too late to eradicate any herpes spores. Since it's empty, I gargle with beer to prevent anything from setting up camp in my vulnerable mouth tissue. It's nauseating to realize her mouth was on Landon's a few seconds ago. This is no ordinary herpes, but demonic herpes whose lesions will sprout hooves and horns.

***

Sunday morning Otis hollers from the hall about coming out to play. We'd planned to hang out all weekend, but yesterday morning I received a call from my boss about how they were replacing the old slicer with the high-tech one I'd fought for, and even though it was a Saturday, I had to go in and revel in my victory. Today Otis is sane, sober, and smells like Tide. I assume we're off to Roseville again for breakfast, but he drives me to a seedy blood bank instead. "Can't I donate twenty bucks instead?" I ask the nurse, desperate to find a loophole. "You're going to give me HIV." My need for a Clorox bath is escalating; I'd even drink it if it could sterilize me from the inside out.

"I assure you, we're all professionals here," the nurse says, leading us inside.

"And I assure you, the idiots amputating the wrong limbs call themselves professionals too," I say.

She ignores my comment as she punctures the surface of Otis' blue vein, his blood vacuumed out through a hair-thin tube that empties into a gurgling sack. Otis is too hypnotized by the sight of his own blood to realize that he's sporting a partial boner in clear view. Apparently, there's something about the sight of blood that gets him off, so the trip here was less about wanting to earn a star for good citizenship and more about using it as a means for cheap arousal.

I don't object when he says he wants to go back to church for another funeral; at least I know he can't do anything screwy in a place like that, although the first thing he does when we sit back against the pew is grab a Bible and cut up lines of heroin on the cover. This time, it looks as if Landon cut it with chocolate Nesquik.

I stare straight ahead, trying to get over the fact that he's snorting heroin in the middle of a funeral and we just came from a blood bank, a place he treated like a coin-operated peepshow. And, no, normal people don't go to coin-operated peepshows, but the blood bank situation makes the perverts who frequent coin-operated peepshows seem normal in comparison.

"I can feel Jesus in my veins," he says in between sniffles. "He's smiling in my blood." He reaches out to hold my hand and runs his thumb over the rugged scales on the back of my knuckles: their surface is flaking and cracked, and there are red spots where the skin grew over my bleeding pores. But instead of saying anything, he licks the face of the Bible and leans his head against my shoulder.

***

At home we lie in my bed, distantly quiet. We're naked, spooning, but nothing's happening. All the time we've spent together in bed mostly consisted of just sleeping and kissing. Doing more than that has been a challenge (sober at least), with his phobia of leaving things behind, and I have yet to get over the thought of his microbes teeming in every dribble of his saliva.

Though last week, I woke in the middle of the night to him touching me, and he stopped whenever I stirred, so I pretended to sleep. He was bold enough to jerk off for a few minutes, but I think he was too drunk, because he fell asleep in midstroke. The following night, he made it over the hump and brought himself to come against my back. I shivered in the air-conditioned room as his warm spurts snaked down my side and met the mattress. It was weird but nice, because no one's ever done that to me before, not that it'd be something I'd admittedly want, but it's nice to know someone thinks of me that way.

"Come with us," he says to me.

Ever since he mentioned that Riot Venom would leave town to tour, I've been waiting for him to ask, even if I had no intention of going. "You know I can't."

"Why?"

"My whole life is here."

"Like what?"

"Work."

"Fuck work, you know you're coming."

"I can't pick up and leave."

"Everybody else is."

"I just got a slicer at work. Do you know how huge that is for me? All those years and no cigar, and now I have a slicer." And though he's been this ethereal glimpse into a strange alternative world, I can't throw my life's work away for someone who doesn't recognize the importance of showering every day. "And how hard is it to keep your piss in the toilet?" I ask suddenly. "It'd be different if you were seven feet tall and there were three feet between your dick and the water."

"What?"

"Nothing."

"Think about it more. This'll get us out of this shithole."

"What do I need getting out of?" I'm not a high-school dropout working in a jumpsuit with my name embroidered on the pocket.

I roll away from him and pretend to fall asleep, but I involuntarily twitch every time he talks, sprinkling my back with spit. "Have you ever thought about getting your shit out there?" he asks. "Like making a book?"

"Writers are shit out of luck unless they're Harry Potter or some self-help douche."

"You're never going to get out of here unless you quit acting all high society," he says. "You really want to be like them?"

"There is nothing wrong with them. How would you know? You don't have parents."

It stuns him. Even I felt the blow. "When you die, everything you write will disappear," he says. "But if it's out there, it'll live forever. Landon says it doesn't matter if only a few people know your music 'cause it's still part of the movement, and after it gets out there, it gets bigger than the person that made it. Everybody out there will fly with it and then write new shit, and that's how everything keeps going. Don't you want to keep shit going?"

"I don't want to dwell on what I need to forget."

"We feel the highest and the lowest. Why would we want to be stuck in the middle and never feel anything?" For a high-school dropout, he can really organize a thought when he wants to. "You come with me and we'll be everything we're supposed to be," he says. "I been off my meds for a while." I don't know what that means. All I really know is that I'm an easily replaceable industrialized slave, and though Riot Venom have an innovative sound and stage presence, it probably won't get them farther than the East Bay, and in five or six months, I see myself walking into Walmart and finding him and Landon greeting me at the door. It's sickening to think I might be somehow involved in a future like that, supporting Otis the way I supported Kree through his decade-long failed pipedream. "Did you hear me? It's just me now."

After everything I've endured over the years, it shouldn't be this hard to go with him, but when he says, "It's just me now," I'm not sure what that means, and it's not enough to make the decision any easier.

Sipping Kool-Aid

Friday night Landon jumps out from behind my car in the parking lot of Safeway. Having lived amid a steady stream of drive-bys, intuition sends me diving over the hood for cover.

"Fuck, you need to be sedated," he says and picks my keys up from the ground, then turns them around in his palm. "What's with the whistle?"

"It's a rape whistle," I say.

"Who the fuck would want to rape you?" He should have punched me instead.

When I unlock the car, he hops into the passenger side and squirms around against the upholstery as if purposely trying to get a reaction out of me. "God, this place was fascist even with the union," he says. "Broomsticks went missing on your watch 'cause they were shoved so far up your ass. I bet you can tell me all about unilateralism and rogue states..."

"Again, what does that even—"

"...but you can't tell me dick about working-class exploitation."

I'm too worn out from a fourteen-hour salaried shift filled with frivolous worker's comp claims, employee relations crap, vendor nightmares, customer complaints, and the nuances in-between (an audit from Cal/OSHA and, subsequently, my boss, who'd come out to check the dust levels on the shelves and the new slicer in all its glory), to care what else he resents me for. At the same time, I don't want to stop bickering with him because once I do, he'll tell me what's happened over the last two days, like what Otis might have done after I told him I wasn't going with him. Or more importantly, whom he's done.

"What do you want?" I ask.

"He's been off his meds for a while, so you'd better be there when he's got the noose around his neck."

At least we've gained one back from the zombie-eyed medicated population.

"Or the gun to his head," he says. "Or a razor to his wrists."

"What are you—"

He interrupts me when he answers his buzzing cell phone. "Is this fake? Or like the time I found out my parents were dead?" he asks. "Okay, okay...I'll be home in a bit." He hangs up, tossing the phone across the dashboard. "He just tried hanging himself in the garage, but there was so much crap in there that he couldn't step off anything to actually hang. Have to give him credit for trying." He laughs.

"You seem to have a pretty jaded view of death," I say.

"Over the years I've learned a shitload about killing yourself. You know you have to cut into the main artery in your neck if you want to do any real damage? And you only lose a pint of blood when you slit your wrists."

"When did it all go downhill? You know, when did you lose your innocence?"

"Don't start that bullshit with me."

"You're just so...bitter."

"If anything, I never had any."

"There's so much out there that dissolves a person's substance..." I can't even remember a time when I wasn't constantly on the defense against people like him, I don't remember a time when I had a comfortable meal at the dinner table with my family and actually ate the food, and I don't remember the last time I was enthusiastic about the people I work with or for. "We've become machines without direction," I say. "The living envy the dead."

"Holy fuck. Don't you have any self-control?"

"Want to know when I lost mine?"

"Please shut up."

"It was probably in college when I started giving too much of a damn. Maybe earlier." I've been staring at the streetlight for so long that when I turn to look at him, all I see is a fuzzy white ball of light in place of his face. "Maybe none of the pieces ever fit, like the puzzle was fundamentally fucked from the start and now it's just a matter of endurance."

"So you coming with us or what?" he asks.

"You weren't even listening."

"I'm not going to sit here enduring your existential crisis unless you fork over ninety dollars for the hour of my time you're wasting. That's the going rate these days; that's what we used to pay Otis' therapist before he *randomly* decided he didn't want to be controlled anymore. You know what it's like when someone like him is off stabilizing drugs? Do everybody a favor and read less Aldous Huxley and more *SF Chronicle*."

I can't intelligently respond when I've never really been sure what "existential crisis" even means. As it is, I barely understand half the shit that comes out of his mouth. *You're a twenty-first-century genuine example of society's misanthrope* this, *that was the most pejorative thing I've ever heard, you raging right-wing* that.

"Evie got a job as a tech, that's the reason she gets to come," he says. "But you, fuck dude, I had to suck so much dick to get you on this tour."

"Really?"

"Fuck, no. I'm saying you laid the dynamite, you damn well better be there when the building goes down."

"I—"

"All you have to do is make sure he's on stage every night." He stalls to flick his tongue over his lip piercing. "I care about him, but I need my own time, and if you're both picking daffodils and making spice cake together, isn't everyone better off?"

This visit of his feels less about me and more about him and his comfort, like I owe him some favor. Not only do I not owe him any favors, but it'd be kind of nice to see him suffer. As much as possible.

***

At home, the answering machine flashes as if subliminally trying to warn me to run while I still have the chance. "6, 6, 6," it flickers. I erase the messages and call Mom before she pounces again. "Are you networking?" she asks immediately. "I hear that's the only way to move up these days."

As she drones on, I cram fistfuls of chocolate chips into my mouth and mentally shuffle through the events of the day from the OSHA inspector dinging my score for the weathered "warning" stickers on the baler to the customer bitching me out for the shortage of fifteen-bean soup mix. I remind myself that it'll all be worth it because Landon will suffer.

***

"Who do you think is the most important member of a band?" Evie asks.

"Unless you're Meg White, it's the drummer," I say.

"And like management, the drummer's the easiest one to replace," Landon says.

It's Otis' last weekend in town, and he invites me to dinner with him, Landon, Evie, and Aunt Zee at their favorite country buffet in Roseville (in other words, a wall-to-wall pit of health code violations and food poisoning). I pretend to eat by cutting up my food and slipping it into napkins while the rest of them voluntarily pack down their platefuls of botulism without hesitation. Landon returns from his third trip to the meat trough and sets down three plates of fried chicken, ribs, and slabs of junk beef.

"You look after that brother of yours," Aunt Zee says to Landon. "You never know when he'll step off a sidewalk and accidentally get himself killed."

"I will," he says.

He holds to Evie's mouth what the restaurant claims is "steak" and observes with an erotic expression as she tears at it like a starved beast. She returns the favor by spooning mashed potatoes into his mouth, removing the utensil after every bite to replace it with her tongue. Then they squabble over a pile of chicken skin. After dividing up heaps of skin and batter, they initiate a countdown before packing the greasy waste into their mouths with their fingers. I shouldn't watch, but that's like trying to look away while a mooing cow is fed into a processor.

"Baby, get more chicken legs," Evie says to Landon.

"Are your legs painted on?" He accidentally sprays potato on her when he speaks, and she scrapes it off her skin with her finger and eats it.

Landon acts confident and egotistical, but he follows her around like a helpless puppy craving affection. Lots of it. Eventually, he caves, gets more chicken, and returns to hand-feed her the skin wrapped around blocks of cheese. The grease drips off their chins in shimmering trails and they take turns licking it off each other without any regard for the rest of us.

"I just got rid of two weeks' worth of stubble and when I lick my face, it feels like a shaved pussy," he says.

"You people make me sick," I say.

"So be honest," he says, "did you vote the Terminator into office just 'cause he's Republican? You know, support your guy even if his career highlight is winning first place at Mr. Universe?"

"What is your deal with Republicans?" I ask.

"I want to beat your elephant ass," he says.

Having been called *fat* for the last time, I use Otis as a stepping stool and lurch for Landon's stringy throat, but before I can inflict any damage, he gets his greasy fingers curled around my neck, and we yank at each other till we're bowed against the booth screaming obscenities. I let go when I realize that neither of us is proving anything.

"I can exterminate you with a clove of garlic," he says.

I turn to Otis for support, but he's doing what he's done all night, spacing out and chewing cattle fat with an unruffled expression on his face. I guess this is Otis, off the meds.

***

After dinner I kneel on the floor of my apartment sifting through the albums we've fooled around to. "*Ixnay on the Hombre, Stranger than Fiction, ...And Out Come the Wolves, The Art of Drowning*." The sight of rib sauce dried in the corners of his mouth makes me smile. "Something Social D?" I straddle him against the couch and run my fingers over his crotch, hoping to spur a reaction. When I reach for his pants zipper, he lifts my hands away and wiggles out from under me.

"I'm getting rid of my apartment," he says. "I'm never coming back to Sacramento."

"Okay." At least I think that's what I said; it might have been more of a crackling choke of inaudible gurgles. "So you're going to live on the road?" I ask. "Permanently? Like that'll be your address? Forever." I'm stumbling and I may sound desperately sarcastic.

"I'll be gone for months. A lot can happen in that time. We shouldn't see each other anymore. We'll make it painless. Like a clean break." There's a calmness in his voice that lacks sincerity, and maybe I've just been thrust into breakup denial, but those sentences, no matter how simple, do not sound like ideas Otis could ever piece together on his own.

After he leaves I sit for a while in the strange silence. The room still smells like him, his natural scent masked in buffet grease. I page through my memory for any advice I might have received throughout the years. Of course, the only voice I hear is Mom's. "Happiness is a choice, so think happy thoughts," she said to me throughout high school and college, but I wish she'd realized that I wasn't trying to fucking fly; I was trying not to drown.

***

"Did you get lost?" Mom asks. "They didn't teach you how to read a map in first grade?" Maybe my problem isn't that I'm easily distracted or that I persistently zone out, it's that I'm so fucking deaf from all the years of her screaming that I don't hear anyone talking to me. I'm late today for the family's summer-end picnic. I sat outside in my car for an hour listening to *The Living End,* hoping to gain some enlightenment or defense that I could take with me to armor myself in this yard filled with cannibalistic wolves.

"You need to apply for a makeover from one of those cable reality shows," Mom says. "It looks like a blind stylist cut your hair with a sickle." It's a struggle to keep up with her as we head toward the backyard. Her elfin figure, though aged into its sixties, is still pole-thin and curveless and has maintained the energy and zing to badger me while power-walking in the opposite direction.

After applying a third layer of SPF 45 and accepting that I will inescapably die of skin cancer, I tighten my hood strings around my chin and step out of the shade into the doom of the sun's radioactive rays. The worst part about being in the midst of my family and their friends is having to feign optimism and pretend to be, drum roll please, happy and satisfied with life. I'm silent at the picnic table, hoping to fly under the radar for the remainder of the afternoon, but it's hard when Mom's at my side jabbing me with her elbow the whole time.

"How much did you weigh again when you gave birth?" she asks my cousin.

"A hundred and nine pounds," she says.

"I get it," I say. "I weigh more than that and I'm not nine months pregnant."

"Imagine what you'll weigh when you are," Mom says.

My eyes roll so far back that I think I strain a tendon. I come from a long line of gymnasts, and rivalry and humiliating comparisons among family members are as natural to our family as hugs and kisses are to most others.

"Do you want a gift certificate to a salon for Christmas?" Auntie asks. "Even ugly people can get help with a makeover."

"Sorry...what?" I ask, thinking I imagined it.

"I said even ugly—"

"Thanks. That's, um, really inspirational," I say.

"Your uncle made you a chicken burger because he knows you don't eat beef," Mom says, placing the burger on my lap. "Eat it." The heat from the burger seeps through the flimsy paper plate and onto my thighs. "Right now." I can almost hear the salmonella seething in the meat juices. "He went out of his way to accommodate you, you weirdo." She of all people knows I don't do chicken, and definitely not group food. "Eat it or you're getting the macaroni salad." She also knows I don't do mayonnaise-based salads, and she's using it as ammunition.

I pick up the burger and hold it to my lips, but I'm bombarded by images of pink, gelatinous undercooked meat dripping with salmonella juices. I don't remember the last time I ate a piece of meat, but I also don't remember the last time Mom hovered above me with her arms on her hips, telling me to hurry up and gorge myself on undercooked meat filled with purple veins (because that's what chickens have, veins filled with salmonella and growth hormones), all because she doesn't want me to "embarrass" her in front of the family. And then she ups the terrorism by threatening me with the macaroni salad, but what she doesn't realize is that there's already mayonnaise in this chicken burger, because my uncle put it in there, or maybe *she* put it in there just to fuck with me. I have to get out of here. I have to escape the eighty-five-pound freaks, the chicken, the mayonnaise.

"Otis would never make me eat mayonnaise!" I shout suddenly.

The yard's conversations stop and everybody looks in our direction. I inhale and hold my breath to keep from combusting again. It's quiet. I figure I better try and fix it because it appears that Mom's about to have an aneurism. I pick up the burger and bring it to my lips, but I don't make it very far because the convulsions overtake my upper half. The only sounds resonating through the yard are birds chirping and my dry-heaving.

***

The chicken burger will no doubt take a permanent place on Mom's checklist of damnations, but I try to appease her by agreeing to meet Newark's former neighborhood Torture Twins for dinner in Danville. It's been years since I've been in contact with either Teresa or Elizabeth. They catch me off-guard at the dinner table with an enthusiastic compliment on how good I look, as if they don't remember preying on me throughout high school. Either they've genuinely matured, or they've found new victims from which to suck self-esteem.

"Oh my God, I, like, totally hit a guy with my car today," Teresa says. "He, like, bounced over my hood, hit the windshield, and plopped off the side. It was freakin' hilarious. I could barely drive away 'cause I was laughing so hard."

"That's hilarious," Elizabeth says. "Was he all right?"

"Someone ran over to help him up, so I figured he was okay."

"You just drove off?" I ask, cranking my jaw back into place.

"He was fine."

"I know, but—"

"So are you still, like, gothic and depressed?" she asks. "I remember in high school you were always dressed like you were going to a funeral."

"I was never gothic, or depressed."

"Yeah, remember that one time Winnie came up to you and was, like, 'You'd be better off if you killed yourself'?" Elizabeth asks.

"I don't remember that," I say.

"You don't?"

"No." I break open my menu, hoping they'll drop the interrogation and open theirs.

"How can you not remember something like that?"

"I just don't." Or maybe I do, but fuck, enough shit goes down in a teenager's adolescence (the standard confusion over life, the misery brought on by parents' sadistic expectations to excel) in addition to whatever else went down in the '90s that could significantly warp an impressionable kid—the Gulf War, the Soviet Union collapse, the Oklahoma, Georgia, and Kaczynski bombings, not to mention Columbine—and I really want to know how uprooting any of this (especially the part where Winnie said that I should kill myself) could possibly do anyone any good when we're all still trying to get over how horrifying our twenties were, much less what went down in our teens.

"Twenty-two dollars for a salad?" I say, trying to change the subject. "It better be garnished with diamonds."

"You don't remember her saying that?" Elizabeth asks.

"No, I remember now," Teresa says. "Winnie came up to us and was all, 'Hazel would be better off if she killed herself 'cause it would do the world a big favor.' She never said it to her face. Right?" She looks to me for confirmation.

"Oh," Elizabeth says. "Hey, but remember how she'd always ask you how the suicidal cult was doing? And she'd chase you around campus screaming, 'Drink the Kool-Aid!' and everyone would call you Hazel Nut Job."

This is why people go into work one day with a shotgun. This is why people turn to the masses and drink Kool-Aid. This is one of the reasons behind Chuck Palahnuik's conceptualization of Project Mayhem. I scratch at my neck, hoping the conversation has run its course.

"So are you still a manager at Safeway?" Teresa asks. "That's cool. You can, like, boss people around and, like, make them do stuff."

"Something like that," I say, wondering how much a glass of wine is. Or a bottle.

"I hear retail is grunt work. It's all about finding a trust fund," Elizabeth says. "You marry that and you can stay home eating Godiva and watching *Oprah*."

"I'd pick up golf or tennis full-time," Teresa says. She drops into deep thought like she's trying to solve the problems with Social Security. "Definitely tennis. The clothes are hotter."

"Hey, have you guys ever seen an uncircumcised penis?" Elizabeth says. "The last guy I went out with totally had one. I didn't even think things like that still existed. It's so freaking nasty. If they don't wash it every day, they get like crusty, greasy stuff collecting in it."

No matter how hard I try to distract myself from the flashes of diseased crust on what I think an uncircumcised penis looks like, I can't. Coffee and chocolate erupt from my stomach. I press my hand against my mouth, but it creates a pressure that makes the upchuck stream across my cheeks. "I have to go," I say. "I need a steam clean or something."

They're glaring at me the way they always have, like I'm some freak of nature they'll talk shit about after I leave. I'm sure they do. I want to ask Mom if this is what she wants me to be: a girl who terrorizes the unpopular kids and only worries about uncircumcised dick gunk and hunting down trust funds. If it is, then I think she's the one who needs therapy.

***

I decide to spend the night in Newark instead of driving back to Sacramento, but I quickly come to the agonizing realization that I'm in the city of Newark, in my parents' house. In other words, I'm trapped in an enclave of an enclave. Mom and Dad are watching *Law and Order* and my brother escaped the cellblock hours ago, which leaves me buzzing alone in my room with a bottle of spiced rum I found wedged in the back of Mom's cupboards.

I wonder what Otis is doing right now, if he's packing, if he's buying travel supplies, or if he's telling some other girl how he jacks off to her. I traded him in for a slicer. A grocery store deli counter slicer. That's the only thing I'll have to tell future generations about. That was my sole impact on the world, my humanitarian contribution: my life's efforts came down to a motherfucking slicer. Something has to give, and it has to be more than a deli slicer.

I ditch Newark so quickly, I think I leave my bedroom light on. A lifetime of never teetering over sixty-five miles an hour, and tonight I careen at ninety up the freeways from Newark to Roseville. Captain Morgan and I almost make the eleven o'clock news when I nearly collide with a street post.

When I get up to the house, I ram my way over the sidewalk and into the yard. A tree stump or car motor or something solid and unwavering boosts the right half of my Camry upward, and the wheels spin without traction. I shut off the engine and force open the driver's side door. The ground is closer than I remember, so I roll off the driver's seat and into a pile of junk. I kick my way through the yard, break a few pieces off a once-white-and-now-blackened picket fence, and trample through a jungle of dried thorn brush toward the back end of the house.

The light from the corner window pours into the yard with the same intensity as the stereo, which is currently blasting The Dead Kennedys, and in between tracks, I hear Landon and Evie going at it. I play back images of that carnivore, recalling how I tried to handle him civilly and how it all collectively failed. I don't think there's anything rational about this, and it may be melodramatic, but as I put my elbow through his bedroom window, in my head I scream the words: "Suburban OCD *this*, you dickhole!"

I clear the remaining glass with my foot and dive headfirst into the cluttered sty. He's on the bed crouched over Evie like a frog, and they're ass-naked slathered in something unidentifiable, something glistening—probably chicken grease. "What the fuck?" he asks. I grab random shit off his shelves, geodes and books and who knows what else, and launch them at his face. "What are you on?"

I make a fist, maybe to try and punch him even though I've never punched anything before, but when I squeeze my fingers into my palm, my forearm muscle snaps and sends a sharp jolt up the length of my arm. There's an open six-inch gash running from the fold of my elbow to the backside of my forearm. My knees give and I flop into a loose ball against the dirty laundry scattered on the floor.

"Not on my Pennywise shirt," Landon says. The laundry shifts under my weight as he yanks something out from under me. "Goddamnit, you're bleeding all over Dropkick Murphys, too. Here, bleed on Paramore."

"Hey, that's mine," Evie says.

I roll away from them and feel my cheek meet the crunchy carpet. When I cough, a cloud of dust hurtles off the floor and settles on a chemistry book a few inches from my mouth. The rum sloshes against the walls of my stomach and I puke generously all over the book.

I want to go to the hospital, but Landon says they'll ask questions, and when I ask him what kind of questions, he says, "The kind of questions they ask a drunk drama queen with her arm slit the correct way."

"Correct way?"

"The way that gets you a 72-hour hold in the psych ward." He helps me into his bed, and although it's over ninety degrees in the room, I shiver at the thought of a million bacteria parading through the breach in my skin. He breaks out his first aid kit (a cardboard box filled with Band-Aids, gauze, and needles), and then sews me up like a dress torn at the seams.

It's a miserable night, mostly spent puking into a bucket against the side of his bed. And not only do the blankets reek of stale chicken and stick to my skin, but I'm covered in a parasitic sprinkle of fleas as they leap around my exposed regions in a blood-sucking parade. I groan as I scratch at the swollen lesions on my arms, neck, and face. I'm slumped against the mattress like a rotten mushroom, and everything about the

86

place reeks: the sheets, the carpet, the air, and probably me. I sleep on and off, and get up only when the heat in the house becomes unbearable.

Landon and I idle on the front porch, staring at my car parked diagonally across the industrial slum of a yard. "You're a Lit song now, meaning you're practically one of us," he says. "Your car is in the front yard, you slept with your clothes on, and you came in through my window last night."

"And I'm gone," I say, finishing off the last of the lyrics. "Fuck."

"You're going to forfeit that pension and go buy a suitcase."

***

It's Monday afternoon. I should have been at work hours ago. As I head back into Sacramento, I sift through all the employee excuses I've heard over the years about being late or failing to show up for a shift: "I overslept" or "I was in jail" or "I am in jail and this is my one phone call, so you should realize how much I need this job and you shouldn't hold this absence against me."

As I drive, my old life seems to fade. I see a picture with progressive movement and sound, but nothing irritates me to the point of an apocalyptic meltdown. Fits of road rage usually surface at the slightest inconvenience, but now I experience a mellow indifference. Maybe it's because I'm too busy planning out the rest of the day, how I'm going to drive to the post office and stop the mail, put in my resignation papers, collect my final pay, buy a cell phone, and clear the drugstore's supply of hand sanitizer, bleach, sunscreen, Clorox wipes, Pine-Sol, Brillo pads, pencils, and Post-Its. And I do.

It's a true test of Zen when I get a call from Mom, who probes about why I took off so fast last night.

"And when are you going to go out with some friends, mole?" she asks.

See, the nagging rolls right off my back.

"And get a tan, albino."

Kind of.

***

That night, Otis and I jump the fence of a Roseville cemetery. We lie between a few cemetery plots, letting the early Indian summer rain pelt against our faces. He fingers the makeshift stitches running the length of my arm and curiously pokes a nail or two into the wound. "You scared the hell of out Landon," he says.

We spend the night groping each other on the floor of the mausoleum, kissing till our lips are ready to bleed, and sipping Slurpee and whiskey concoctions. In the parking lot we outline each other with soggy chalk and creatively tag our positions with titles like "Suicide by Cop," "Speedball Overdose," and his favorite that he made up for himself, "Death by Sodomy." As I lie on my back, outlined as a puke drownee, he dangles a tarnished locket above my face. He's torn off its front half and in its place he has glued one of his molars—still intact with crusty remnants of gum and blood—that he ripped from his mouth sometime in middle school.

"Did you know teeth are the last thing in your body that decays?" he asks.

I examine it in the dim street lighting, run the pad of my thumb over the ridges of the tooth, and close my hand around it. I have no job, no health insurance, and I'm about to leave the confines of Northern California with a bunch of musicians; but I have his tooth, a big one, and in my palm it feels like more than just collateral—it's comfort.

Part III

Self-Titled

Back on the first Tuesday of September, we drove to Santa Rosa, met up with the other lineups on the tour, and boarded a monstrosity of a bus. We inched down the edge of California, heading through San Jose, San Luis Obispo, LA, and Long Beach, and played venues ranging from bohemian and modern to ghetto and primeval.

Now, a week later, I'm in the middle stall of a truck stop bathroom somewhere on the outskirts of San Diego when it hits me: there's no easing into tour life, nobody circulates a handbook outlining what to expect, and there isn't a disclaimer sticker on the creaky tour bus door that says, "warning, leave all expectation of privacy, sanitary shower and bathroom opportunities, and uninterrupted sleep behind."

Everything's sprawled out in public display, from where I'm expected to sleep (I share a bunk at the back end of an exhaust-filled bus with Otis), to where I'm supposed to...go (public rest stops, where wind drafts blow between my legs as I attempt to concentrate). Evie has no trouble concentrating, of course, nor does she have any sense of privacy or boundaries, because right now, she's on the other side of the wall, attempting to strike up a conversation with me as we piss. "Landon won't let me be a SuicideGirl 'cause he doesn't want a million guys spanking it to me," she says. "And he won't let me work at the porn rental store 'cause he said everything I touch will have some douche bag's screw juice on it, and he said I was covered in enough of that at the sperm bank. And he wouldn't let me be a cocktail girl at the Indian casinos 'cause he said he didn't want a bunch of drunk asshole gamblers grabbing my ass."

I wish she would stop trying to talk to me while my pants are at my ankles and the muscles in my thighs are twitching from holding myself in a squat.

"I keep telling Landon we'd save so much money if I worked at the porn place because I'd get employee discounts," she says. "This one time, we paid a shitload to get this one with guy-on-chicken action, and it went to waste 'cause we couldn't get into it. It was too freaky."

Chicken porn. That's just asking for a salmonella and avian flu outbreak.

"It was so kinky, even Otis watched it. The poor thing probably died from being rammed for so long. I wonder if they cooked it up and ate it afterwards, spooge and all."

At first impression, Evie comes off as vicious and unapproachable, but she's really more of an air-headed indie rock princess covered in spikes, makeup, chains, piercings, and a sprinkle of tattoos, all of which are fueled by an outrageously perverted mind that Landon feeds off of and vice versa. "You into tromboning?" she asks. "Like, where you eat out his ass and reach around the world to jack him off? I can teach you how to milk the prostate. Landon showed me in high school."

I give up on pissing, pull up my pants, and hope that the human body can somehow reabsorb its fluids if held in long enough.

There's novelty in escaping Sacramento until I realize I traded in a steady paycheck, group insurance, and privacy to become a road zombie holding in bodily fluids, enduring graphic descriptions of Landon's sex life, and going days without an opportunity to shower (aside from an occasional Clorox Disinfecting Wipe scrub-down). The entire experience has created an anxiety that is consuming me whole, and though it's a comfortably warm morning in San Diego and we're outside of a truck stop, I feel like I'm in a cardboard box in the middle of Death Valley on a summer afternoon.

"I think I'm having a heart attack," I say to Otis.

"It's anxiety," he says.

"I'm combusting or something."

He pulls me against his body for a hug, but his arms feel like forceps.

Back on the bus, he holds out his fist, palm down, and drops three pills into my hand that I kill with coffee in one swallow. I figure even if it's some date-rape drug, at least I won't have to hear about chicken sex or deal with the cardboard box feeling for much longer.

Over the next half hour, the cloudiness seeps from my thoughts and I feel myself drop through his arms and dissolve into the bus bench. The air folds around me like warm silk and I'm no longer treading against a riptide, just drifting in fuzzy jubilation.

"Babe, tell me when it gets that bad," he says.

***

I have a lot of time to myself because Evie's working and the guys are doing sound checks or radio shows. I get bored sitting on the bus alone, so in Phoenix, I zip up my hoodie and head into town for the cold medicine aisles. I mess around with cocktails of Benadryl and Nyquil, garnished with a Tylenol PM or two, but I can't recreate that particular quiet I experienced with what Otis told me was Xanax and Valium.

On the road it's weirdly easy to find any (if not every) drug. The drum tech, Andrew, carries around a drum case filled with everything from heart medicine and multivitamins to pot and crack. He sells me a plastic bag with about forty to fifty pills, a medley of Xanax, Valium, Vicodin, and Percocet.

The Vicodin goes down easier than chocolate. Three on an empty stomach induce muscular delirium, and I spend the afternoon eating Saltines and vegetating in a warm bath of disinfectant in a San Antonio roadside motel. In the evening before the show, Otis bursts in, buzzing about a new song they wrote, but I can't comprehend much of anything through the thickness of the fog. "Are you still going home?" he asks.

"I don't know," I say.

"When?"

"I don't know."

"How come you don't like it here?"

"I don't know."

It's a chore to break from the Vicodin's effects and listen to what he's saying. He asks another string of questions, and I shuck out a few more "I don't know"s, but then he mentions something about a "literary agent" and sending my writing to "some lady who knows a shitload about books."

"I don't want you to go home," he says. "I thought if you got published or something, you'd figure out your shit and be happy and stay with me."

My concentration returns with a vengeance (meaning my buzz is thoroughly ruined), and so it seems that the motel room we paid for will go to waste: instead of using the privacy to screw around, I use it to yell and interrogate him. "Are you insane?" I ask, standing up to towel off. "What's wrong with you?" I scream. The motel walls are so flimsy that we hear Landon scream at us to shut the fuck up.

"How do you know if you don't try?" he asks. "Just call her and see what she's got to say."

I stare at the razor burn splotches on his throat and chin. It sickens me to think that there's someone out there ruthlessly combing through my writing. But maybe it's not about that at all. I've become proficient at failing what *others* have asked of me. It's become so easy to just sum up any disappointment with a simple, "Well, I didn't want to do it in the first place," but failing at my own initiatives just seems so much scarier.

The following night, during Riot Venom's show in Fort Worth, my cell phone lights up with the number of the agent Otis contacted. Her name's Sarah, and I answer, unsure how to respond to her cryptic mentions of "unsolicited manuscripts" and "slush piles," nor to the sounds of her licked fingers sifting through the pages. "It has potential," she says. The licking continues, the same wet sound she might make if she were trying to dislodge pieces of soggy tuna fish sandwich plastered to the roof of her mouth. "But I have one word for you: editor."

I get the same nausea people get when they hear the word "lawyer." The idea someone will hover over my work with a sadistic red pen fills me with such anxiety that the only way I can successfully skate through the rest of the night is to raid my pharmacy for a few Valium.

***

I hadn't really noticed the ever-increasing amount of booze Otis has been burning through every night, but it becomes apparent when we wake up in Louisiana and can't get him out of the bunk. He wallows in a paralyzing hangover all day, missing their afternoon interview and subsequent sound check. An hour before they're supposed to appear before the crowd, Landon force-feeds him beer, and twenty minutes later, Otis crawls out of the nook, humming Danzig, almost as if he hasn't been a human bedsore all day.

After their set I make the effort to catch him in the middle of his perfect buzz, those final moments before Plasterville. We take a cab to a nearby cemetery, and I swallow a combo of pills on the drive. It helps me ignore the rancid cheese stench radiating off Otis' scalp, and I care a little less about the sweaty foot stink of the cab seat.

Together, Otis and I spend the night surveying old headstones that date back to the 1800s and messing around on the grass, sloppily kissing and rolling around between plots, something he refers to as "porn for the zombies sleeping under us."

"When did *you* lose your innocence?" I ask him as he cuts a line of heroin on the surface of a flat grave marker.

There are so many things he could say: the drugs, attempted suicides, one-night stands, drunken one-night stands, coked-up one-night stands, doped-up one-night stands, and because of his eccentricity, he might even talk about pulling his own teeth. "I didn't," he says between sniffles.

At dawn the sun rises and warms the air, and it's so comfortably pleasant that we doze off in the shade of a miniature mausoleum. I lie back and let him gnaw on my throat like a chew toy. Over the last week he's ornamented my neck and collarbone with black bruises, swollen raspberries, and shallow holes from the sharp ends of his teeth. It's always the day after, when I'm dousing the wounds in dime-store rubbing alcohol, that images of flesh-eating bacteria consuming me in leprosy-like horror flash through my mind, but I can never bring myself to stop him midbite, and for some reason, it feels kind of nice.

And—no different than the day when Kree shat upon my state fair experience—Mom calls. I don't want to answer it, but I know if I don't, it'll give her something else to scream about. So far, it's been easy to continue the façade of working and living in Sac, but this morning she calls because I didn't answer the intercom to buzz her into the apartment complex. "I drove up because I haven't seen you in weeks," she says.

I sit up from the grass, choking on spit, hoping suburban guilt has caused me to imagine all of this.

"You better not have ballooned up to a hundred and twenty pounds," she says.

But that's as real as it gets.

***

I board a flight to the Bay Area. It takes a lot of Xanax to get me on that plane because I've been shivering in a chronic sweat from fear of contracting SARS or avian flu from some host spreading the seeds of disease into the air supply. I arrive in Newark in the late afternoon and the first thing Mom does is drag me to the mall because my jeans are covered in mud dust and it "nauseates" her.

At the department store I stand idly beside her as she fleeces the rack of jeans, lecturing me on how it's offensive to be around someone who looks like she hasn't washed her face in days. "One of Dad's sisters just passed away," she says. "I refuse to go, though, because the funeral is in the middle of the Berkeley hood and they just had another drive-by. But you need to go: I hear there will be singles there. Wear a good suit with your Mikimoto pearls. I don't want to hear from anyone that you showed up looking like a street rat." It takes all my willpower to contain the profanities ready to fly from my mouth like vengeful dysentery. "Oh, and remember what I told you about sitting between Dad's twin nieces." Her theory: 110 pounds seems smaller when wedged between two 300-pounders.

While she busies herself in the high-end stores of Santana Row, I walk across the street to the bank to make a withdrawal for the road. I ask the teller to withdraw two thousand dollars from my account.

"Would you like it in one-hundred-dollar bills?" he asks.

"Thousands," I say.

"We don't have thousand-dollar bills," he says. The patrons behind me snicker.

"Which of your branches does?"

"There's no such thing as a cash denomination of a thousand dollars."

"In the state of California?" I ask.

"No, in the United States of America," he says. "Would you like hundred-dollar bills?"

"Five hundreds, then."

"This country doesn't mint those, either. Denominations come in hundred, fifty, twenty, ten, five, and one."

Behind me, the snickering grows into full-fledged laughing.

"My aunt sends me a two-dollar bill every year on my birthday," I say. "You mean to tell me that she's been scamming me with Monopoly money for the past thirty years?"

"No, ma'am, two-dollar bills do exist, they're just not common in circulation," he says.

Louder laughing.

"Can I just get my money?" I say.

And I'm just glad my family isn't around. As it is, "You majored in finance? Do you even know how to file your taxes?" is still a standby punch line whenever there's a conversational lull at holiday dinners.

***

Later in the evening, at Mom's dinner table, I fidget around with my food and wonder how much longer I'll have to be here, if the truth will come out, if it should come out, if Mom will scream at me till I'm legally deaf. She's already picked me apart for the last twenty minutes with her usual topics—my appearance, job, marital status or lack thereof—as if she's trying to make up for her lack of opportunities over the past month. My brother and Dad just sit there nibbling, as if it's a pleasant break for them to have me here, taking the brunt of her barbs. "Why aren't you eating my chicken casserole?" she asks.

"I don't do chicken," I say.

"Since when?"

"Since ten years ago," I say. "You know that."

"What?"

"Again, with the surprised façade. Get over it."

"Ever notice how your face is always shiny? Like you use Crisco for foundation?"

"That's exactly what I do."

"You smell like the trunk of a car. What is your problem?"

I don't know why I'm here. I should have ducked out earlier; then she would never have spotted the scabs and scaly scars dotted down my throat and collarbone. She jumps on a sleuthing path for information, and since I haven't opened my mouth yet, she makes the ludicrous assumption that I'm on drugs. She is halfway out the door and headed to Walgreens for a home drug test when I decide to save her the trouble. "I quit," I say.

"Quit what? Quit drugs?" she asks.

"My job." I say it softly, but I know she heard me. "To tour the nation with some guy's band."

Her temple vein throbs as she attempts to absorb the information, and by the looks of it, she's on the brink of hyperventilating herself into a hot flash. "Why did you break up with Kieran?" she asks. In other words, Kree (who Mom never approved of) seems like a safe route now. "This is about a man, isn't it? Tell me it's a man and not something else."

I don't know what it would take to gag her just once, and it doesn't even have to be about sex. Just one thing that's my way for once, one motherfucking thing I'm allowed to do. Eating a Twix in front of her or wearing my comfy Vans out to dinner or—

"Just let me put sugar in my coffee!" I scream.

"You are too old to be living in a fantasy world," she says. "What kind of psycho is still in a band at your age?"

"He's—"

"Are you pregnant?" She's always given this question a negative connotation, sort of like, "Did you just simultaneously ruin your life and mine?" or "Have you finally tarnished the family image with a child conceived out of wedlock?"

"How do you go from accusing me of being gay to being pregnant?" I ask.

"Have you looked in the mirror lately? You've let yourself go."

"I've been letting myself go for the last thirty years. Let me do this," I say to her, and it's almost as if I'm fourteen again, arguing submissively in a futile war.

"What is the matter with you?" she asks. "Why has it always been so darn hard for you to be like everyone else? Just be normal. Don't you want that?" The tone of her voice rises exponentially with each nipping question, and she has so much barreling authority and confidence that I understand now why opposition has always been so hard. The ironic thing, though, is that it seems like the only person who would ever be able to win the war against her, maybe even sneak in a few hits below the belt and walk away feeling a shitload better about himself, is Landon. "How hard is it to be a normal part of society?" she asks. "It's like you go out of your way to stand out like a total whacko."

"I don't—"

"It takes no effort whatsoever to just be normal."

"There are alternative forms of life out there," I say. "And they have nothing to do with this suffocating conformity which seems to be your definition of normal."

"What happened to applying for district manager?" she asks. "This is the worst time to be out of a job. Companies have stopped matching 401ks, pensions are long gone, and you're on your own with social security."

"I get that, but—"

"Whoever this riffraff is, he's riffraff, because that's all he knows. Just because he's a loser doesn't mean you should let him take you down, too."

"It's not like that."

"You've been brought up better than an hourly worker, better than just a high school graduate. You want to be a street rat, mooching off tax-sponsored social programs? Is that what kind of life you want to marry into?"

"I don't want to have to do anything."

"Well, there's a surprise."

"There's nothing left of our planet, anyway. The only thing I can do is take part in what's still alive and thriving." I feel guilty. I've never said it aloud before, and now I realize that the last thing I want is to see her sincerely hurt over something I've done or become.

"What you're doing now will screw up your entire life."

"I have the rest of it to worry about getting on track. I was never on track to begin with, anyway."

Everyone has a different idea about the American Dream. I don't know what mine is, but hers seems to be having a daughter who's a 90-pound gymnast Olympian with a degree from the University of Southern California and some executive job in the heart of Mountain View's business district, and maybe an upper-class husband who can afford a nanny for their *Gattaca*-created kids.

"He doesn't have any tattoos or piercings," is the only thing I can really think of saying about Otis. Of course, the lack of tattoos and piercings isn't really a choice; he can't stand physical pain. He whines for hours over paper cuts and hangnails till Landon gives him something to shut him up.

"Just remember," she says. "Your kids will resent and hate you forever if you bring them into a dysfunctional world."

There are so many ways I could respond to a declaration like that.

***

I board a plane to meet up with the tour in Alabama, and I spend the flight writing on Post-Its to escape my manic thoughts. It's an experimental, maybe even avant-garde, short story about Otis meeting up with poetic images and random anthropomorphisms.

When I see Otis waving at me on the other side of airport security, I suddenly feel sedated, though it may have something to do with the Xanax I dropped midflight. He welcomes me by cramming his beer-soaked tongue into my mouth, then feeling up my chest. I hand him the stack of Post-Its and he flips through them before reading the opening sentence out loud: "'It left me without a liver, with a broken heart.'" It takes a few seconds before he comprehends the meaning, but when he does, he breaks into the animated giggle of a thirteen-year-old after a first glance at porn.

Throughout the week he reads and rereads it, making other people on tour read it so they can discuss it with him. It's kind of invigorating to hear other peoples' interpretations and perspectives on something I've written, and it motivates me to head out in Jacksonville, Florida, in search of a cheap computer. After buying a second-hand (and, more than likely, first-generation) laptop, I hook up to an Internet connection in the lodge of our motel, download Sarah's file, and muster the courage to read what her good friend and editor, G.A. Laws, had to say.

When I open the attachment, I am literally bludgeoned by all the graffiti and strikethroughs. The document is busting at the margins with vermilion comment balloons filled with terminology and concepts I've never heard of before. He talks about having "author responsibility" by knowing a scene from floor to ceiling and characters from toenail crust to dandruff flake, and that I have to "build credibility" by cleaning up inconsistencies, and that I should know exactly where I'm going with a plotline and what it's trying to prove and how I have to relate everything back to the novel's major focus. His side notes bury me in a tsunami of perplexing questions:

What is your central conflict, exactly?
Have you raised feasible stakes?
You raised these stakes but how do they relate to the central conflict?
How will you use this scene to raise the stakes for your protagonist?
How does this secondary character raise the stakes for your protagonist?
Where's the scene opening?
Where's the character development?
Where's the dialogue introduction?
Do you even know what your central conflict is?

Are you cramming in a bunch of unnecessary words to hit a certain word count?

Why are you making the reader do all the work?

That was a weak and underdeveloped opening line, what are you going to do about that?

Did you think fiction just happens?

Holy fuck. I thought editors filled in missing commas and fixed misspelled words; I never thought they went through and raised the sort of questions that I have no answers for, much less the luxury of time, privacy, or patience to formulate.

I shut the creaky laptop, trek onto the bus, and chug through Otis' emergency beer stash, intermittently swallowing a Vicodin or two because I can't soberly handle getting tanked over by all this unexpected literary expertise at once. I'm glad Mom isn't here to see the life—a tour bus, a used laptop, and a bleeding manuscript—I was trying to convince her was "alive and thriving."

Humpty Dumpty

When I stopped mulling over everything I'm not, I naturally became someone I could stand to be, but that's easy on the road because nothing is real. The only things we have to worry about are finding Laundromats and all-night grocery stores that sell cheap generic snacks, sodas, and discount liquor, and from time to time, a way to stitch up the occasional cut. Tonight, for instance, I find Landon backstage, sewing up Evie's forehead after she took a mutilating stroll through the mosh pit. "Welcome to the world of no health insurance," Landon says.

By this point in the tour, everyone's come knocking on our bus door for his services. He hauls around a duffel bag packed with rubber gloves, bandages, surgical tape, needles, saline, iodine, syringes, and tiny vials so he can numb and sew people up if they need mending. He'll sew himself up if necessary, he'll make a splint when someone breaks their arm, and he's CPR-certified, so whenever someone goes stale, he's at their side bringing them back. He has the equipment and skill to put IV lines into Otis' arm for "instant hydration" after a bender, and every morning he takes everyone's blood pressure with a gauge and stereoscope.

I've never witnessed anything like this. It's some fantastical dimension where everyone's sovereign of conventional dependencies and expectations, and where they can afford to blow off all reservations for self-indulgent instantaneous gratification, as long as the music is still worthy.

As for me, my body is quiet. The insatiable appetite looming in every cell is asleep and for the first time in my life, I'm satisfied. A week ago, I stopped eating dinner: either I was too busy messing around with Otis, or I was rocking in the soothing arms of a Vicodin fog, and since then, I've slowly lost my taste for solid food in general, existing solely on coffee, energy drinks, alcohol, and whatever pills are lying around. Lately, Vicodin has taken the place of meals, Xanax has replaced snacking, and Valium has become dessert. They are remarkable tunnels, taking me to places I could never experience otherwise, requiring no effort... I just sit there and fly in my own body.

I've always thought drugs were the candy of losers, but there's something extraordinary about their ability to transform me into a different person. When I'm on a combination of any or all of them, there's a quiet that hushes the usual internal typhoon of anxiety that asphyxiates me. I only know it's always been there after experiencing what it's like when all that unrest and self-loathing is muted. I can keep a conversation going. I can approach people, introduce myself, listen to them ramble, and even when I don't give a shit about what they're saying, I no longer have trouble faking it. I think back to all the times I judged people, thinking they had to live pitiable lives if they had to reach out to artificially induced forms of entertainment like drugs, but I know better now. Who was I to judge how anyone dresses, what anyone listens to, eats, drinks, snorts, shoots, whoever and however anyone fucks?

***

It's a week till Halloween, and everybody's flying on candy or whatever else they're flying on. We'd planned to crash a local Rapid City house party after the show, but Otis barricades himself inside the venue bathroom. Four hours go by before Landon hurls his body into the flimsy plywood door to break it open. Inside, Otis is curled between the wall and toilet, hypnotically rapping his forehead against the wall, his eyes staring catatonically into oblivion while saliva pours from his mouth into a pool on his lap.

"What's wrong?" I ask. After putting up with this bullshit question for years, it has now just slipped from my mouth like soap across a prison shower.

It takes a half bottle of whiskey and a fistful of Xanax to get him out, and then he lies on a couch backstage, whining gibberish into the armrest. I try to pull him up, but he slumps against the bench like a bag of cement.

Landon appears beside me. "Isn't he the life of the party," he says.

"Should I call a cab?" I ask.

"For what?" He burps and chugs whatever was left of his drink.

"The ER."

Otis pukes and the convulsions wake him up. "It got in my hair," he says as he tries to wring out the ends.

"If he's coherent enough to know that, then no," Landon says.

At first, Otis' weeping seems like a joke because here he is, the frontman of one of the top bands leading this tour, and he has tears dropping off the end of his chin. In the hopes of salvaging the last of his self-respect, Landon and I haul him around the side of the venue, through the parking lot, and onto the bus, where we dump him on the floor of the tiny bathroom.

I kneel in dried piss to hold his hair out of the toilet and out of the line of fire of his hurling, which continues to create an echoing orchestration against the surface of the metal bowl. After three substantial heaves, he leans against the wall and rips at his hair till clumps fall against his lap. He worms into a limp pile on the floor, barf still dribbling from his mouth, and when I try pulling him up, he thrashes me into the doorway and trips away, planting the tread of his boot on top of my neck with his first step. Before running very far, though, he trips and hits the ground face-first.

"Lannie, I need to do it." He sprays Landon with snot and blood, screaming curse words he invents out of frustration, and it takes the combined effort of Joey, Landon, and Evie to wrestle him to the ground and hold him down. It's haunting how prepared and well versed they've become at dealing with something like this. Landon sits on the ground holding Otis' head in his lap, while Joey restrains his kicking legs, and Evie wipes the blood bubbling from his mouth. Eventually, Otis simmers into cryptic rambling, which finally fades when he passes out.

Everybody—excluding Otis, Landon, and I—goes to the party. Otis spends the night puking into a bucket perched on the side of his bunk, and Landon and I suck on warm forties, blast The Smashing Pumpkins, and every so often, make back-and-forth cracks at each other that tend to escalate into smacking fights.

Around 5 a.m., I pull Otis into the bathroom and balance him over the toilet as he continues to puke, half-conscious. "So how does it work?" Landon asks from the doorway. "You sit there for a thousand hours writing? They teach diligence like that in charm school?"

"Leave me alone." I'm desperate to breathe air that isn't polluted with the pungent stench of puke, second-hand smoke, or Landon's verbal abuse.

"This is what you do." He squeezes into the bathroom and sits down, lifting Otis' face out of the toilet. "Rest his mug against the edge of the bowl. That way you don't get tired of holding him up while you're waiting for those chunks to fly." He wiggles his spidery legs around Otis' back before collecting the loose hair out of his face.

I offer him the last few ounces of Otis' Grey Goose.

"I don't drink vodka. So, am I doing your cover? What's the title? Some tree, right?" He picks at his lip piercing before exhaling a cloud of smoke away from me.

I try to change the subject: "Why aren't *you* vocals? You sing good and write everything anyway."

"It's 'you sing well.' Fuck, I can't believe you went to college. Twice. And you want to be a writer? A real writer that writes shit people are going to read?" This heckling continues for the next few minutes, the highlight being, "Listening to you is like watching an episode of one of those SoCal bimbo reality shows." But after exhausting himself of punch lines, he admits that he started on lead vocals, but in order to counteract any more lame suicide attempts, they let Otis give it a crack.

"You let him have his way so he wouldn't kill himself?"

"Worked for a while." He nuzzles his face against Otis' back, then exhales a stream of smoke down the arc of his spine. "Ever read Norman Maclean's *A River Runs Through It?*"

"Through what?"

"You probably read about existentialists going on about the human condition, huh."

"Last thing I read was an article from Harvard Business School," I say. Coincidentally, I read it for ideas on how to get *Landon* to fall in line at work. There was a time though—back as an undergraduate, before I became a salaried manager with no chance of ever seeing a lunch break again—when I used to read real fiction: Douglas Coupland and Kurt Vonnegut and Haruki Murakami. Now, I don't even read the HBS; I read the labels on Otis' pill bottles.

"So I got this idea for your book cover," he says. "I did some design and font crap in art school before I had to drop out when you fired me."

"Thanks...I think."

***

With the help of Vicodin, I suck it up and attempt to conquer the challenge of nursing the manuscript to health. Though a fistful of pills may be holding my hand through the process, it's still painfully arduous, worse than ripping an infinite number of pubes from my cooch with tetanus-laced pliers. Even if I try to conjure up some answer to Laws' proposed suggestion, I have no idea if it's a good answer, much less the right one. And it's hard to stay on task when everyone else on the bus is drinking and watching movies, or when Otis has his hands in my pants.

Andrew helps me out by prescribing something he refers to as "extra-strength Adderall," which feels like motivation in a pill and sustains a spontaneous thought process for hours on end. Tonight, I chased a few of those with a couple of energy drinks, and through my solid brick wall concentration, I hear Otis call to me from his bunk. I'd lost track of time and didn't even realize that it's almost 7 a.m. I shut off my laptop, and in the dim light, feel my way to him.

"What do you like best about writing?" he asks.

"The unreliable nature of a writer," I say.

"I like it when you talk smart."

"Hey, do you know what the American Dream is?"

"Like getting to do your own shit, you know. Pursuit of happiness?"

I've spent my whole life denying that I've wanted a counterpart, and now that I have one, I don't know what to do with him. Call it commitment-phobia, but I want to test him to see if he will fold or get stronger. I want to do something for him that will resonate and hold his attention, even when he's fully engaged in something else, even when he's onstage.

In the afternoon, while he's off rehearsing and sound checking, I swallow a bunch of Vicodin for the pain and Valium for the nervousness. I line up bottles of Listerine on the edge of the bus bathroom sink, and soak some mom-and-pop-store pliers in a pan of alcohol. After two hours alone on the bus, I fend off the feverish sweats, gargle the last of the Listerine, insert the pliers into my mouth, and wiggle a molar till it's loose. Though deliriously nauseated, I zip out of the bus, into the venue, and down a corridor, where I find the band waiting for their sound check. Two yanks and a confident twist, and the tooth skips like a restaurant mint against the floor, leaving root prints of red as it hobbles to a standstill. The blood comes quick, overflowing past my lips and draining down my throat. I feel myself fading, but I lurch for the tooth and press it into Otis' palm, then unintentionally puke on him.

The ER doctors can't put the tooth back in because I won't open my mouth and Otis refuses to give it up. By the time I'm coherent again, I see that he has set the tooth in a platinum Claddagh and is wearing it on his ring finger.

***

Since Otis popped his cherry on fits, it's become a routine to simply endure his freak-outs, then pull him from the motel bathtub or corner of the tour bus, then put him to bed in his moldy smelling bunk that reeks of toenail fungus and pump him full of Xanax and liquor. It's a blind experiment every night, like a game of Russian roulette, estimating how much it'll take to get Otis through his set without tail-spinning him into an episode, since he's always in a different state of mind and it's difficult to gauge what substances are already circulating around in his system.

Most nights he'll pass out at the venue and we'll have to carry him out while he pukes. Just follow the Hansel and Gretel trail of chunks and we'll be at the end. I used to strip off his clothes and hose his corpse down before bed, but lately, I've been leaving him in the aisle of the bus. He's like a human Zamboni, picking up miscellaneous crap in his hair. Last night, I pulled a silver-dollar-sized dead roach from his tangled locks, although it may have crawled in alive.

Every night before closing, I have to ensure that there are at least three beers on hand for Otis in the morning so I don't have to mosey out at some vampire-toxic hour of the day to hunt down a liquor store. I thought it was dysfunctional up until recently, when I found myself waiting in line in a crowded coffeehouse—twitching from caffeine withdrawals—ready to scream at the workers behind the counter to hurry the fuck up and inject me with a triple shot of espresso before I jump the counter and snort the grinds.

November comes and goes, and somewhere in there, Obama is voted in. We tour our way into the Northwest, up the coast, heading in and out of a countless number of cities, states, and even another country, Canada, jumping from one venue to another, interrupted only by the loading and unloading of the bus. The scenery and subcultures change, but everything becomes a blur of scheduling and planning around Otis' behavior. He's either drooling in a catatonic daze or throwing an epileptic suicidal tantrum, and each episode seems to draw out longer than the last.

There's an expectation that I'll deal with it, like I'm the one who should be at the front lines getting blasted by his vinegary bile, the one who's supposed to be judgment-free when it comes to him doing whatever he wants—like guzzling a bottle of Jack or playing quarters all night till he can't sit up straight—and then I'm supposed to be sympathetic to the aftermath and understand that this is just the way he is, that I should accept mopping up his puke, missed piss attempts, and talking him down from his wig-out like it's my job, because that's the way everyone treats me, as if I should have known what I was getting myself into.

But I didn't, and I wonder if this is the life Otis had in mind when he first asked me to come with him.

Margaritas : Tequila ::
Holidays : Dysfunction

It's the start of a frosty December, and over the last month, I've gained the smarts and experience to predict which kind of night Otis'll have the moment his foot meets the stage. If he interacts with the crowd and doesn't miss his cue, then he'll put on a decent show and I'll get to sleep through the night. If he scream-sings and can't tell up from down and needs help finding his way offstage, then I know he'll go rabid and I'll be awake with him into the next day.

Tonight in Edmonton, I already know what's going to happen. After his mediocre performance, he blindly feels his way off the stage, through the dark, to clobber me against a wall. He rambles on behind a wall of excess spit that he sprays against my forehead before turning around to slam his nose into the opposite wall. He goes on like this for an hour, pacing the venue hallways, bleeding all over, before we can calm him down enough to get him on the bus. We're lucky he cooperated this time. Most nights, he's so unmanageable that we can't get him to sit still long enough to get a tranquilizer down his throat, and he'll linger in corners of rooms, lashing out at the walls, at tour managers, at anybody who goes near him.

In Saskatoon, Evie and I watch as he rolls across the stage, screaming a chain of curse words, and the crowd eats it up. They don't know that we'll have to see an encore in a few hours, that we'll get the VIP treatment of being showered in his vomit and snot, and that I'll get the added VIP treatment of having to sop it all up.

Otis spends the next morning with his head bobbing in a roadside Porta-Potty pisser. Since I refuse to brave its conditions, I wait on the curb sipping booze with Landon. We watch Otis crawl out on his hands and knees, puke dribbling from his lips. Somehow he manages to pull himself up, but almost immediately topples face-first into the dirt, unconscious. We stare as he lies there like a comatose bum until those who still have sympathy and respect for him run to peel him off the ground. I exchange the last of my rum for the last of Landon's Scotch, and we cringed simultaneously after the first bite of a different booze.

***

A few days later, outside Winnipeg, he actually wakes up functional, and the band decides to take a chilling polar bear plunge at a hotel pool. I smile at the spectacle of his pale skin reflecting the minimal sunlight, and Evie chases him around the edge before they both run into the water. His evident lack of buoyancy makes it difficult for him to stay afloat, so he paddles with all his might. He huffs around in the water with a childish smile on his face, his tongue sloppily hanging off his lips like a puppy's. He giggles, circles around Landon who's effortlessly treading water, and it's there that I realize how Otis doesn't have an angry bone in his body. He never gets mad or upset at anyone, never casts blame or spiteful criticism. He's just a happy sad person.

***

At a rest stop in Montreal, Landon rips off my sweatshirt hood to reveal my vulnerable skin to the sunlight. "Idolize the Unabomber?" he asks. I pull the drawstrings on my hood and tighten them around my forehead and chin. "I'm going to get you an umbrella for Christmas so you can walk around like Michael Jackson."

I'm about to kick him in the shins when he hands over a sketch he drew with charcoal and chalk. It's a concept illustration of a girl whose hair grows upward into a bare persimmon tree with fruit dangling off its skeletal branches. It's black and white with orange speckles, and so eloquently symbolic that it's difficult to stifle my animosity and cough out a compliment. I kick him in the shin anyway.

"What the fuck was that for?" he asks.

"I don't know." I just couldn't think of anything else to do.

"Now everything's done for you, so hurry up and edit your shit."

We hover over the wrinkled drawing, flittering in the arctic breeze. He probably expects me to hurl an insult and I expect some comment about how his work shouldn't be depicted on the front cover of some piece-of-shit contemporary fiction novel, but I think he knows from reading it that this is the right answer to whatever could have been. It's eerie, because this is Landon standing two feet from me, sucking on his cigarette, rubbing his shin, and I'm turning seven Vicodin over in my stomach and maybe it's just the seven Vicodin, but it feels like we're floating in the eye of the storm and everything outside the surging walls doesn't matter anymore.

"Hey, someone help!" Joey's shout breaks our momentum. He's running around the front of the bus with Evie's unconscious body in his arms.

She hit the asphalt after smoking a joint laced with Angel Dust, Joey tells us as we're driving to the hospital, and there was nothing in Landon's duffle bag (nor in his medical knowledge base) that could help her. In the ER waiting room, Landon goes on a warpath of blame, but none of us can take his amplified insults personally. After all, Evie's been his girlfriend since he stepped off the plane at eleven, freshly spat out of one of Massachusetts' most isolated towns. He failed his last two years in high school so he could stay behind to be with her, he names every one of his guitars "Evie," and though I can't say for certain, if he had to choose, he'd probably ditch Otis before ever leaving her. Some asshole from a wannabe-Ramones band sold it to her, and over the course of a few days, revenge is all Landon talks about.

In Vermont, during the band's afternoon sound check at a local venue, he finally confronts him. "You nearly killed her," Landon says.

"She was begging for it. And so's that Rain Man brother of—"

And who would have thought that a bony 117-pounder could throw a punch? Of course, it isn't like the movies where we all do nosedives to break them up, nor do we circle around rooting for a particular side. Neither of them appears to have ever been in a fight before, so members from both bands, along with a few roadies, stand around and watch them clumsily attempt to inflict pain on each other. They scratch and pull at each other's hair, both uncoordinated when it comes to wrestling or slugging, or whatever it is they're trying to do. Eventually, Landon gets a wallet chain looped around his throat and, because he's stacked on top of the other guy, they sway side to side like an overturned turtle.

Since it doesn't seem like anyone's going to intervene, I reach for the back of Johnny or Dee Dee or Whichever-Ramone-He's-Trying-to-Be's neck and pinch like a pair of pliers. He lets go of Landon, but gives me a boot across the face.

It isn't fair. Landon walks away with a few chain hickies and I'm left with a snaggletooth smile. I feel officially deformed since the left side of my face is still swollen from my tooth fairy adventure, and now the right side of my face throbs from the steel toe of that asshole's boot. Everybody on this tour is in Vans, DC, or Converse, but the one asshole that punted me in the face had to be wearing steel-toed boots.

***

I spend the post-fight afternoon in a Vicodin stupor, bobbing around a motel bathtub of plain hot water since I ran out of bleach and detergent weeks ago. While inhaling the steam, I obsess over all the cancerous maladies I could have accumulated over the course of this tour from all the power line exposure, gasoline fumes, second-hand smoke, tour bus exhaust, and drug aerosols.

High on whatever he's always high on when not comatose, Otis kicks open the bathroom door and jumps into the tub with his clothes on.

"What the fuck, no," I say, but because of the Vicodin, it's all gibberish.

"When you take a bath, you're wallowing in your own dirt anyway," he says.

"I showered before, and now your parasites are wiggling their way through my pores."

He laughs. "You're in way too deep, babe."

He frisks his coat pockets (not taking into account they're submerged underwater) for a spoon and a small plastic package filled with beige powder. I watch glossy-eyed as he fills the spoon with bathwater and sprinkles in the drugs.

"Isn't it more sanitary to snort it?" I ask. "You'll end up like Cobain."

"Fuck Cobain, he was murdered anyway." He gets a Zippo going with the jerk of his thumb and heats the underside of the concoction till it fizzes into a brown sludge. "I got enough for you, too."

"I get addicted easily. I can't get off coffee or carbs."

"Those are Martha Stewart addictions."

As he tightens his belt around his biceps, I wonder who gave it to him. If it wasn't Landon, then the ratio of heroin to baby powder is probably a lot higher than usual, and I'm dealing with more than enough of Otis' shit right now without the Mark Renton habit.

"You know..." I start, but falter because it's all trying to come out of me at once:

Why is it, when someone uncaps a bottle of beer, it's like ringing Pavlov's bell with you?

When are you going to learn how to take care of yourself?

When are you going to get your shit together? Let's start with that first.

Quit drooling on me.

More importantly, quit puking on me.

Fork over the Xanax before I think myself into a nosebleed.

It takes him four or five tries before he finds a vein, and I know he has to be high or drunk already, because he would never be able to stab himself like this while sober. He injects and drops back against the wall of the tub with a neutral expression on his face, as if he were sleeping. He lets go of the needle in the process, and it's still bobbing in his arm, held up only by the walls of a cerulean vein.

***

Christmas is ten days away. People have been mass-producing their own eggnog, and after OD-ing on Landon's last week, any whiff of the creamy slop makes me bow over hurling. To add to the queasiness, my intestinal track throbs from abuse after I went on a vitamin C and Echinacea binge, popping them every hour, on the hour, for three days, hoping I could build up a defense against the wasteland of diseases circulating from person to person. Maybe it's Otis' dark side, maybe it's the swollen infection that's invaded the slimy pocket in my mouth where a molar used to be, maybe it's the chronic exhaustion coupled with all the eggnog nausea, but I can't remember why I chose discomfort like this over a consistent paycheck, group insurance, sterile bathrooms, and a warm bed to stretch out in.

In Boston I'm on the steps of the bus' doorway when Landon approaches me with an eggnog mustache and a red cup in hand. Three Valium (and the water they were swallowed in) shoot past my teeth into a streak near his feet. Evie recoils, but he doesn't flinch. I shiver from the taste of the stomach acid and lean my cheek against the bus door. I want a searing shower, bleached sheets with an allergen-free comforter, and a hot cup of gourmet coffee, all of which I haven't had since I left Sacramento.

"Punk's a man's world," Evie says and strokes my hair. "But someday I'm going to move to Jersey and start a hardcore band called Girl Kicks Boy." I'm a breath away from telling her to leave me the fuck alone and ride someone else. Otis' demons have kept me up for four days straight, I just puked up my only daily dose of relief, and the last thing I want to deal with is her enthusiasm. "You want to be the angsty chick that thrashes around on stage and throws stuff at people?"

"Sure," I say.

"What do you want for Christmas?"

"Otis' shit to stop."

"That's a wish upon a star."

If I had a wish upon a star, I wouldn't piss it away on Otis; I'd use it to take back what I did last night. In a stout, Vicodin, and maybe Xanax and/or Percocet combo fog, I called Newark at 3 a.m. and asked Mom if I should come home for Christmas. Maybe I called for the rejection, hoping I'd then know that I'd finally reached the end of the line and could quit feeling bad for the shit I've done, become, and will inevitably turn out to be.

"Are you pregnant?" she asked.

"Do you want me to come home or not?"

I think I was waiting for her to say something about missing me, being worried about me. "I guess," she said.

***

I wanted to go home because I thought I owed those people something, but as the days progress, I remember that this entire tour was *supposed* to be my "FUCK YOU" to the family. A "Look what I'm doing. Look what I've done. Look who I've done. I'm different. I'm not you people anymore. I'm not your personal punching bag, an accessory for you to derive gratification out of butchering. I'm completely different. Fucked from the inside out different." So on Christmas Eve, when Mom opens that fucking door to her house, Otis and I are going to be standing on her front porch like two vein-ridden erect middle fingers.

That's what I imagined, anyway. However, when he and I pull up to Mom and Dad's driveway, I can already sense the tension radiating inside. Right now, someone is probably complaining, yelling, or ragging on someone for something they've done or were in the process of doing. It's a constant stream of overexpressed opinions mashed together to create a ridiculous super opinion that no one can scrub off when they leave the house at the end of the night.

"And if you think otherwise, you'll be damned out of town," I say when Otis turns off the engine. "You agree for the sake of agreeing. That's how they poison you; that's when you change."

"Nothing bad's going to happen," he says.

On the porch, I comb out the kinks in his hair and adjust his tie. It's been awhile since I've been in a normal social environment, so I can no longer gauge what is normal versus what is bizarre. Otis rings the doorbell and my confidence morphs from a vengeful beast into a fearful titmouse. I wish he would have laced my dress tighter before we left my apartment, but he said corsets are sexist, so he wouldn't touch me. I was on the bathroom floor for an hour lacing and re-lacing, and he'd been waiting at the door, jingling his keys.

"Do I look fat?" I asked him when I came out of the bathroom. "Am I fat?"

But he didn't say anything. He put down the pecan pie and backed me up against the kitchen counter and said to me: "You're going to come on me."

He pulled the dress up around my hips with one hand and yanked the laces of my corset loose with the other. I felt his unwashed fingers slide up my fishnets to my panties where he moved them to the side before squirming a digit into my dry interiors. I wasn't lubed up, but when he pinched my clit between his thumb and forefinger, the walls melted.

I slid my tongue up the side of his face and behind his ear. There was a lasagna-like layer of brackish paste composed of rancid sweat, dirt, and grime, all crunching between my teeth. I unbuckled his belt and jammed my hand down the front of his pants, and the guilt of knowing we should have been at Mom's place over an hour ago made his dick throb in my palm like a telltale heart. "Come for me," he said.

I did and left a gooey mess on his hand that he licked off before forcing his tongue into my mouth, an act that smeared my lipstick across his face. I flush when I recall how I tasted in his mouth: slimy, brackish.

Back on the porch, Dad opens the door and Otis holds out the pie. "We brang pecan," he says.

Dad thanks him, shakes his hand, and leads us inside. Maybe I don't give these people enough credit. After all, they are family, and they wouldn't blatantly ostracize me in front of a guest, but as I hear Mom and Auntie descend the stairs, their footsteps hammer against the floor like nails in my coffin.

"Hey, hermit, where were you this morning?" Mom asks. She called eleven times this morning in the course of an hour, kicking off the fest at 5:30 a.m., almost as if she knew I was indisposed and wanted to probe for evidence. She used to call like that in college, like she expected to find me in a booze or sex-induced stupor. She never did, and I think it disappointed her when she didn't have anything to yell about. "Nice outfit. Did you get that in a whorehouse lost-and-found?" she asks.

Moving through a house filled with my extended family is a lot like speed dating. I go from one station to another: the first was at the front door, exchanging insolent dialogue with Mom, the second is the hors d'oeuvres spread in the living room, where an uncle asks me to remind him what size I wear. "Six petite," I say.

"My receptionist is giving away her pre-gastric-bypass clothes," he says. "You're the only one in the family I thought could fit into them."

I wonder why they aren't making cracks about my unemployment or about Otis, who's fishing maraschino cherries from the punch bowl, loading them into his cup.

I head for the beer and wine station, and Auntie and Mom sneak up from behind. "I don't get how you can go out with someone like that," Auntie says.

"He's gross," Mom says.

"He's intellectual," I say.

"Hey, babe?" Otis hollers across the room from the punch station. "Do you want a smoothie? Your brother's blendering some." Slurp.

He appears to be having a snapdragon of a time discussing musical influence with my brother, who adores similar bands—Black Flag, Atreyu, and Thursday—but after a quarter bottle of Absolut and a fistful of muscle relaxants, Otis could be having a snapdragon of a time if someone was whittling off his nut sack with a dull table knife.

"His hair is offensive," Mom says, jabbing me in the kidney. "I can't tell which of you is the boy or girl. God, is he gay?"

There are only two kinds of people in her eyes, and if they're not her vision of perfection (someone straight out of an Abercrombie & Fitch catalog, rather ironically), then by default, they're gay, fat losers. She could walk in on Otis, his dick heaving inside me, and she'd still doubt our sexuality. And call us fat losers.

"At least Al Bundy had a job and somewhat of a work ethic," she says. "This guy here looks like he needs help getting dressed every morning. You need to think right now. Do you really want to ruin your figure with stretch marks, hemorrhoids, and an even wider butt by having *his* inbred kids, who will—at some tender age—have to watch their father go through a sex change? They'll be drawing pictures for the school psychologist of their two mothers and whatever freak that she-male dates next. And what if the next freak decides to go through a sex change, too? Your children will have three mothers, and then whatever creature *you* get involved with next. Think hard, Hazel. Right now. Imagine the reality of your future and the severe social consequences."

Sadly, I think Mom lost it sometime before I entered high school, when the World Health Organization deleted "homosexuality" from its directory of classified mental illnesses.

"I think you have Stockholm Syndrome," she says.

Onto station four: the dinner table. I try to keep a low profile, but it's difficult when Otis slurps for the fourth time in minutes, and after smacking him and quietly scolding him, he primitively resorts to wiping his spit on his sleeve. With the extra company, there aren't enough dining room chairs, so I'm sitting on a folding chair with my chin against my plate, white-knuckling Otis' hand for support. I refuse to let go, so he is forced to cut his meat one-handedly.

"So, you quit your job?" Auntie shifts the room's blazing attention to me. "I can pull some strings and get you a job ushering at the Pavilion."

"No." I didn't go to college to haul my ass up and down a stairwell in a blue blazer, holding out a flashlight like an extension of my body.

"In this economy, with your negative qualifications, you have to take what you can get."

I clench Otis' hand tighter, and I don't realize I'm hurting him until I feel a few joints in his knuckles pop. It makes him yelp. I try changing the subject to something that doesn't revolve around my deficiencies. "Otis and I have seen North America in just a few months," I say.

"I've had so much trouble sleeping lately," Mom says.

"We even went to Canada."

"Hazel was a colicky baby. All she did was cry. That's probably why I have so much trouble sleeping now. Sometimes I wake up in the middle of the night from nightmares of her unbearable screaming. It's driving me to drink."

"Otis is playing The Catalyst in Santa Cruz soon," I say.

"Try Ambien," Auntie says.

"One time I came home from work and found Avaline on the toilet eating pizza," I say, hoping the shock of this random detail will swing the conversational focus back in my direction.

"Ambien? Does it work?" Mom asks.

It passes through them like corn; I don't even get a weird look. I'm screaming at these fucking people to pay attention to me, to the new developments in my life, but it's like they've found a button to fade me out.

"Cider, please," I say to Otis. He picks up the bottle of Martinelli's and as the lip of the bottle touches my glass, Mom turns in our direction.

"She doesn't need the calories," she says to him. "And I better see a ring on both those fingers before a pregnancy. I'm so afraid, Hazel, you're going to come home one of these days with an illegitimate kid named Blanket."

"Landon says I don't have to worry about getting girls pregnant," Otis says. "'Cause he says my sperm is so suicidal all my kids will abort themselves."

"Why? Why would you say something like that?" I ask.

The table undulates with laughter, the low utterance of judgment passing from place setting to place setting.

"You're in a band?" Mom asks. "How long have you done that?"

"Since I was sixteen. My brother showed me everything about music when we moved to California." He hasn't paused in a while to slurp up his excess saliva and a few drops slink over his bottom lip toward his chin.

"Your brother's in the band too?" Mom asks.

"Mom, don't," I say, because I know where it's going.

"That's like New Kids On The Block," she says. A guttural moan involuntarily scrapes through my throat. "Hazel, remember you used to listen to them?"

It opens up the floodgates to Otis' laugher. He doesn't even try to hold back.

"I was only, like, seven or something," I say.

"No, you were in middle school by then."

Otis hits his fist to the table in such hysterics that it makes the silverware jump.

"So, where did you go to school?" Mom asks him. It makes my hypothetical ulcers throb.

"Massachusetts," he says. I bet he can't even spell Massachusetts.

"What did you major in?" she asks.

"That's where he went to middle school," I say, distracted by the sight of him trying to hide the snail tracks on his sleeve.

"So you went to high school and college in Sacramento?"

"I—"

"His parents are dead." I can't help it; if everyone knows he's gone through some horrible trauma as a kid, maybe it will explain why he turned out the way he has.

"That's unfortunate," Mom says. "Have you been making sure to keep your gas tank filled?" she asks me, then looks at Otis to say, "A few times she called me screaming about how her car broke down in the middle of the highway, but it turned out she was just out of gas." I chug my glass of diet soda, hoping the chemicals will spontaneously blow out my liver and kill me. "Oh, and our scale has been off by four pounds all these years. Meaning you weigh a hundred and fourteen pounds, not a hundred and ten."

I would rather have had her reveal in front of everyone that, due to a shotgun wedding, I'm really a year older.

"I have toenail clippings that weigh more than that," Otis says.

I don't know if I should be flattered or offended at his remark. He cuts his massive talons every few months, but only when they're an inconvenience, like if they're cutting through the front of his Vans or like that one time when we were taking a bath together and they were extending toward me like raptor claws, yellowed with sludgy fungus and chalky nail rot.

I refuse to suffer through dessert and coffee, so I force Otis to get up and come with me to the coat and shoe closet. Mom follows us to the front door because it isn't officially a holiday if she can't get in the final blow. "Whatever you do," she says, "no tattoos. I don't want you coming home looking like Yakuza."

If I had a choice between coming home and cleaning out someone's colostomy bag, I'd take the colostomy bag. No, I take that back, I'd choose to meet my demise in a sea of leaky colostomy bags. There was no "FUCK YOU," no rebellious acts that shocked or disturbed any of them. And I've never heard Otis laugh that hard before, not even during *Jackass* reruns.

***

It's a long night. I'm up for most of it, trying to prevent Otis from raping Jack Daniels since we need to be up early for breakfast in Roseville and he has to be functional enough to get on a plane for Philadelphia shortly thereafter.

When we get to Aunt Zee's in the morning, Evie and Landon are pulling their idea of a Christmas tree through the front door. They brag about snagging it for an unbeatable price, but it's probably because it's russet and dead.

The burn of yesterday dissipates inside the house when I see that the list of hijacked street signs above the mantle has grown since my last visit.

Zelda Way
Landon Lane
Evelyn Lane
Otis Avenue
Hazel Avenue

"We're both avenues in Sac, just like Landon and Evie are both lanes," Otis says.

It's always interesting to see how other people spend their holidays. Kree's family used them as an excuse to throw a neighborhood keg party and spend the day smoking and drinking in the backyard. Today in Roseville, we decorate the Christmas tree by shrouding the branches in cobwebs, fake spiders and bats, and Otis' collection of rubber body parts, and Landon tops the tree with an anarchy sign made from the yard's scrap metal. Aunt Zee cooks up a carcinogen-laced, honey-burnt ham, and bakes a spread of casseroles garnished with cat fur and gray hair. We eat out of coffee mugs because there aren't any clean dishes, and Landon and Evie sit at the table shirtless, shivering in the cold, because their Christmas gifts to each other were their own names tattooed across one another's shoulder blades. I wonder how impossible it was for the artist to tattoo Landon's pustule-infested back since the needle had to be hitting land mines of zit puss.

"So, Scrooge, what's Christmas like at your place?" he asks. "Is it all mimosas and fighting over who's got the bigger gun?"

"You must be hungry, babe," Otis says. "You didn't eat last night."

"I'm afraid my mom is putting Prozac in my food," I say.

With a plane to catch, we hurry through the meal and move on to our gift exchange. Otis hauls mine in on a dolly, and it drops like cement against the floor. "This is only the first part," he says. "The second part is coming, 'cause I still need to put a down payment on it."

I rip through the newspaper wrapping and stare down at a stereotypically shaped tombstone engraved with "RIP."

"Is that a bat?" I ask, pointing at the small cutout in the upper corner.

"Yeah." He drops to his knees to admire it more closely. "Your name and dates can go here." He outlines my invisible name with his fingertip. "And I had them put cup holders on top so people can light candles or put in little pumpkins at Halloween."

"Or rest their beer in, right?"

"Hey, that's a great idea."

"Um... what if, and this is hypothetically speaking, years from now, I don't want my tombstone to say 'RIP' and..." I turn my head to examine the atrocity in greater detail. "And that looks like the Batman symbol."

"It's not Batman," he says.

"Maybe we could exchange it."

"You can't. It's personalized."

"It says fucking 'RIP' with a cartoon bat on it. If I use this, everyone who walks by is going to think that's where Batman is buried."

"It's not Batman. There's nothing about this that has anything to do with Batman. It's wicked evil." His arms are tensed against the sides of his body and he won't look at me when he yells out his responses in short spurts.

He probably thought it was supposed to be an expression of affection or ticket of acceptance into his world, but... "How many times have you seen a headstone with 'RIP' on it?" I ask. "What if I wanted it to say something like 'Wife and mother'?"

"You can put that at the bottom."

"I think Batman might distract from that." He's probably more hurt than upset by my reaction, but I stand behind my initial hunch: it's fucking Batman. "Well, what's the second part?"

"It's the grave to go with this."

"Like a grave in the ground?"

"Yeah, at the graveyard down the street that we went to."

"That's awful."

"It's supposed to go with the headstone."

"It's not like buying earrings to match a necklace. And what if I don't want to be buried? You ever think that I might want to be put in the mausoleum, juicy, or have one of those tombs built around my carcass?"

"I'm not made of fucking money."

"There you go. This is the same inconsiderate logic you put into the Batman headstone."

"For the last motherfucking time, it wasn't Batman."

It's our first serious argument and it had to be in front of Landon, who's rolling off the couch laughing at us. We almost miss our plane to Pennsylvania because Otis locks himself in his room, downs a bottle of Scotch, and spends three hours kicking his walls. If he loses it like this when he's trying to express affection, I'd hate to see what he'll be like if things ever go south.

Part IV

Transgressives

The band has been going back and forth with a major label, and their gig playing on the roof of a New York bar on New Year's Eve in a week will result in a final decision by the execs. On the surface, I've expressed a mellow indifference about it all, but in reality, I hope they suck hard. I hope Otis trips on a cord, takes down the rooftop setup, pukes all over what doesn't collapse, and loses that potential record deal and sponsored tour opportunity because I can't continue living on the road.

Our plane lands in Philadelphia late Christmas night and we crash at a motel, wherein Otis comes to bed with a knife, slicing me up like sashimi from my shoulder blade to ribcage. I think he does it on purpose, but it's hard to get mad while lost in a haze of Vicodin. I understand now why Landon's so afraid of hospitals and ERs. Without group insurance, my tooth extraction cost me more than I've paid for that insurance in the past three years, and Otis' carving would probably cost just as much, but with enough isopropyl alcohol for the wound and Valium for my nerves, I'm comfortable enough to let Landon fix me for free. I lie face-down on the starched motel sheets, letting him swab the wound with alcohol-soaked gauze while Otis takes Polaroids.

"You are starting to creep people the fuck out, Sid Vicious," Landon said.

"It was an accident," Otis said. "Like *Edward Scissorhands.*"

Not only is his behavior volatile, his mind is showing signs of advancing deterioration. Sometimes, he'll only shave half his face, or he'll take a sip of beer and get up to buy another, forgetting that he still has one in his hand, or he'll complain to someone on his cell phone that he can't find it but forgets he was looking for it before realizing he was talking on it the whole time.

This coupled with the butchering incident inspires Landon to start grinding up antidepressants in Otis' food, an idea that (ironically) he took from Mom, but two days later, they still haven't kicked in, and as a last resort, we try eliminating alcohol from the equation. Then AA throws him out of a meeting, because apparently he has to quit cold turkey and can't attend meetings partially buzzed. It's bullshit anyway. Hooking up two alcoholics and telling them to motivate each other is like hooking up two suicide cases, and if I was looking to get my life straight and overcome addiction, the last person I'd want as a sponsor would be a perverted whacko who can't put the bottle down long enough to finish puking.

***

The night Otis gets kicked out of the AA meeting, everybody is outside playing cards or quarters, so I'm left alone on the bus with him. He's trying to skewer me in between his hips and the miniature bathroom sink, but I'm not into the idea of being naked right now. I can feel Landon's amateur stitching pull taut in my back, even tearing through parts of my flesh, so the last thing I want to do is feel Otis' dirty fingernails digging into the raw openings between each stitch.

"Let's borrow Evie's porno," I say, thinking it might get me in the mood.

"I'm not watching some poor girl get jackhammered by some prick," he says. "It's disgusting."

"She said you watched the chicken one," I say.

"That's 'cause it was a chicken."

"How is that different?"

"I'm not a fuckin' vegetarian."

His thrusting does nothing for me, but he gets off in seconds from watching the long stretch of stitches ripple down the length of my back. While he cleans up, I dress and head outside. I shimmy between the buses and gag myself to empty my stomach of all the sloshing whiskey and beer for which I would ordinarily pay the price in a few hours. While bowed at the waist, I overhear Landon's inebriated laughter: "I fucking swear the Axis Powers are still around. You think it's coincidental that the best cars come out of Japan and Germany?"

I stand up to shout at him for being such a goddamn conspiracy theorist, but Otis stops me when he sloppily gropes me in the dark from behind. He presses me against the bus and manually clamps my hand around his dick, which is out and ready. He yanks at the sides of my pants, sliding them down my hips. His rugged fingertips feel up the stitches on my back as if he were reading them like Braille, and every once in a while he jams a nail or two into the open flesh. His dick aim is off, so he ends up thrusting between my legs, and before I can correct him, I feel his warm jizz gush over my thighs. He grapples my body down to the asphalt and dozes off with his mouth open and dick hanging out of his zipper.

***

"Babe, let's go bar-hopping," Otis says to the back of my head. They have the night of December 29th off before their last two shows, one in Jersey City tomorrow night, and the New Year's Eve performance in New York. Landon planned to pass out in his bunk and I planned to conquer a chapter or two of the manuscript. "You can edit later, can't you?"

No, I'll be holding his face out of the water of some Jersey Porta-Potty so he won't drown. When I look at him, I see irritation marks ringing his throat, perhaps indicating that he's just tried hanging himself again. "Why do you keep trying to kill yourself?" I ask. He shrugs like a thirteen-year-old scolded about neglecting his chores. "If you don't stop this, they're going to lock you up and you're going to die an old man in there."

Tonight he's somewhat functional, and though the situation is different from normal in theory, it'll all be the same by the end of the night. I mash my face into the seat of the bus as he sprints up and down the aisle singing and headbanging to his Walkman. He's insistent on going bar-hopping but none of us are in a mood like his, so we piss on the idea, which pisses him off, which pisses us off because he's the reason we pissed on it in the first place, which pisses him off because he realizes he's the cause, and the whole pissing contest ends with him locked in the bathroom again.

"Fucking shit!" Landon kicks the door before cussing into it. He isn't cynically comedic anymore. Now he's just chronically pissed off. "You need to get over your rich psychosis and fix the shit you've caused."

"Fuck you."

Enter the screaming accusations and blame: "I know exactly what you are with your crappuccinos, gas guzzlers, 401ks, and your ridiculous phobia of getting some pussy disease from a public shitter." It's like he practiced for the sake of flawless delivery. "Get over yourself."

"I drive a Camry hybrid," I say. "And I don't believe in 401ks because I never planned on living that long. And..." I wish I had the resilience of his tongue. I could go places with a talent like that. "You think you're such a rebel? You worked at Safeway, too: a resource-wasting capitalistic unionized grocer."

"Don't pretend to know who I am, you spoiled fucking brat," he says. "We have real problems, unlike the ones you people create, counting calories the way we count fuckin' food stamps."

"Then don't spend all your fucking money on tattoos. How do you expect anybody to take you seriously with 'vaginatarian' on your arm?"

"Who the fuck are you to lecture me about money? Don't you think if I had it, I'd pay to fix the goddamn heater? You don't know how fucking cold winter is without heat."

"Yes, I do," I say. Who wants to voluntarily die in their sleep from carbon monoxide poisoning?

"Oh, this from the neocon whose parents put her through college."

"Your idol, Dexter Holland, is an Orange County-bred USC grad. The epitome of—"

"One, you're not Dexter Holland, and two, you're the crazy bitch he writes about in his songs. And at least he's not some aristocrat looking down his trunk at us."

"I've never treated any of you different because of your...socioeconomic situation."

"You don't have to say it out loud. You being here is enough."

"That doesn't make sense," I say.

"We're just entertainment to you, right?"

"This is your idea of entertainment?" I ask. "Sleep deprivation, getting puked on, living on a bus?"

"Yeah, so at the end of the day, you can go home and brag to your friends and family about how you gained perspective when you went slumming with the lowest dredges of society."

I don't possess the mental acuity to even conjure that up, and if I wanted to gain perspective, I'd rather invite a piss-smelling insane alcoholic bum to sleep beside me every night, not put up with this bullshit. I desperately dig for the only thing I have left: "Maybe there *is* something wrong with you people. You're the only ones I know who didn't go to college."

He charges at me and backs me up against the bathroom door with both hands. "Look at where we are. We're everything we should be. We're part of the resistance. And what did your pansy-ass degrees get you? You learned how to put people down to feel better about yourself." I heard it's possible to kill a person with a ballpoint pen. I need to learn how to do that. "I always knew he'd end up with some psycho fuck," Landon says, "but he could've at least found one who's treatable. You can't cure spoiled rich bitch."

"Fuck, Landon." I force myself to swallow. "You're supposed to be on my side. We're supposed to band together against all that bimbo ditz Orange County bullshit."

"What side have your demented delusions put us on?"

"Punk." And I know I've backed myself up against the flypaper before saying it.

"That's fucking hilarious. Hey everyone, Veruca Salt here thinks she's *punk*."

I should have seen it coming. All Landon ever does is slam everybody unlike him for what they are, where they grew up, what they eat, what they buy, who's musically hardcore, who isn't, who will never be. It's not good enough to be a Democrat; one has to be a registered independent voter, a sovereign thinker outside the masses, outside even the subculture masses. It's not enough to play in a band, one has to hit the right balance of political and social commentary backed by original musicality. It's not enough to participate in change, one has to drive it in some subjectively fucked-up self-sacrificing way. In his view, it isn't about being thin, pretty, or rich enough; it's about being punk enough. Anybody not conforming exactly to his definition of punk is just a poser. I knew all of this before muttering one of the most controversial and debated words of our generation, but it was all I could manage. "Ask me what I believe in," I say. "Ask me what I am."

"You're a motherfucking cunt, that's what you are."

"Ask me about religion and politics and all the other social bullshit you're always going on about."

He chews on his lip and maybe I've cornered him for once, maybe for a split second he's scared shitless that I might be less of everything he's always accused me of being.

"Ask me something."

"Don't tell me what to do."

"Who gives a shit about where we came from or what we've had to do because of it? Who gives a fuck about the differences between a Republican or Democrat? Whatever the mess, it's still a mess, and in the end, we're all going to suffer and we're all going to have to clean it up." I wait for a glimmer of understanding from him, that maybe he understands I'm no ultraconservative princess or dumb-fuck American. But there's no recognition in his face at all.

"You're awful," he says. "Indifference is so much worse."

Before I can defend myself, Otis opens the bathroom door and shoves between us for the front of the bus. We tried bickering in private for his sake for a time, but after a while we stopped giving a shit and our screamfests made very public appearances.

Landon and I spend the rest of the night waiting for him to come back. For all we know, he could have thrown a tantrum somewhere in the state of New Jersey that landed him in a jail romance, the psych ward, or shanked in some back alley. Around 2 a.m., when the bus engine kicks on, he climbs onboard with the jerkoff who sold Evie the bad pot. They share headphones, harmonize David Bowie, and flip through *Alternative Press* like conjoined twins. He associates with the enemy for the rest of the day, laughing and pointing back at us like he wants to punish us for caring about him.

On stage, he opens the set in Jersey with a monologue about how the kids out in the crowd shouldn't feel bad if they feel fucked up and alone because he's more fucked up and alone than all of them because nobody gets him. It's kind of like watching an immature sixteen-year-old passive-aggressively blast the authority figures in his life. I wish he'd just grow the fuck up and act somewhat like the seasoned thirty-three-year-old he's supposed to be.

***

Riot Venom's New Year's Eve performance is anticlimactic. They play the same set the same disastrous way that I've had to put up with for the last four months, and yet everybody from the crowd to the band to the record execs thinks their inventive sound and image is the best thing since the meningitis vaccine.

I should be excited I'm in New York, the epicenter of the music industry, on New Year's Eve, but I don't give a shit. Otis is drinking by himself in a dressing room and I should prevent alcohol poisoning, but again, I don't give a shit. Trying to take beer away from him is like trying to wrestle a sack of garbage away from a rabid raccoon.

Minutes to midnight, I head out back for the portables to be with him anyway, and as I walk, I realize I've gone days without brushing my teeth. There's a slimy film on them that tastes like stomach bile fermented in a rain gutter, and it's encrusted with the stain of coffee and stout. Halfway to the dressing rooms, Landon calls my name from the second-floor balcony of the bar. He pukes over the railing, then comes down to meet me. We trek side-by-side to the dressing rooms, both so drained we don't even notice the awkward silence.

"Heard Christmas at your place was rough," he says. "*Joy Luck Club* rough."

It's hard to be civil after being at each others' throats two days earlier, but I make the effort since he does. "Something like that," I say.

When we get to the dressing room, we stall at the door and stare at our vapor-breath, puffing like cinder from our lips. Out of obligation he turns the handle, but I wish he hadn't. My jaw drops through the ceiling of hell and winds back around to kick me in the ass: I see a girl bent over Otis' lap, his shriveled cock in her hand. She wiggles the tip of her tongue over his mushroom head, then envelops it with her lips.

"Oh, good God," Landon says.

Of all the things I should be thinking—whore, slut, tramp, bitch, groupie ho, low-self-esteemed groupie trash, groupie nympho, home wrecker of the feeble and defenseless—I can only dwell on how exotic she is. Svelte, her complexion untainted by a single freckle, mole, or blemish, beyond lustrous hair that frames her face in black, silky waves. Flawless makeup, Halloween-exaggerated, but perfected to make her look dead, just the way Otis would like it.

I'm unsure if I should open up with guns blazing or try to shuffle her out civilly. I sift my memory for a similar conundrum I might have read about in a magazine, but I don't think anyone's done an advice column on how to handle finding your drugged-out comatose boyfriend with his dick through his pants while a stray dog gives him head that he doesn't know he's getting, or maybe he knows he's getting it, but he wants to pretend that he's so wasted he doesn't know so that it won't technically count as cheating. Then again, I doubt he has the understanding to devise such logic.

"Do you mind?" she asks us.

I hesitated too long and I'm left without a reasonable defense. I look for Landon, but he's slunk outside with his cell phone. I pull a bottle of rubbing alcohol from my bag and douse Otis' dick from head to base, then attempt to tuck it back into his pants, but she worms her fingers into my hair and yanks at my roots till I'm candy-caned backward, staring upside down at her. Though thin, she has a large skeletal build and launches me face-first into the wall. I bang and scrape the side of my cheek against the unfinished plywood, and the only concrete thought I can formulate in the seconds I have as she charges toward me with her claws extended is a line from Brad Listi's *Attention. Deficit. Disorder.*: "Quit being a pussy, you lame, sheltered, weak...suburban piece of shit."

She sacks me against the ground, straddles my chest, and pounds me in the forehead until it feels like one of my eyeballs dislodges and rolls around somewhere in my skull. I drag my nails down her creamy cheeks, instantly wishing I hadn't, because she goes for my hair, ripping out as much as she can, and then she stands to stamp my torso with boot treads. My only bragable victory is crawling away with the same twenty-six and a half teeth with which I entered the fight.

I can't feel which way gravity's headed, so I roll against the floor moaning melodramatically, hoping Otis will wake the fuck up and help me. He doesn't, but Landon's not far off, and after peeling me off the ground like roadkill, he pulls me into the alley behind the bar and insists that I learn how to defend myself since I'll eventually come across other psychos who will inevitably be attracted to the psycho in Otis.

"Can you just give me some Percs or something?" I ask, trying not to draw the attention of the clusters of people on the curb.

"Don't be such a wuss," he says. "Now, you're going to want to go for the stomach, and when they're bent over whining about it, pop them in the face or throat. If it's a guy, it's always the nuggets then face. Okay?"

"No."

"Here, practice on me, but don't really touch me."

"Ugh."

"Didn't they teach you shit like this in charm school?"

I pummel my shin through the space between his thighs and send his balls toward his chin, and while he's on his knees gasping for air, I club him in the eye. It's quiet as the onlookers watch him go down against the asphalt, holding his crotch. He threatens to inject garlic into my veins when I'm asleep, but it's so worth it.

***

Otis wakes up with an irritated lap, the two of us hovering over him with black eyes. I can't be pissed: after a bottle of gin and a prescription of tranquilizers, he barely remembers which side of the nation we're on. So we grab breakfast at a local buffet, and at the table, Landon chews him out over the incident. "One of these days, you're going to pass out and nobody's going to be around to prevent some pervert from shredding your asshole."

"I drank a lot. Take it with some salt," Otis says through a mouthful of sausage. He leans over to kiss my forehead but gets me in the eye with his slimy, sausage-juice-ridden lips instead. I try to rub off the greasy moisture before it seeps into my tear ducts.

"Next time you're going to say 'I was drunk, that's why I ended up licking all those herpes-ridden fur-burgers,'" I say. "'I was wasted and I tripped and my dick thrust repeatedly in and out of some crack whore's cunt and she gave me leprosy of the dick.' Or, 'I was plastered. That's why I let her infect me with super-AIDS and passed it to you.'" It's only when the entire buffet turns toward us that I realize I've lost all sense of propriety.

Two weeks from now, we're supposed to hit the road again, internationally this time, but I'm done being the psychologist/personal assistant/companion who has to pull his face off the floor and make sure he doesn't accidentally step off the curb in front of a carrier truck. My interest in Otis is decreasing at an exponential rate, and I end up sniveling over the phone to one of the most unlikely people: the editor. "It's like a mafia of gangsters. You can't get out alive," I say.

***

New Year's Day, we fly home to Sacramento. The agony of a failed suicide attempt (or a string of failed attempts) is equivalent to the agony of blue balls. It throbs and aches, and Otis mopes around at home in Roseville; he doesn't even pick up the drink. At night he wraps Landon's car around a telephone pole, but we all know he wasn't really trying to kill himself; he had his seatbelt on. And he totaled Landon's car, not his own, walking away from the incident without consequence because (as usual, in Landon's eyes) it's never Otis' fault: it's always mine.

The next day, I drive down to San Francisco at Sarah's request so she can nag about how I'll never get the manuscript picked up by a publisher if I don't finish (or start) editing it.

She looks different from what I imagined. On the phone she always sounds harebrained and unorganized, like she's tripping on meth. In person, she's composed. Petite but confident, faultless posture, disarming and modest expressions. She has soft crescent eyes, a slender, arched nose, and purple streaks in her chestnut hair, framing subtle dimples.

While she rambles on about missed editing deadlines, I wolf down her desk bowl of jellybeans without regard for the millions of germs that will soon gnaw away at my stomach lining. "You know, there's piss in restaurant mints?" I suddenly feel compelled to say. "Fuckers don't wash their hands after pissing and they grab a mint on the way out. I bet there's piss in this bowl right now and maybe a little shit. And did you know when you smell something you're smelling little pieces of it? For example, when you smell a lemon, you're inhaling little pieces of lemon, so that means when you smell shit, you're inhaling little pieces of shit."

She maintains a smug smile as if everything is passing right through her, so I continue. "And speaking of jizz, I found out, having accidentally opened a thesaurus and dictionary the other day, the word 'ejaculate' has two definitions, the other meaning to exclaim forcefully or passionately. Same with 'orgasm.' It means a climax of emotionally intensity. I blame it on the sexual revolution. Nowadays I can't write dialogue like, '"Oh, yes!" he ejaculates.' Or, 'Sir, this is a library, would you please refrain from all your vivacious ejaculations.' Or, 'She orgasmed when the juices from the sausage squirted into her mouth.' 'Cause then everybody will think I'm just a perv."

Still nothing. "Why don't we get some surf 'n' turf?" she asks finally. "My treat."

"I don't do bottom feeders," I say.

"What about a nice salmon filet?"

"Cross off seafood completely and blame it on rising mercury levels."

"Everything in moderation is okay."

"That's what the government makes the FDA announce in press releases. They don't want the fishing industry to fold. You want to get mercury poisoning, that's your prerogative. And don't get me started on that continent-sized garbage island of plastic in the middle of the Pacific. There's plastic in the food chain because of it. You're eating plastic."

"You're a super-duper special kind of killjoy, aren't you? You need to stop taking everything so seriously. You're going to give yourself a heart attack one of these days." Then she asks me about the "moment of weakness" I had with her best friend Laws, making me wonder how he, an editor, would describe a full-blown mental breakdown.

After the meeting, I drive back to Sacramento but make a detour to the county jail to bail out Avaline since she was arrested for "assaulting" her BMX-biker boyfriend. She stabbed him with a spork, and I've yet to decide what is more ridiculous: the spork, or the fact that the shithead called the cops because she stabbed him with a spork. "Was it a plastic spork?" I ask her.

He refused to let her talk about anything other than modeling, sports, and sex, because he couldn't stand the fact she was so fucked up. After the third hour of listening to her whine on my couch, that doesn't seem very inconsiderate.

She stays through the weekend, though, and I spend most of that time lying in bed in a stout-and-Vicodin haze. I know I need to get moving with edits, but I've come to realize that I've grown out of the story, the style of writing, the voice, the immature concepts. Trying to edit it feels like I'm performing some intricate and time-consuming operation on a dead corpse. I want to move forward and create new stories, not go back and analyze ones I'm no longer connected with.

On Monday, after a weekend of being home in Sac and away from Otis, I make the pilgrimage to Aunt Zee's house out of guilty obligation, but mostly because I'm out of Vicodin and I'm sick of the panic attacks I get when I think too much about Otis' parasites winding their way into my eyeball tissue for a conjunctivitis party. Also, I recently found out there exists such a thing as ocular herpes.

Inside the house, Landon's at the table perched on an elbow, his hand limply holding the cigarette to his mouth. When I sit across from him at the table, he glares but says nothing, as if silently formulating some jackass remark to hurl at me. I haven't seen or spoken to them in days, and I expected to hear about Otis OD-ing or finally killing himself, but there's nothing.

"What's he been up to?" I ask.

"What's he been up to?" Landon mimics behind his cigarette, motions that cause the ash from his cigarette to plop down into his cereal. Over the last few months, his corpse-like features have intensified. His bones seem shrink-wrapped in gray skin, most of which is concentrated under his eyes. That's all he is now: a mangled mess of bags, bones, veins, and skin that shiver in once-snug clothes.

Aunt Zee breaks our glaring contest when she sets a bowl of cream of wheat in front of me. When she's safely back in the garbage-ridden caverns of her kitchen, he tells me not to eat it. I pick up my spoon and part the sea of milk. Pill-shaped clumps break the surface of the grainy muck, and I don't get the chance to register exact details because I involuntarily keel over to hurl my M&M-and-coffee breakfast. The bile milkshake detonates out of my throat and nasal cavities, splattering on the linoleum beside my feet. I spit out the last dribbles of puke, swallow the residue on my tongue, and sit up teary-eyed in front of Landon who, to my surprise, isn't gawking, just solemnly exhaling smoke as if bored with the visual.

I can't shake the image of maggot bodies suspended in my stomach had I eaten it. It's burned into my eyes, and when I shut them, I still see the outline of the wigglers. Something brushes up against my ankles, and when I look down, I see two cats lapping at the regurgitated puddle.

I trip from the table, through the living room, and down the hall to the bathroom, but the door's locked; I kick it in and bowl over to heave into the sink till my stomach walls grind against each other. The cats follow and whine for attention, but midpuke, I reach down and chuck those bitches into the hall and wedge the busted-slab-of-wood-that-was-once-a-door in place to keep them out. I ransack the counters for antibacterial soap, overturning liquor bottles and beer cans, but there's nothing. I only notice Otis in the bathtub after I snatch his whiskey away to disinfect my hands.

"Jesus fucking Christ," I say as the whiskey dribbles off my fingers. "It's a Third-World country in here." He peers up at me with bloodshot, shitfaced eyes. His belt is tightened around his right biceps, there's a live syringe teetering between the pads of his jittering fingers, and a cigarette dangles limply in the corner of his mouth. "When did you start smoking?" I ask.

He turns away and exhales without answering. It looks like he's literally been wallowing in this bathroom sty all weekend, as there is a weekend's worth of cigarette butts, alcohol containers, and heroin residue to vouch for it. I'm not sure what I should be more worried about: E. coli, maggots, cat saliva, lung cancer, the fleas, or being swallowed whole by this biohazardous slum.

"You want to get in with me?" He motions to the empty tub.

"Not really," I say, forgetting how a single asinine response can blow everything out of proportion.

"What the fuck do you want?" he asks. "Hmm?"

"For fuck's sake, give me a chance to answer." I wipe the remains of regurgitated coffee from the corners of my mouth and clear the drug paraphernalia from the toilet cover.

"Why'd you take so long? You were out there like you were talking shit about me. What was Landon saying?"

"Calm down, you're acting—" We both know what I meant to say.

"I am fuckin' crazy. Is that what you want to hear? That I go to a fuckin' shrink? That it's ninety dollars 'cause we don't have any fucking insurance like you people?" He trips over his words, chokes on his saliva, and descends into a coughing fit. "You should've known."

"Known what?" I ask.

"I'm fuckin' crazy. You said it's weak to go. I'm so fucking weak. I was tired of it killing me. It hurt so bad. I don't want to fuckin' cry anymore." His face shrinks into itself and he drops into a prolonged wail.

"Stop taking me so seriously."

"It's killing me. I need to fucking die."

"Please stop crying," I say. We're home now, but nothing's changed.

"Don't look at me like that." He points up at me. "Stop looking at me like that."

I don't think he knows who I am, just that there's someone in the room passing judgment. "Like what?"

"Like I'm a fuckin' joke."

"I'm not."

"Like I'm the only one who's fucked up."

"What are you talking about?"

"You ever wonder why your hands look like the Crypt Keeper's? Or why you're up for weeks on speed?"

It takes inner poise I never thought I had to fend off the fury building in my skull. "I'm not on speed."

"Bullshit. You ever count how many pills you take just to go to sleep? Landon says you probably puke up your food, too. Bet you want a drink now, huh? He's got Valium. And Vicodin. And Perco-something. You want OxyContin? You always drank those with a forty."

"You're hurting me."

"Good," he says. "Do you know the shit you've put me through?"

I mow through the crap on the floor, force myself to ignore the scattering silverfish and roaches, and kneel to lift him against me. He smells like rancid liquor, stomach acid, and damp cigarettes, but I squeeze tighter. He feels foreign. I didn't notice when we fucked, but I feel it now. He's frail, breaking apart at the joints.

"Why don't you write anymore?" he whines into my chest as I kiss his greasy head, hoping to dissolve his paranoia. "You never wrote a poem for me. Write me lyrics."

"Come home with me," I say. I don't have any armor here; everything's in my sterile apartment where I can regulate the microbial population.

"Talk to me about Avaline." He shoves me back against the toilet. "Tell me what she's doing. Hurry."

"Don't worry about her, worry about yourself." And yes, I said it. This is the kind of bullshit people used to force on me, and now I'm cramming it down the throat of the last person I should be lecturing.

"Lannie was fucking right," he says. "You were never on meds because you didn't need them. You say they fuck you up, but you never needed them. What if I did? I'm different from you." He kicks the tub walls and moans about medicine being the only thing that's worked and all I've ever said was how it was wrong. "I'm fuckin' sick. It's in my fucking head and heart."

"We'll go to my place and do whatever makes you feel better," I say, but this is the rationale of an idiot who has no idea how to fix this. Irony: the misunderstood has become the ignorant.

"You don't know what it's like," he says.

"Then tell me."

He covers his face with his arms and sinks deeper into the tub to cry. I don't know how much more of this I can take. If he isn't throwing a tantrum, he's accusing me of some failure to understand. "What took you so long?" he asks. "How come you didn't come sooner?" I clench my lips shut but he continually provokes them with questions about why I didn't call, come over, get here sooner to be with him, or in other words, take care of him. "What were you doing being gone so long?" I reach for his hand but he retracts it defensively into his chest, scowling with unblinking eyes before diving into a paranoid fit about how we're all conspiring against him. "You left me for so long. You didn't even fucking call. You don't give a shit about me."

"I had shit I needed to do," I say. "I gave up my life to follow you around like a dog. You can't give me a few days?" I name off errands like cleaning, paying bills, and sleeping to validate and humanize my absence, but I didn't do any of that except spend a few hours a day with my newest friends Dictionary and Thesaurus. Come to think of it, I don't know what I was doing; it was just so liberating to be somewhere that wasn't the tour bus or bathroom floor. "I don't belong stuffed in a cheap tour bus that reeks of rotting flesh and backfiring exhaust." I wasn't meant to live on wheels enduring the atrocities of truck-stop shitters and Porta-Potties all over the nation, sleeping in a cesspool of a thousand motel patrons' worth of skin cells, piss, jizz, and saliva, eating nothing but hormone-injected fast food and disease-ridden buffet entrees.

"What were you doing without me? You fuckin' disappeared," he says.

"It's like you liked it better when I didn't have a life." The bitterness is bubbling to the surface like so many maggot bodies.

"Get the fuck out of here," he says.

"What do you want from me?" Kree badgered me with this same question every time our arguments went on too long, but I finally get where he was coming from. "I gave up everything to come with you and you don't even see me."

"'Cause you don't know what it's like."

I'm so tired I don't feel myself saying shit I can't take back: "I don't. I don't get what it's like to have everything given to you. You just got done touring with a major record deal lined up. You get to do what you want. When do I get to be what I want?" Put two of the most self-centered and volatile people in the same room and they won't destroy each other, they'll destroy themselves. "You're always going on about what Guy Picciotto has to say about doing something constructive with your pain. Take a lesson from Trent Reznor. 'If you want to kill yourself, do it; save everybody the fucking hassle. Or get your shit together.' You have the opportunity to put on the best motherfucking rock show, but you flop around on stage like a drunk retard. The crying and being miserable, that's not what music is about."

"Who the fuck are you to tell me what music's about? Go the fuck away. Leave me alone."

My fucked-up wisdom momentarily makes me believe that launching another torpedo will fix this. "So you can attempt to attempt to kill yourself?"

"Fuck you."

"You don't mean that."

"Fuck you."

"Do you know who you're talking to?"

"Yeah, so fuck you."

"I can't help you," because I don't know how, but I wish I did, so I wouldn't have to know what it's like to be the frustrated dumb shit watching on the other side.

I shout for Landon and he busts into the bathroom like Otis has already killed himself. "What's he taken?" I ask.

"The usual," he says.

"Babe, come home with me," I say, trying to pry the miscellaneous drugs from his fingers. I lurch for the heroin-filled syringe against the wall of the tub, but he gets me by the hair and accidentally rips a significant clump from my scalp. I slap him in the face, and he slinks down to cry into his chest.

"Just let him have it." Landon wrestles the syringe from me, and I let go because I know we both want Otis to stop.

As he tightens the belt around his arm, I study a scrawny body that's spent months wasting away on bathroom floors and in motel tubs. His face isn't a round pumpkin that smiles anymore; it's gaunt, angular, sunken into itself. He's metamorphosed from someone wholesome, real, and alive, to something brittle, sick, and unfamiliar. We watch as he injects and loosens the belt around his arm to let the poison meet with the rest of his body.

***

The thing is, self-medicating with TV, Internet, video games, diet soda, and three pounds of chocolate won't kill a person, but a combination of prescription drugs, booze, and hardcore unadulterated substances will. We end up in the ER because there's nothing in Landon's first aid kit that reverses a heroin overdose.

"We should buy stock in one of those heroin antidotes," Landon says.

"At the rate you're enabling, we just might have to," I say.

"What the fuck's that supposed to mean?" he asks.

"It means it's time for you to quit dicking around with the fucking coke and set an example."

"Last I heard, Adderall was an amphetamine and Vicodin was a narcotic."

"I don't contribute to illegal drug delinquency."

"You justify it in your head 'cause yours come in the form of a prescription? At least we're open and honest about who we are."

"I'm not the one who put the needle in his arm."

"You don't fight or yell at someone who's ready to snap."

I know where this is going, he knows where it's going, and if we weren't such jackasses one of us would end it. "He was yelling first."

"Then you let him yell. Fuck. You walk around like your problems are bigger than everyone else's. They're not."

"Everything was fine before the tour." Before the grimy motels, grueling concerts, and heroin and booze. There weren't any shitfaced tantrums, shitfaced suicide episodes, or shitfaced cocksucking sessions with skanky groupies.

"Yeah, because he had a therapist and expensive meds keeping him alive, and then you came around preaching all that *Brave New World* bullshit."

***

I buy a ridiculous amount of vodka and orange juice and drink my way through it. In the heart of my deepest inebriated state, Mom calls, but she doesn't notice how fucked up I am because she's too busy dominating the conversation the way she always does.

"Dump the retail," she says. "Although, I doubt anybody outside that industry would want to hire you with your qualifications. And when you go for interviews, wear skirts. You didn't sell all your good clothes and jewelry for drugs, did you?"

It's disorienting to go from the chaos of the road back home to Sacramento, where I'm forced to deal with the uncomfortable return of reality. On tour, the daily agenda's pretty set: wake up, get Otis up, make sure he gets through the interview and/or sound check, get him on stage, get him back on the bus, get him to sleep, mop up the puke and piss, and if I'm lucky, sleep for an hour, then do it all again.

But the momentum of that reality is different from the reality asphyxiating me now. I have to worry about groveling my way back into the job market, paying bills I've gotten behind on, and the drugs don't flow the way they did on the road. The withdrawal enhances every inconvenience and pain, from bill collectors to Mom's nagging to job applications. I don't know if it's the withdrawal from Otis or from the Vicodin; maybe it's both.

I wallow the week away in a mindless routine of TV, screwdrivers, and Xanax I stole from Avaline, trying to divert the guilt from all the bills, responsibilities, and other realities decaying on my doorstep like an abandoned, murdered, and maggot-stuffed rape victim. In between it all, I wonder if I am responsible for Otis' demise, or if he's responsible for mine. Whichever it is, our next steps both seem pretty dismal.

Eat Out the Exit Wound

It's Friday night, and after only a week of being back in Sacramento, I'm already lying in bed eating from a five-pound tub of Red Vines, chugging gin and tonics (or maybe just the gin), obsessing over how we dissolved without even going through the motions. We were fucking against a motel sink one morning, in separate sheets the next. I hate this new reality: cleaning an empty apartment, sleeping in an empty bed, and checking an empty voicemail box. I miss the chaos of the road, and even though it was mostly shitty/incoherent/out of control, I miss Otis.

Saturday, Riot Venom show up for their gig at The Catalyst in Santa Cruz, so I know for sure that Otis hasn't yet killed himself. I buy a ticket, get myself marched on by a crowd surfer, and stand in the faceless crowd as if it's my expectation, maybe even a necessity, to see him play the show plastered, miserable, and hysterical. But I see no evidence that he is distraught over our breakup, that he sucked off Jameson till borderline unconscious, nor that there is any anxiety shivering at the edge of his voice. In fact, I've never seen him so composed.

The show lets out and they take off from the venue before I can fish myself from the crowd, so I soon find myself outside, at a payphone, debating whether it's better to get brain cancer from my cell or tuberculosis from the public phone. I settle on cancer.

Evie coughs up directions on their whereabouts, but warns me in the subtlest of ways that I shouldn't come. "He's with someone," she says. I should have expected her to say something like this. Though Otis persistently reeks of musty puke and piss, there's never been a shortage of snatch circling him the way those inner-city park pigeons circle around puddles of bum barf, pecking away at whatever it is that bums eat.

I need to get him back.

I drive to the house party and in my head it's a hardcore porn fest: close-up shots of Otis coming, a myriad of glistening cunts, each jump-cutting to the next as if he is some sexual superhuman blessed with an infinite amount of nut fuel.

When I arrive at the party, Joey steps into the doorway to block me. "She just started hanging around," he says. "She's a SuicideGirl and does vocals for some SoCal chick band, but if you ask me, they suck." The words sputter sluggishly from his mouth in uneven intervals as if he's stalling, but I veer past him and into the next room, where I see that Otis is with someone, but not just a no-name someone; it's someone who probably recalls very distinctly how she kicked my ass in New York.

"Hazel." Landon latches onto my arm.

The party's a people maze with very little visibility, but I see Otis' lips responding to hers and it doesn't matter if he's teetering on the brink of unconsciousness and has no idea what he's doing, it's the fact that he knew hours ago—before the seven shots of Jäger—that he'd end up doing it.

"Don't do this." Landon's fingers clamp around my arm so tightly that his nails burrow into my skin. "Just leave them alone. They're in their own little drugged-out world together. She's on hardcore shit like lithium. It's like looking into a mirror for him."

I claw at my chest, thinking I might convulse from arrhythmia, so I push through the crowd and jerk at her beanstalk arm, hoping to yank hard enough to dislocate something. Joey probably remembers how I came out last time, so he dives on top of her, and with the beast contained, I crawl onto Otis' lap and grind my face against his familiar stubble. I inhale his scent, feel his silky hair kissing the grooves of my fingers, and I'm instantaneously balanced again.

"Let go," Landon says. I slap Otis a few times, hoping he'll wake up, but he whines and flops over the armrest. "He is staring down a loaded gun and his finger isn't on the trigger. He needs to be with someone who gets that."

"I get it," I say.

"No, you worry about bacteria."

"So I'm not crazy *enough*?" I'm right here being what I've always been because that's all Otis said he needed, and thrashing on the floor is Courtney Love's evil twin, and he chose her. I can't help but feel somewhat inadequate.

144

"Go home to your mother," he says.

I lurch for Otis' unconscious, pathetic, alcoholic corpse and roll him onto the floor to tenderize his stomach. While pounding with one fist and fighting off Landon with the other, it dawns on me: I've turned into the psycho, launching into a bitch fit in public.

I feel the wind knocked out of me—Joey has lost his hold on the groupie, and she rams me against the dusty floorboards. She gets in some hearty smacks and scratches before Landon and Joey pry her off. "Get out of here," Landon says. "Just stay away from us."

"He came to me," I say. "He noticed me."

"He was so starved for a cock pocket, he would've fucked Anna Nicole Smith's corpse." He screams it, but it's not the sarcastic screaming I can use as kerosene to burn him back; it's the kind that spirals me into a new dimension of inadequacy.

The rubberneckers drop against each other laughing, but they don't realize that he just carved out a piece of me that'll never grow back. The monster that treated me like fly-infested shit, lived to make my job a cesspool of intimidation, and made it clear he never had any intention of accepting me as good enough for his psychotic brother just crushed my last toe of submissiveness.

I scrape myself off the floor. Landon is holding down the groupie, which puts his nose at an easily accessible level for my fist. I feel it break long before my knuckles throb.

He lets go of her and brings his fingers up to his face to survey the damage as if he can't tell by the way the blood coats his upper lip like a mustache. He takes two strides and I watch passively as he returns the blow with knuckles adorned in silver rings. When I hit the floor, I pep talk myself into believing that it could have been worse, that he could have meatloafed my face entirely. "That's the last time you hit me, you fuckin' bitch!" he scream-gurgles in choking sputters, like he forced the words out just as a river of blood went down. He hacks up mucus and blood, spits into my face, then grabs Evie and walks away.

I squeeze my eyes shut to prevent his slime from dripping in, and crawl for the door when I realize that nobody is going to ask if I'm okay. Outside on the lawn, I drop face-first into the grass. It's cold and smells musty like it's just been watered, but who knows? Maybe I'm wallowing in a cold puddle of beer and piss.

***

Now, if I were a cop and the car I'd been tailing for ten minutes was driving erratically, and after pulling it over and interrogating the lunatic inside, I noticed that the driver reeked of beer, was scream-singing Fiona Apple through a mouthful of blood, hitting the dashboard with her fists, and couldn't walk a straight line because of fallen arches, I'd arrest me, too.

Six months ago I was sitting in my room, packing away candy and diet soda, while Kree sat in front of the TV getting fatter and dumber, and now I'm sitting in a bona fide small-town jail cell while a few cops gorge on square-shaped burgers from Wendy's and bicker with each other about my fate.

Though my situation is highly uncharacteristic, I don't want—after passing the breathalyzer test with a blood alcohol level of 0.00—to be driven back to my car on the side of the road; I don't want to go home alone. I understand now why Avaline does what she does. Once or thrice she set off her apartment alarm while she was home and pretended someone was trying to break in so the sheriff would come out and take down a report. She even went as far as setting a kitchen fire so the fire department would bathe her in attention. Not only did she get sympathy and pity, but her model face and figure made off with a handful of phone numbers.

Since I don't have the energy or creativity to pull off such a cry for help, when I get home from Santa Cruz, I lie in bed obsessing over what I could have done differently, and no matter how insignificant, I want to take it all back, knowing that if I'd just let it go, we'd still be together. I'd let Otis play the explicit ballads of The Misfits while we fuck. I could even live with the Batman headstone, or more correctly, die with it. Without him, there's no faith in my writing, no point in sex. Jerking off now feels like a chore, like flossing my teeth.

***

For the rest of January, I fall back into old habits such as sugar, cleaning, and retail. After shitting on the industry, it's hard to take myself seriously as I pace the narrow, filthy, and disorderly aisles of a Walgreens. Not only is this a demotion in rank (I'm an assistant manager in a store that feels like the size of my 900-square-foot apartment), pay (I'm making half what I made with Safeway), and theory (everybody knows what a Third-World dump Walgreens is), but this institution will never be as sterile or controlled as my Safeway, and the workplace filth follows me home. The walls, carpets, and countertops of my apartment swell with the plague of Walgreens patrons. I breathe it. Consume it. It never leaves my skin or dissipates from my bloodstream.

After work every day, I throw my dirty clothes in a bucket of disinfectant at the doorway. I decontaminate the walls, even if I've done them in the morning. I sanitize the shower, toilet, and sinks after every use and wash the dishes and silverware even when they're unused. My hands whittle away to crumbling and bleeding extensions of my arms, so at work I hide them in latex gloves.

After my second week of training, I hole up in my apartment with the Hostess children and Jameson. I must have spaced out somewhere between the overlapping hours of Aimee Mann, because I stand beneath the store's general manager, who waves a complaint form at eye level. Apparently, when there's nothing left to sue over, the American consumer will complain about stock boys not having enough enthusiasm for their jobs, and my boss tells me to coach this minor about exhibiting more passion.

In my mind I snag this kid by the collar and scream at him to run from the shackles of retail while he's still young. In reality, I linger at the end of the aisle and watch as he painstakingly pushes his flat bed of generic snacks toward the shelf. When I finally kill the last of my free will, I approach and tell him that maybe he should think about smiling a little more. The words dribble from my mouth like piss from behind a kidney stone. I wish I could tell him that this inane request could only happen in America. Afterward, winded by the situation, I lean against the shelves and grapple down the soda to the linoleum. "Are you okay?" he asks.

My brain feels like a dried sponge, fried and porous from all the alcohol and pills I've downed over the months. Lately, I've been experiencing light-headed episodes that drop me to the floor and it takes a few minutes to get the world to stop bouncing me around. I tell people I suffer from narcoleptic episodes that turn violent if anybody disturbs me. I've tried to counteract the sickness by adding a few shots of Bailey's to my morning coffee, and although it hasn't helped much for the dizziness, it's sure made it easier to deal with shit like this:

"Your store doesn't sell adult diapers for big-boned people."

"Safeway sells these Magnums for ninety cents less, can you price-match that?"

"My son just slipped and fell in your aisle. What are you going to do about that?"

"I'm going to kill myself," I say.

"What?"

"I said, I'll take care of it myself."

***

In just under a month, I've probably downed enough chocolate, diet soda, and booze to sustain a relocation camp through winter. I'm tempted to sloth through the last weekend in January, self-medicating at the Pepperidge Farm, but I decide against it, and instead make the drive to Laws' office in SF. Over the past three months, I missed his original deadline for the first chapter, and then I missed the one that he pushed back, and I may have missed another one independent of those first two. It all blurred into a tick-less timeline since I didn't have a thought to myself outside of Otis.

At the end of the tour in New York, I delivered a broken and anemic first chapter, torn up, cut and pasted, missing punctuation, missing words (and probably whole paragraphs and concepts), and according to our incompatible word processors (mine was a generic piece of shit that came with the second-hand archaic laptop I bought in Jacksonville for fifty bucks), the document that he received on his end was a blank page sprinkled with alien font characters that I think he took as my idea of a sick joke. Today, I bring a hard copy of that mangled first chapter.

When I get to his office, I am a miserable specimen of society, physically drained, emotionally hung-over, and craving a tall glass of vodka. I have to tape-record his comments because my knuckles are so dry from the disinfectants that I can't bend my fingers without my skin splitting open.

"You're improving," he says. "Did you get a thesaurus for Christmas?"

He never means to come off asinine, but it irks me nonetheless. Laws is clumsily tall, six and a half feet high or more, and if he walks with his head down hoping to avoid kicking or stomping something accidentally, he'll hit his head on a low overhang, but if he's watching out for the overhang, he'll inevitably kick or stomp something. His build is overwhelming, visually intimidating (his fingers are bulbous and branchy, and he could strangle me with one hand if he had it in him), and if he stands up or leans across the table, it feels like the space in the room shrinks. But he's also timid and humble, a fifty-something bachelor who seems open to exploitation in most regards, except when it comes to literary proficiency.

He mumbles quicker than a cracked-out auctioneer about what needs to be reworked, rewritten, or cut out. There's always some form of what he calls "constructive criticism" prowling in the shadows of his chicken's feet, and he starts most of his sentences with "don't take this personally." Example: "Don't take this personally, and this is something that copy editing would catch, but duct tape is not spelled like a quacking duck."

Okay, maybe that was common sense, but that's beside the point.

"You alive? You haven't disagreed yet," he says.

I nod. It's so quiet I can hear his eyelashes beat against the lenses of his bifocals.

"You know..." He pauses as if to let a colossal wall of criticism build in the back of his throat. "People like Otis never really click with life. Look at Ozzie Osborne and Axl Rose. I bet they still haven't figured *it* out."

I gaze at his bland face and wonder where he a) gets his information, b) thinks Otis is anything like Ozzie Osborne or Axl Rose, and c) thinks I'm begging for life lessons.

"No relationship is equal," he says. "One is always more invested than the other, so someone always ends up hurt."

I don't get what he means by that. Maybe he's saying that I was the loser dog in the relationship, pining away for Otis, that I really am a mutt because I gave up my own identity to follow him around and sop up his puke and piss, because I let him pull me around on a leash that I couldn't break away from because I was too busy measuring out his drugs, finding him booze, and talking him down from psychotic episodes. Then he traded me in like an old clunker for a tax break and a shiny, upgraded dick magnet, and—through his brother—dumped me. I feel used and duped, and above all, fucking stupid, and I can't believe Mom was right; she was fucking right, and maybe I knew this whole time that something would give, but fuck, I just needed to experience something different.

"Maybe you're the loser dog in your relationship!" I shout across the table.

His eyes drop from the wall behind me down to the manuscript, and I expect him to say something like, "I'm not putting up with a freak show like you, get the fuck out of my office," even though he's probably never said or typed the word "fuck" in his life, much less thought it.

"I didn't mean that," I say. "I should go." I push my chair away from the table and turn toward the door.

"Hazel, I have a nephew," he says.

Fuck.

"He's a couple years younger than you, but he's passionate about music and literature. He was always going on about how nobody understood him, either. I know he really likes punk music, bands like P.O.D. and MxPx. His favorite is Slick Shoes."

I attempt to change the subject with an editing question: "Is 'nut sack' two words or one? And is it possessive as in 'nut's sack' or no possessive but plural as in 'nuts sack' or is it both possessive and plural 'nuts' sack'?"

"Maybe you two can go to a concert or something," he says, as if the topic of nuts never came about.

***

The first Friday in February, Mom forces me to go to a foundation benefit dinner in downtown SF where I'm introduced to Patrick, a project manager for a water cooler/office politics/cubicle corporation. He's six foot something, every blond hair on his scalp cut to precision, his suit seemingly custom-carved to his athletic form, and he commands attention in his facial posture, holding his chin at an exact forty-five-degree angle. "So, what do you do?" he asks. I can already tell I'm not good enough to hold a conversation with someone like him. Since he won't lower his chin even a few degrees, his eyes strain to peer down at me, and after a few seconds, he gives up and pans the room like he's trying to catch bits of other conversations.

I chased the last of Avaline's Xanax earlier in the bathroom and followed it with three Jack and Cokes from the open bar. Somewhere between the teriyaki skewers and the silent auction table, I went under, and since then, I haven't cared if chili-induced diarrhea is detonating from my mouth and splattering all over these aristocrats and their designer silks. "I drive a bus," I say. "And I run people over." I bowl over at the waist laughing, but he doesn't walk away.

150

"What company are you with?"

"Microsoft."

He laughs, then asks: "Should we do dinner and a movie tomorrow night?"

I object to the movie, saying it'd cut into our time of getting to know each other. In reality, I haven't done movie theaters in over a decade. I read somewhere that people put HIV-laced needles in the seats and unwary patrons don't realize they're getting an ass full of death.

***

I meet him for dinner at the Zinfandel Grille, knowing I need to change something about my routine before I spiral out of control and end up behind chicken-wire glass. I derive confidence in knowing that someone like him, someone who, at first impression, is a stereotypical metrosexual yuppie who swallows women whole in his bed, would ever take a second glance at someone like me. Though his crater-ridden face has endured more than a few years of raging zits, he seems whip-smart and business savvy, as if he could work any room to his advantage. He could have anybody he wants, but he drove over an hour into Sacramento to have dinner with me, and I figure I've had such bad luck with the mellow and apathetic, the artistic and insane, that maybe arrogant and educated will work this time around.

"I'm sick of hearing about all the donate-to-Katrina-victims bull," he says. "One, that was three and a half years ago, and two, why didn't those idiots evacuate when they were told to? You see a circle of wind headed for your state, get the hell out." He motions with an aggressive jerk of his thumb. "You have to be a complete moron to voluntarily live in a region where you know destruction happens every year. I mean, why subject yourself to disaster over and over? Who does that? You have to be some kind of a sick masochistic freak or something."

The only way to skate through his obnoxiously offensive opinions unscathed is to nod.

"I got two calls from telemarketers today," he says. The first wanted money to research infant death, but I told her that it's population control."

An ass full of HIV doesn't seem half bad anymore.

"This other guy wanted money to enforce seatbelt laws, but I told him people who don't wear seatbelts are too dense to live."

And I drink. I go through three-quarters of a bottle of wine by myself before dinner arrives.

"So are you a conservative like the rest of your family?" he asks. "Your party drove this nation into the ground. Still does." I laugh and rub my forehead because there's nothing else I can do in place of gouging out his eyeballs with my fork. "By the way, you have really great DSL."

"I'm still on dial-up," I say. "I only word process."

"It stands for 'dick-sucking lips.' And dial-up? Geez, how archaic are you," he says. "So, I hear you've been out 'finding yourself' over the last year." He quotes with his fingers. "A lot of 'sex, drugs, and rock and roll'?" Again with the fingers. "Did you get it on with other chicks?" I can only imagine the rumors my family is spreading about me. "What about threesomes? Come on, you're not that ugly; the opportunity must have presented itself." He slides over to my side of the booth, and the cologne radiating off him burns the inside of my nose. It smells like someone chemically bound together gasoline and grandpa aftershave. "You into breath play?" He shivers like he's turning himself on. "Or being burned?"

"What?"

"With wax, cigarettes, things like that. Quit being a cock tease. I've seen the scars." He moves against me till I'm backed up against the wall of the booth. "I know that's not thyroid surgery."

"Hey, hazelnut." The tension and discomfort of being cornered by Patrick is broken when I look over my shoulder and see Kree; but a newer, polished version of Kree. It feels like a pelvic exam, when the probing instruments are pulled out of one hole only to be shoved into another.

"I haven't seen you in forever," Kree says, presenting himself to me for a hug. Maybe it's the restaurant's mood lighting, but his eyes are fiercely blue, he has a facial complexion he hasn't had since the womb, and he's dressed like a page out of a Macy's catalog: white V-neck sweater, fitted jeans, black pea coat. "You've really cleaned up," he says. "What are you up to these days?"

"She's at Walgreens," Patrick says.

"Oh, yeah? I thought you'd retire with Safeway. You—"

"Nope. Assistant manager at Walgreens," Patrick says.

"You look so good, hazelnut," Kree says. "So you're not gothic anymore?"

"Can we talk about something else?" I say.

"So you're not with that goth anymore?"

"What about you?" I don't know why I turn it around and ask if he's seeing anyone; maybe I'm hoping he's pathetically single.

"I'm with this girl who techs for musicals. She has this refreshing upbeat attitude about life. I finally found a keeper," he says.

"Totally happy for you." I haven't faked it this much since he was on top of me.

While he goes into detail about his "keeper," I dump the last of the wine into my glass and gulp, tuning out both him and the sarcastic expression Patrick has had on his face for the last minute or so, likely because he's been making mental wisecracks about Kree this whole time. "How's your romantic life?" Kree asks.

"This is my romantic life," I say as I give him the finger. Well, I don't do that, but I really should have.

"Did you hear I moved to LA? I got someone to work on a movie with me. It's not big or anything, but it could hella kick ass if we work hard."

"You have a movie deal?" I choke on wine as the pillars of envy shit green turds from above. Wait a fucking minute. Seven months ago, he was on his ass watching daytime TV, eating Ramen, and drinking beer at 10 a.m., and now he's thirty pounds thinner and somewhat attractive with a movie deal and a functional relationship?

"I wrote this script and got someone to put up some money to produce it."

There's something wrong with the success factor here. This is Kree. He passed college entry-level English with a D-. From then on, I wrote all his papers to ensure he wouldn't be a seven-year undergraduate.

His friends holler at him from the restaurant door, which is strange because I don't remember him having too many friends, much less friends who ate at places like this. As he walks through the exit, a gust of wind pops up the collar around his neck.

"Where was I?" Patrick resumes his interrogation. "Oh, S&M. Your mom described your ex to me and it sounds like he was into hardcore S&M."

I end the date there, figuring I'd better get out before I find myself sodomized by a piece of his IKEA furniture or something.

***

I'd feel inhumane if I went out with Patrick and didn't give Laws' nephew one decent conversation, so several nights later, I'm on another date.

"You have to try the sausage in my jambalaya," Laws' nephew says.

"No, thank you," I say. The night has consisted of mild-mannered conversation, filled with stiff, interview-like questions that go nowhere.

"You have to," he says. "I've never tasted anything like it." He stabs a giant, sweating globule with his fork and holds it near my face.

There are so many things wrong with this situation that I don't know where to begin. "It's been stewing in your cootie soup," I say.

"This isn't sixth grade. I don't have cooties," he says. "You'll thank me after you taste this." The pressure in my veins has grown over the last minute. "Come on, open the hangar." And I don't know how much longer I can contain it. "Don't leave me hanging." He pushes the boiled-flesh blob inches away from my lips. "It's seasoned really well."

And here it comes: "You people get grossed out when Hannibal scarfs skin, but you wolf down *processed meat* like it's a matter of survival? Take a field trip to a processing plant and watch them toss entire mooing, oinking, gobbling animals into the grinder, but not before ripping out their intestines because their own puréed flesh seasoned with cancer-inducing nitrates needs a skin casing, all in the name of sausage." I didn't mean to unload my hostility toward Patrick onto this innocent guy; I just couldn't hold it in any longer, and after two glasses of Zin on an empty stomach, it busted through my seams that much easier. And it wasn't like I didn't warn him with the initial "no."

"You have a lot of problems, don't you?" he says. "All of them would be solved if you just accepted Jesus Christ into your heart."

That was the last straw, but I should have seen it coming.

***

Mom drives up to Sac to visit, and she spends her time flittering around the apartment, ransacking every room, and dumping shit left and right. The trashcan is filled with nail polish, hair dye, and anything Otis left behind—razors, CDs, rubber body parts, paintbrushes, pill bottles. There's a pile of my Dickies clothes and tour hoodies in the middle of the living room, and the only thing Mom hasn't done yet is set it ablaze and dance around it with a pitchfork.

Since I blew off Patrick, her comments about how I'm going to die shriveled, alone, and pathetic are not in short supply.

"That's the last real man you'll ever see."

"Get used to seeing 'Just For One' TV dinners in your freezer for the rest of your life."

"You need to put up a profile on those mail-order bride sites."

I am way too sober for this.

"It's all about perspective," she says. "You have to get up in the morning and say to yourself, 'I'm going to be the best person I can be.'"

Way too sober.

"You come from a good family, and all you've done is waste it away."

She's right. I'm bred from one that's never, not in all our generations, seen a divorce. No one suffers from substance abuse, no one ever beat me, and no one sat me in front of the television to let MTV raise me, although now that I think about it, that probably wouldn't have been half bad.

"If you laid off the carbs and stopped listening to that horrible music you'd be so much healthier and happier," she says. "That racket gives a person indigestion."

"Yes, Mother, sugar and punk are the root of all my problems," I say. But fuck, maybe she's right.

"So are you and that she-male broken up for good?"

"For this life," I say.

She sleeps on the couch now. She used to share the bed with me when she visited. She won't put her toothbrush in the same cup as mine, and she insists on having her own soap in the shower, keeping it in a tall-walled soap dish. I did the same with Kree, but that was Kree. I never expected Mom to fall into that pattern with me.

In the morning, she makes plain oatmeal that sits like dough at the bottom of the bowl, thicker and more of a drag than I remember as a kid. When I lift the spoon out of the slop, it picks up the contents of the bowl in one massive and overbearing plaster blob that, if eaten, would sit in my stomach for days. I put the bowl on the coffee table and lay against the couch, half-consciously watching music videos on TV. She dusts around the surrounding furniture, doing her best to purposely block my view. "You should call Elizabeth and Teresa and see if they want to go for lunch," she says. "So did you call them yet?" she asks, even though I haven't moved from the couch since she mentioned it three seconds ago. "Aren't you too old to be watching music videos?"

"Can you get out of the way?"

"Oh, stop being such a mole. The only people who like stewing in their own misery are masochists."

***

Saturday morning Avaline nags me into going with her and her boyfriend to Lodi, California, for Valentine's Day wine tasting. We walk the winery property in a tour group of retirees, wealthy couples, and ladies of leisure, and her boyfriend continuously interrupts the tour guide with his little tidbits of knowledge. "The fruit was good this year," he says as we sip samples. I gaze at him and even though my eyes are glossy and inattentive, he continues to talk to me.

I rub my kidneys and liver, knowing that soon they'll blow like grenades from my body. I've killed nine cases of diet soda over the last week, countless bottles of hard liquor, and I've demolished over ten samples of wine on an empty stomach.

The drive back to Sac does nothing to sober me up, either, and although Avaline and I are ready to hurl, she takes me to her afternoon support group, "Lean On Me: A Place for Manic-Depressive and Bipolar Sufferers to Come Together," or in other words, AA for the suicidal. It's hosted in a middle-school classroom, and there are people of all ages sitting in a circle, fidgeting, bored, inattentive. The moderator seems to mean well. He goes around the room and asks each of us how we're holding up, subsequently offering us gum, but if any of these people are anything like Avaline, manners and gum aren't going to do shit.

"This is Hazel," Avaline says with a slur. "She gets butt-hurt easily, so be nice."

"Hello, Hazel. Why don't you tell us about a recent low point in your life that's really tested you," he says.

"I can't really think of anything," I say, distracted by the sight of the ceiling fan circulating in the reflection of his polished head.

"Last week, we discussed our biggest fears. Most of us fear we'll pass our disease onto our children," he says. "What's your biggest fear?" All eyes are plastered on me and it's making me tense up even more.

"That the only sex I'll be able to get is fat-fold sex," I say.

"Don't take her seriously. Hazel's an angry nineties chick and she just broke up with her boyfriend," Avaline says, revealing to the public truths I've taken considerable care in hiding from myself. Bitch.

"I didn't break up with him. He dumped me for the third element of the periodic table."

"Now, now," she says. "Marilyn Manson cheated on Dita Von Teese, the Queen of Burlesque and Bondage, with that little girl from the Green Day video. And that skuzzy Billy Bob cheated on Angelina. And Ethan on Uma. Those disgusting guys don't appreciate the beautiful women they have. It happens to the best of us." For a second, it really makes me feel good. "Although Ethan's a beefcake and I'd have his babies any day."

"You're ridiculous," I say.

"It's been way over a month. You need a good fuck buddy to help you get over him."

It dawns on me that we're not too different: she has an address book of fuck buddies; I have a grocery list of carbohydrates.

"If you really want to get back with him, invite him over to talk," she says, and the moderator's mouth is gaped open as if searching for the right words to end this. "Mix him a sweet drink and dissolve in two Viagra. You could throw in a hit of E if you want to warm things up. After he drinks it, come out of the bathroom in your skivvies and push play on your DVD player that just so happens to have lesbian porn in it."

"That's your advice to me?" I ask.

"Wait a minute," some guy says. "Straight chicks watch lesbian porn? Can I watch you two—"

"I think, um, we're getting off track here," the moderator finally says.

"Say the Viagra and porn don't work," Avaline says. "Slip him a mickey, drag him into bed, and fool around with him while he's out cold. You'll wake up together naked and he'll have to take you back." The room goes mute aside from a fly buzzing overhead and a few clearing throats.

"That's motherfucking rape," I say. (For the record, she's the type that would give her kids cough syrup at night to shut them up.)

"You can't rape a guy," she says. "Really, you can't. It's our double standard as girls. It's considered rape for them but not for us. And I've never had to roofie any guys because they always fold after the Viagra. Rohypnol just got a bad rap 'cause everybody called it 'the date-rape drug,' but it's really just another benzo."

I wonder if anyone would notice if I slid under the table and crawled toward the door.

"Unless you're some fat-ass heifer, no straight guy is going to turn down punani with two Viagra in his cock," she says.

"Can we not use the term 'fat-ass'?" I ask.

"Hazel," the moderator says. "Um, are you suffering from a mental illness or grief from your breakup? You know, there's a difference." He hurls out a bunch of inquisitive questions about my "clinical diagnosis" and my "combination of medications," so finally I tell him I have none because I'm undoubtedly not batshit insane. He asks me to leave. I could put up a fight but I decide against it.

On the way home, Avaline tells me that I should have faked it so we could have at least stayed for the hot chocolate and cookies break, but listening to her about something like that would be like going to Liza Minnelli for marital advice. Maybe I should join a cult. At least they do everything in their power to prevent their pledges from leaving. But after being rejected by the punks *and* the crazies, I doubt I'll fit in anywhere.

***

It's impossible to ax someone who was so deeply integrated in my life. I don't understand what I'm supposed to do with all my free time and trolling emotion. Parts of me have disjointed. My outer flesh runs like an android, accomplishing what I need to do to get by in life—paying bills, cleaning the apartment, putting up with work bullshit—while my inner parts hemorrhage for him. I miss his smell, taste, the heat of his body asleep against mine, his delirious laughter enveloping my head when we're flying, and the way he looks directly into me when we're fucking. And thinking back makes me sadder because the memory of him doesn't belong to me anymore, because he doesn't belong to me anymore.

I miss his flaws the most: the metal fillings in his teeth, the zits all over his back, and the way the veins pop from under the pallid skin of his portly hands, engorged as if feeding them like distended tumors growing off the ends of his arms. I miss the way he can't stay on the bed and how it got so bad that Landon bought him one of those portable bed railings for Christmas so he wouldn't bang his head against motel nightstands or the bus floor anymore.

I miss the stupid shit, like how his feet are a size thirteen but he doesn't have half the dick to account for it, the way his stubble rubs the inside of my thighs raw, and how he refuses to fuck me in any position which puts me on my back because he says that's how most women get raped. I miss the way he wipes his runny nose and mouth on his sleeves, how he has to constantly slurp at his lips, how he even slurps into the microphone during radio interviews and creates deafening static that makes the disk jockeys roll their eyes in irritation.

I miss the way he can't eat animal crackers or gingerbread men because it makes him sad. That he chooses Polaroids over digital, cassettes over MP3s. That he can't type—once when he fiddled around with my laptop, he asked: "Why are all the letters mixed up? A and B aren't near each other, and C is between them, kind of."

I lie awake in bed, and all I see are that groupie whore's pink nipples protruding from her tits. Her nipples shrink into tight points as he flicks his tongue over them and finishes with a pinch of his lips. They're probably parked right now on the shoulder of some shady New Jersey turnpike, boozing it up in the backseat while he goes down on her. It's burned into my retinas, and all I hear is her irritating giggle as his nut gravy drips out of her pussy. It's driving me fucking insane and makes me scream out in random places at random times.

I regret reaching out to Mom, but right now the words are coming out of my mouth and I've never been good at hitting the brakes, especially when fueled by a half bottle of Smirnoff.

"You'll feel better in the morning," she says, somnolent like she's in bed, the phone propped on her face. "Make friends and quit sitting inside all day like a groundhog. You're the color of an anemic. Read my copy of *Reviving Ophelia* and figure it out yourself. And did you make an appointment with the dermatologist like I said? Your pores are huge."

"I'm tired of feeling this way," I say.

"Hazel, you need professional help." Click.

And that was *her*. She hung up on me. My own mother hung up on me after saying one of the worst things a person could say to someone, and it must mean something when Mom of all people no longer has the energy to hassle me.

Right House, Wrong Fetish Room

I've squandered away the first two months of 2009, spending every night hammered, every morning hung-over, always teetering between staunch nausea and violent hurling. Rock bottom gets old. Not boring, just excruciatingly intolerable.

I spent a lot of time trying to get Otis off bar floors and bathtubs, and maybe I've done the same since we split. I've sat on my manuscript since October, done nothing to ready it for publication, and somewhere in there I even alienated Laws with the nephew/jambalaya incident. It's Sunday morning, but I call Laws anyway to see if he'll meet me.

When I get to his office, he throws on a coat and suggests we get out and walk the Golden Gate, and though I want to go on about UV rays and metastasizing melanoma lesions, I don't want to let him down again. The city's warmer and more temperate than Sac, but on the bridge, when the Bay wind hits us from every direction, it gets cold very quickly. Wind and traffic noise make it difficult to hear each other, so we don't talk much. Then again, I can't think of anything to say. We walk for twenty minutes, stopping halfway to study Alcatraz in the distance. From the corner of my eye I can make out bits of thick silver weeded through his dark hair quivering with every wind stroke.

"You know," he hollers above the wind and car engines and it sounds more like a question than his usual introductory hesitation. "You don't have to use a load of profanity to make dialogue pop off the page." I smile when I realize he's talking about the manuscript. "Just like you don't have to rely on graphic sex to make the interaction between two people darkly intimate." He pauses to wait out a foghorn. "And you don't have to rely solely on sex, drugs, and rock 'n' roll to make your characters anarchic. It's all excess, and I think you're enough of a writer without them."

I lift my shoulders to my ears and hold them there. His words feel like aged whiskey warming me from the inside out.

"Without *him*," he says.

Constructive criticism tagged with a slight compliment. Maybe that's all I've never needed.

***

I head home with hard copies of his detailed analysis that I study line by line, realizing that he went through each page and uncovered all weaknesses, inconsistencies, indistinct details, put them under a meat lamp, then dissected them by asking *why this?, why that?,* coupling his inquisitions with *develop this, change that, set the scene, amplify this voice by adding more dialogue,* and *tone down and create vulnerability.*

I work with him daily, going back and forth till a decision is rendered, the scene's set, the dialogue's authentic. Where it reads rough, he demands refining, where the dialogue is too clean, he wants it broken up. It's painful to face my weaknesses, like organ surgery without anesthesia. I'm awake and enduring every slice and dice, prod and poke, but in the end, I almost enjoy it.

He makes me aware of things I never thought about when reading or writing, like how callous terms of judgment will kill any sympathy for a narrator. His most recent criticism went something like: "Don't just say he's a washed-up crackhead, show me what makes him a washed-up crackhead. Is he an Oakland crackhead or a New York crackhead? Those are two very distinct and different types of crackheads that hail from completely opposite ends of the nation, and the reader must get a feel for what type of crackhead you're talking about."

Periodically, Avaline comes over, but most of the time I'm too focused on edits to notice she's on my couch eating chocolate. It's nice to have the company, though, sort of like a dog that nuzzles up on the couch.

***

Summer comes and goes. I finished editing in April and turned in the final manuscript for Sarah to pitch to publishers. I've been eating food made out of natural ingredients I can actually pronounce, and in the process, I've lost about ten pounds, most of which probably consisted of processed chemicals and trans-fat residue in my veins. Autumn arrives, and by the time the sun starts to set earlier, my skin looks darker, and lean.

I take frequent walks with Avaline. She tells me about her recent conquests, most notably the psychiatrist who dumped her as a client to be her boyfriend, then dumped her as his girlfriend. Sometimes it's hard to tell if she's gone through more psychiatrists than boyfriends, but still I listen to her. She listens to me, too. I tell her about the multiple round of edits I've completed on the manuscript, from the global to local to the copyedit, and all the minor rounds in between. She seems mildly excited for me when I tell her an indie publisher picked up the manuscript and we've been going back and forth with details like galleys, marketing plans, and design. I even tell Avaline about pitching Landon's artwork for the cover, despite our falling out, since it's so fitting for the novel.

"It's like this whole other world I never knew about," I say to her during one of our walks. "And I'm contributing to it."

"I just found out about a whole other world, too. It's called a 'play party,'" she says. "People go over to their neighbor's house and do bondage with the entire block. A suburban orgy. Who knew?"

***

The second Saturday of October, Avaline and I attend a monthly event where artists, musicians, and craftspeople display their talents on the downtown streets of Sacramento. Five minutes after she drops me off at home, my complex doorbell rings. I buzz her in, assuming she's left something in my apartment, and I head into the hallway, teasing her out loud about being an airhead. I round the corner and expect her to tease me back, but when I look down the stairwell, it's not her sliding her lanky fingers up the railing: it's Landon. His emaciated hand twitches against the wall, and when he looks up at me, he pins his lower lip beneath his front teeth.

I e-mailed him about a week ago, putting him in contact with the publisher since they needed a release to use his art for the cover. I assumed he'd either turn it down flat or sign their contract without my involvement and that'd be the end of it, but it's apparently inspired him to show up at my door.

For the first time in over six months, I recollect how easily Otis wrote me out. After all the things we put each other through, all the long conversations about music and literary influence, all the times I pulled him off the floor and mopped up his puke, there was never a single phone call, text, or e-mail, never even a single cryptic phone call, text, or e-mail from an anonymous source. There was nothing. The raging wave of resentment is back. Whoever knows the secret to purging it completely from their system must have pioneered the murder-suicide.

Landon climbs up the rest of the stairs and shoves his way into my apartment, but I hope that if I ignore his offhand comments long enough, he'll lose interest and leave. "God, how can you stand it in here, it reeks of fucking bleach," he says, picking up personal effects to examine them in detail. "*The Sheep Look Up,* hm." He pauses to read the back of the book. "You're really into all that dystopian downer shit, huh?" That familiar screech of his voice makes goose bumps form down the back of my neck.

"What do you want?"

"Sorry, am I interrupting an International Coffee moment between you and your Barbies?" he asks, now rummaging through the kitchen cabinets. "You're either a heavy drinker or really into tonic water."

"Quinine fends off malaria," I say.

"Where's your gun collection? And all your 'Palin in 2012' paraphernalia?"

I head toward the closet for sponges and Resolve, and along the way, my bare foot squishes in one of his crap-stamped footprints.

"Okay, breathe," he says. "It's just a little mud, maybe some dog shit."

"It smells like shit."

"Probably is."

My hands are shaking. I bolt and ditch him for the bathroom. And while scrubbing the bottoms of my feet under the bathtub spout, I hear Otis' studio-edited voice resonating from the living room stereo. I stop the faucet. I haven't heard their new album up until now: they're refined and mature in comparison to what they used to scream-thrash on tour. It's bizarre to hear him in a different production, under these circumstances.

"What do you think?" Landon asks from the bathroom doorway.

"It's...disturbing." I turn the water on again, and resume scraping my heel with a pumice stone.

"You hear what the album's titled? *Without a Liver, with a Broken Heart.* It's a concept album and I'll give you one guess who thought it up and what it's about."

"Dipshit."

"I was going to say *you*, but yeah, I guess."

I'm not sure if I should be flattered or offended.

"We're going to be headlining in a few weeks. Did you know that?"

"Yeah, it's in my daily routine to look up what you dickholes are doing," I say.

"You need to chill the fuck out. One of these days, you're going to give yourself hives."

I dangle my feet in the bathwater and keep my back to him. Months have passed without any thought about their chaos, but seeing him now makes my head throb like the night he punched me. "Why are you here?"

"'Cause he doesn't talk to me anymore. He used to tell me everything. Now the only time he ever says anything is when he's wasted and rambling about missing your color."

I look down at my shins and remember how my sun-starved translucent skin revealed every vein, vessel, and follicle, and how Otis liked to stare at me in the bathroom light. He liked the gray splotchy scars the garlic left behind, and he would say that I was so fucking surreal, I had to be made just for him. He said these unique things with such an eerie innocence and honesty that it melted away some of the ice that had always been in me.

"I'd rather lick a whore's herpes than say this, but it might be in everyone's best interest if you came back," he says. "You're in pain, he's in pain, let's mow it over and you guys can resume doing whatever the hell warped shit you do." He clamps a cigarette between his teeth and sifts through his pockets for a lighter.

"You can't smoke in here." But he lights up anyway.

"One night, he was a step away from throwing himself off the hotel roof. Then he slit his throat. I was on the curb holding in his Adam's apple while Joey was in the middle of the street screaming for a cab. This place in Australia banned us 'cause at the end of the show he slit his wrists and sprayed it all over the kids up-front. And those were the serious ones. The

164

bullshit attempts happen every day. He's going to become another Nick Traina. Only fatter and much less attractive."

I don't believe him. In an online web interview I caught in June, Otis looked happier than a pervert in a downtown sex shop. Landon, on the other hand, seems to be suffering. I didn't think it was possible for him to lose any more weight, but he's pushing kwashiorkor. The second generation of bags under his eyes has sprung two more generations, giving him the appearance of a loosely skinned corpse. I'd be lying if I said that my stomach wasn't doing a jig at the sight of him standing in the doorway of my bathroom asking me back. If anything, I've fantasized about it more than a good book review (even a mediocre review). But it wasn't a sustainable lifestyle, and it was never fair.

"I can't," I say, although sometimes it feels like I was more successful in that world than I'd ever been in my own.

The room is silent for several minutes. He doesn't leave. I don't know what to do, but I know that if he stays here any longer, I might just crack. As fucked up as it sounds, I wish Mom were here to boot him out of the apartment.

"Just suck his dick when he needs it and hold him when he's ready to blow his head off," Landon says. From his waistband, he pulls out one of Otis' journals. It's been scribbled over, drawn on, and filled with miscellaneous lyrics (which, for the most part, look like hieroglyphs). There are Polaroids of wounds and bruises and scraps of paper scrawled with poetry and random obscenities written by Otis' shitfaced hand. The cluttered and warped pages smell rancid, like he puked beer on them. Anyone else would toss this into a fourteenth-century bonfire with metal forceps, but to me it's artistic.

"He needs someone to keep an eye on him. He's naïve and doesn't know any better. Lately, people have been taking advantage of that. Hey, did you know that for a while he thought you were really a vampire till we finally convinced him that you're just a freak?"

"Was he cut off from oxygen at birth?" I ask.

"Is your last name Limbaugh?"

"Fuck, just get out."

"What'd I say?"

I shut off the bathwater and it's quiet except for a few final drops hitting the surface of the water. "You people, whatever you call yourselves—neo-punks, wannabes, posers—you're the tight-asses. You're the hardest people in the world to fit in with."

"Are you coming with us or what?"

"And you don't realize it, 'cause you're too busy breaking everybody else down for not being like you."

"I'll cover your drugs for a month."

"You're not even listening to me."

"Two months."

"No."

"Why?"

"'Cause you punched me."

"You punched me twice."

"You said I was fugly."

"I've never even said shit like that behind your back."

"You said no one would want to rape me."

"And that's how you interpreted it? See, that's why people fuck with you. They know it gets to you."

I shut my eyes and lean against the shower wall. I don't have the endurance I used to have on tour, and it's exhausting to remember what it felt like to put up with his shit every day.

"Get this: couple weeks ago he was trying to beat off in the shower, but he slipped and fell on his dick. He was screaming about how he needed to go to the gynecologist for a cast. And then he passed out in a Boston truck stop with his pants open and mud fleas or bed bugs or something had a suck fest all over his pork 'n' beans. For a whole week he was scratching at his crotch on stage, but everybody thought he was just pulling Michael Jackson moves." He laughs at stories that probably weren't funny at the time, if anything, were pathetic pains in the ass, but laughing now eases the aftertaste. "Come back with—"

"No." I interrupt him because I'm afraid I'll fold if he asks again.

"No one can sit alone with an Aimee Mann collection and a box of razors and expect to be alive in the morning." He slides the carton of razors off the counter and into the trash. I only use them to scrape mildew off the shower tile, but I don't have the energy to explain. He rattles his pockets for sound and pulls out an orange bottle filled with Vicodin. I stare at the pills fighting for space against each other, a mountain of them glowing in the dismal bathroom light. He holds them out to me with his twiggy fingers. "C'mon." He shakes the bottle lightly. "This is so much better for you than chocolate."

I reach up to take it from him. "Just go," I say.

On his way out, I can hear his feet pounding the hall stairs as if he's taking out his fury on them, but this is the first time I've had the upper hand and it's surprising just how damn good it feels.

***

The landline rings and rings until Mom's overly enthusiastic voice blares through the answering machine and electrocutes me into a smoking crust. I head toward the phone to pick it up, but I'm distracted by a crumpled, wrinkled, and stained stack of papers on the countertop. It's a hard copy of the publisher's contract for the cover art, signed and dated by Landon. Earlier today, I could have sworn I had inner poise, I no longer gave a shit, but now all that familiar loathing toward her, Landon, Otis, and everything else is soaking back into my pores.

I park it in front of the Fuse channel with a tub of Cool Whip and a box of Oreos, the first time I've done this in months. Around midnight, while inhaling cookie crumbs, Otis' pale complexion sucker-punches me through the TV. "Riot Venom has drawn an underground following in the mainstream," the TV says, narrating a live clip of a Riot Venom performance.

Underground following in the mainstream? That's the most fucked-up oxymoron I've ever heard, worse than seeing "premium meat" stamped on a package of hot dogs or "upgraded" on the neon sign of a Motel 6. Underground following, whatever. They don't know anything past the stage wings. They don't know that when Otis passes out drunk, he pisses and pukes in his sleep. Or that one of his favorite things to do is to have conversations with homeless people. Or that after a discussion with him, I leave covered in a membrane of his saliva, and after sleeping with him, I'm blanketed in his sweat.

Fuck.

After all this fucking time, he still feels like mine; that's what makes it so hard.

***

I survive another holiday season and the first few months of the new year—of the new decade, to be exact. Walgreens promotes me to store manager and places me on the fast track to district manager. My novel release date is set for Monday, March 15th, 2010, and I've been busy with pre-book release promotional activities.

For a while after Landon's unexpected visit, I received random text or voice messages from him, but it got easier to ignore them, and I finally changed my number altogether. But then he shows up Monday night at the book release and interrupts me before I even open my mouth. "This cover art is fuck-tastic," he says from the back of the bookstore. "The artist must have gone to art school for at least a month before dropping out." I don't have to look to know that there's a line of his fans swelling around him. I should have realized something was going down when clusters of would-be Riot Venom fans filed into a bookstore.

***

Whoever isn't waiting for Landon to sign their book jacket is waiting for me to explain what he meant. I look around the cramped aisles of the tiny store for Sarah and Avaline, hoping they'll do something, but one's jabbering into her cell phone, while the other hits on a kid that can't be any older than seventeen.

I back away from the mob and head toward the exit hoping no one notices, and no one does until I'm two feet out the door. "He's not here, you know," Landon says to my back. I turn around. "He's burning bras with the rest of the feminists in DC."

"Why?" I ask.

"He's a feminist. How did you not know that?"

I step inside to get out of the downtown foot traffic. "So he's a feminist even though he's a guy that uses words like 'tits' and 'cunt butter,' listens to The Misfits, and instead of laying a jacket over a street puddle, would more than likely splash around in it for shits and giggles before realizing he's soaked me from head to toe in leptospirosis and worm eggs?"

"Dude, if I'd gone to school with you, I would have wailed on your ass every fucking day. And maybe he's as much a feminist as you are punk. Hey, we're touring Europe soon. You have to come. Evie and I are going to see how many escargots we can pack in our mouths."

"No," I say, revolted by the image of them incorporating snails into their fuck fests.

"What are you doing nowadays that's so special?"

"I—"

"Hm?"

"It's—"

"Besides being a bubble girl and talking to Boddah?"

If we weren't in public, I'd snap him into kindling.

"Yeah, I know all about you," he says. "I know everything there is to know, and you know what? When I found out, none of it surprised me." He pulls out a folded piece of paper, and I sweat, thinking that it's the paperwork that proves my adoption. On second thoughts, that wouldn't be half bad. "Double-majored as an undergraduate. MBA. Accepted two years ago into law school. Fluent in three languages, you know four instruments, and you're proficient in computer apps I've never even heard of. What the hell is a GIS?"

"Where'd you get that?"

"Outside the agoraphobic germaphobe with an eating disorder, you're this whole other person you never mention."

"I am a state-educated UC reject."

"Fuck you. What I would do with your education. No, you're so egocentric you keep yourself in those shit jobs and this shit city. As long as you keep yourself down, you can blame everyone else, right?"

I try to step outside but he snags me by the arm. "Let's go over your social resume."

"I'm doing okay," I say. I was so sure of it before he showed up at my apartment. I can suffer in silence, I've turned it into an art form, but this act of going back and forth between my reality and his is separating the meat from my bones.

"You have no friends." He says it like a public service announcement. "Your hobbies include Clorox and avoiding natural light. Your family treats you like shit."

"I'm different now," I say.

"You're already a social failure to them. Always have been, always will be. There is nothing else to lose from them."

Everything was so tranquil in the months leading up to this. I went to work, came home, edited, wrote, hung out with Avaline, and I never had to deal with being cornered and called out, much less by someone like him.

"Come with us. You could be so much more than you are sitting in your room talking to your walls like Howard Hughes."

"Let me go," I say. But I could be kissing Otis in the cramped confinements of a bus bunk, waking up in the middle of the night with him clenched around my body like a koala on a tree, and cradling his round stomach against me every night instead of a pillow, which, when I think about it, has probably set a new low for suburban losers.

"Last week he was in the bathtub shaving part of his head," he says. "And he had a gun. There's no going back after the trigger goes off. You don't even get a chance to try. He's literally going nuts. He bleaches his skin to get it whiter and paints his eyes with blood before every show." The words spatter out of his mouth in bunches, like he's graphically visualizing the sight of Otis with a partially shaved head standing in front of a mirror applying blood to his face. "He's been reading a lot of Faulkner lately, so if you don't want him killing you and fucking your corpse, drop the attitude and get on that plane."

"No."

"Stop being such a masochist."

"He should be the one coming to get me."

"The world doesn't revolve around you. He's going to paint his brains a Jackson Pollock against the wall. Is that what you want?" Maybe. "I know I'm on your shitlist, but he is not going to make it, and I've had it. He's on three different meds and we got a shrink traveling with us, and God, that fucker's a tool, but you're his Achilles' heel."

I have a life now. I have a job, an apartment, health insurance, a clean bed, a best friend.

"Come on, Yoko, you're breaking up the band. Do something constructive and fix the shit you caused. You're so fucking selfish. You'll never want anything more than your fucking misery." I should have stopped this before it started. "Hey, don't walk away from me, you fucking twat. No one's lined up outside your door willing to put up with your Purell bullshit. You'd be nothing without us. You think that agent would have looked at you without the band's support? We shopped for her like a restaurant lobster. That editor didn't come cheap, either, nor was he nonrefundable."

"What?" I ask.

"You think your cheap symbolism would get you into a store like this with followers like those without my work on the front?"

His admission carves me into a pile of junk meat against the floor. I don't understand how I'm still standing. I want to think it's bullshit, but it's so specific, and it all makes sense. I don't know if I was being used or if I blindly used them, but I feel manufactured.

"Look at me." He wraps his lanky claws around my shoulders, squeezes. "I lost him. He's gone. I tried everything to get him back and you are the last thing I have. If you don't work, I have to put him away. And that will destroy me."

He won't let go of me, and the people around us are swelling in bunches, including Sarah and Avaline, one even screaming at Landon for being a dick while the other is now holding hands with a seventeen-year-old.

"Just come back with us," he says.

I'm dizzy and sick.

"Just be with him," he says.

I'm thirty-one years old, living alone in a two-bedroom apartment, and I'm a slave at Walgreens for forty-seven thousand a year.

"Don't leave like this," he says.

And I can't even spell duct tape.

Rock bottom isn't where I remember it being. Now, it feels limitless.

Part V

Trifecta

One night back in elementary school, when I was watching *A Charlie Brown Christmas Special*, I remember asking Mom: "What's 'psychiatric help, five cents'?"

And she said, "When you need someone to talk to."

But I think it's too late for that. Maybe I can plead the Twinkie defense. Because somehow, I've wound up in the worst situation imaginable: waking up in a hospital the morning after an overdose. Sitting on the edge of the hospital bed over from mine, there's a guy (whose discomfort and fidgeting make him seem years younger than me) flipping through a clipboard. I tell him I need a place to shower with bleach, but he claims there isn't any. "And you are..." he says, flipping through paperwork. "Hazel. I remember now."

My throat burns when I swallow. It's swollen and raw.

I worm over the edge of the bed and hit the floor in a huff. I attempt to cross the room to the hand sanitizer dispenser, but my body creeps as if underwater. A well-proportioned nurse snatches me off the floor and chucks me onto the bed like a used Kleenex into the trash. She breaks out the IV and I scream.

"You're giving me HIV! Fire! Fire! You're killing me!" Knowing they're introducing all sorts of viruses and mind-controlling drugs into my blood, I contort against the mattress and scratch for freedom. "Fire! Fire! This is *Brave New World! Brave New World!*"

The starched hospital sheets grind abrasively against my skin, so I stop squirming. My limbs feel like lead anyway, and I can barely muster up the force to breathe.

"How do you feel?" the guy with the clipboard asks.

I roll on my side to turn my back to him.

"I talked to your mother. She's worried about you."

I grunt.

"She said that over the past few years, you've been...troubled more than usual. She said your last relationship involved a lot of drugs and abuse." His words are like darts, each aimed at a different place on my body; some even hit bone. "Physical and sexual."

I shut my eyes and roll them under their lids. "Do you believe everything your mother says about you?" I ask.

"At least I have you talking."

Fuck.

"Were you trying to hurt yourself yesterday?" he asks.

"No."

"What happened?"

I'd rather have Mom harping on me right now. "I took some Tylenol," I say.

"It was Vicodin. And it was about sixty."

Asshole. "The first few didn't work, so I took a couple more."

"A couple twenty more?"

"You're such a dickhole." I sound like iron but feel like ash.

"What were you trying to get them to work toward?" There's an unruffled composure in his speech, a generic and apathetic tone that he's probably mastered throughout years of dealing with hospital patrons.

"What are you trying to get me to say?"

"What do you think I'm trying to get you to say?" He scribbles in his folder as if it's so easy to pass judgment on an alleged masochist.

"Well, I wasn't," I say.

"Okay. What were you wasn't-ing?"

"You're ridiculous."

"Why?"

"Why does anybody do anything? It's to stand out and be different."

"I think that's pretty normal."

"I am normal."

"I don't think anyone's really normal."

"You aren't making sense."

"Neither are you."

I come to the unsettling realization that I'm trying to convince a stranger to accept me in all the wrong ways.

"What happened?" he asks.

"Virginia Tech."

"Do you identify with what they've done?"

"No, but I'm sure people fucked with Ted Kaczynski, too," I say. "And wasn't he trying to make a point about globalization? And maybe Jeffrey Dahmer had some eye-opening mission statement. You know how the media blows shit out of proportion and everybody believes whatever they're told. Blame society, and..."

Oh, fuck. My skin is spackled with sweat.

"I'm not sure what you're trying to tell me," he says.

I don't know, either, much less what happened to make me speak out in defense of criminal insanity. "Shit," I say. "I've become one of those douche packers bitching about how video games make kids take uzis into the schoolyard. Or those book banners damning *Catcher in the Rye* for the Lennon thing. Fuck. I have to get out of here; I have to get my shit straight."

I sit up and look at him. He's settled into the back of the chair, now more engrossed in pushing back his cuticles than anything else. When he sees me looking at him, he uncrosses his legs, sits upright, and clears his throat, like he's trying to convince himself of his composure. "What are you going to, um, do?" he asks.

And there's a vulnerability in his adolescent physique. Maybe he's an intern or apprentice, or some smart-ass hospital visitor fleeting from room to room for a cheap thrill and doling out random diagnoses. I instantly think of Landon. "Go home," I say.

"You want to call someone?"

"No."

"Anyone?" He says it incredulously.

"No."

I drop my legs over the edge of the bed but stay seated. I want to rip out the IV for a second time, but I don't feel like being hassled.

"It might seem like you're alone, but there are people who care about you," he says. Oh, here comes the ninth-grade counselor again, advising me as if he knows anything about being fourteen. "Do you remember Landon?" he asks.

Of course. I had a "moment of weakness," not a fucking lobotomy.

"He broke his arm and a couple ribs trying to break open your door because he was so worried about you," he says, and the enthusiasm in his voice is mechanical. "Help me understand what's going on. Help us help you get back on track."

"I can't win, so just tell me what you want to hear."

"It's not about winning or losing," he says.

"I'm going to leave here with you thinking I'm a pathetic pill-popper or a suicide attempt."

"What if you're neither of those things? What if you're something else?"

"What if it's just personality and you're punishing people for having the wrong ones? Feeding them anti-asshole pills and calling it therapy?" Maybe their reasoning is that it's easier to take the bitch out of someone than it is to put a good person in.

"What was going on in your head when you were swallowing all that Vicodin?" he asks.

I was thinking about how Otis' shins constantly looked like overripe bananas from all my night kicking and his throat and face were covered in scars and scabs where I'd scratched him, but he was never angry about it. I was thinking about how graceful and light I felt in his arms when I was high as all hell and we were going at it upright in some motel bathroom. I missed the way I was always soldered to him when we were together, either with his stomach grinding against my back or my stomach scraping against his. Sometimes, when I was on top in bed, I'd come mildly and doze off without compensating him, his dick shrinking out of me while he gently scratched at my scalp and brushed my hair over my back. I should remember what it felt like to be with him, but I only remember the shrinking and scratching. The moist breath. Nails scratching. Dick shrinking. Dick disappointed? Balls blue? Maybe, but he never broke the mood by asking me to get up and finish him off. That's just the way he was.

"Why'd you do it?" he asks.

I finger the scars on my neck and realize I'll have them even when I'm ready for them to disappear. "To feel different," I say.

"So you weren't trying to kill yourself?"

"Something like that."

***

Landon's skeletal frame leans against the nurse's station, and he chats with the staff without any concern for the fact that his face is gruesomely disfigured with bruises and scrapes. I think about hitchhiking out of town, but he sees me and waves. His face is worn and sullen but it smiles somberly in my direction. I don't know why he won't just get the fuck out of my way. Or die. Seeing him is a relentless reminder of how living outside the anal-retentive box of suburbia ended in fatality. I should've known, of course—like skydiving without a 'chute was supposed to result in some artistic statement and not a bug splatter against the asphalt.

It's unnatural. He opens the door and helps me into his car, then points at a coffee he picked up for me on the way over. I don't pull my legs in; instead I hack up a mouthful of random pills they gave me before setting me free.

"Hey, those mighta been good," he says, pointing at the puddle of colors bleeding into each other. I drop against the seat and let my jaw hang. "Evie and I cleaned out a room for you at her house. You'll have to put up with her bitch of a mom preaching about how the Well seeds are going to give birth to the Antichrist, but she'll take care of you."

I wish he'd just shut up.

"So, I hear you've always been into green politics," he says.

Since he keeps talking, I grind the soggy pills into the pavement with my heel and shut my eyes.

"That's a total mind fuck. Why didn't you ever say anything? You never defended yourself; you just sat and took it. The reason I gave you so much shit all the time was 'cause I thought you'd voted Bush into the White House. You're actually a lot more interesting than I thought. I mean, unless you voted Nader in 2000." He finishes with a slight laugh. "You didn't vote for him, right?"

I want to walk home. Right now.

"Fuck, you did, didn't you?"

I let the quiet answer for me.

"Hey, but maybe you could make it up by going into business with me," he says. "With your background, you could help me launch my green condom idea."

Maybe it's knowing that I'll always and inevitably work at a shithole like Walgreens, but making a living off green condoms doesn't sound like such a bad idea anymore.

"Just keep in mind who you'd be working for," he says, fleecing his pockets. He pulls out a tin box and pops the lid: it's filled with cocaine and there's a razor buried in the middle of the heap like a shovel in a sandbox. He holds it closer to my face, but I decline with a grunt, the resonations in my throat rattling against my skull like a steel ball shaken in an eggshell. "C'mon, the psych ward didn't loosen you up at all?" he asks.

I thrust my palm upward and knock the tin out of his hand. It hits the ground in a clanking puff of feathery particulates, and I half expect him to pound me in the face again, but he doesn't say anything. Instead, he gets into the driver's seat beside me and puts his keys in the ignition, but he doesn't turn them. "Avaline's going around with Joey now," he says. "They sort of hit it off when we were outside your door the other night." He trips over the last few words. "Didn't require any wining and dining. He just whipped out his cock and jerked it in the backseat of the car when we were...driving here..." He sputters again. "At least they act like they're going around. All they do is fuck. If that's a relationship, then—"

I cut him off with a wheeze.

I can't believe it. I can't fucking believe it. Avaline is supposed to be my best friend. She's supposed to understand what these people did to me and shun everything about them. She's supposed to be the one who called the hospital multiple times asking when I'd be released so she could come and get me. She's supposed to be the one sitting here in the parking lot talking me down. After all the times I've been there to bail her out of jail, bring her home from the hospital, or save her from a bridge railing, she's such a narcissistic self-indulgent whore that she chose a fucking drummer over me.

"Yeah, for a while there, we all thought you were a schizo, but she's real. You know that saying about people not having anybody upstairs? I always told people you had too many, or that it'd be fucking hilarious if your alter ego had an alter ego." He laughs but trails off after a few moments. "I guess it's not that funny anymore since she's real."

Fucking shithead. And cunt.

"Look, I know I go on about how easy your life is," he says. "But I know everyone's got shit on their plate. I was thinking the other day that people don't think about how much they like being touched and held. You're held most of the time as a baby and everyone assumes you grow out of it when you start running around. But everybody still needs that affection; they just don't admit it 'cause then they'd look like a pussy. Aunt Zee used to hold Otis all the time. He was this twenty-one-year-old man-boy crying in her arms while she hushed him, and then one day she walked in on him ass-naked in the tub slitting his arms. Her hospital bill was higher than his that day. She hasn't touched him since."

It just happened, I guess. I've taken handfuls of pills before and have never woken up sick. On tour, I remember days, hours, and minutes blurring together in a distorted fast-forwarded standstill back-tracking time warp where I'd drop nine Vicodin with three Guinness Extra Stouts, only remembering I'd done it when I realized I needed focus to edit, and a couple Adderall were halfway down my esophagus dissolving in a mixture of energy drinks and coffee before I realized later that I'd screwed myself out of the opportunity to sleep, so I'd top off the downer and stimulant sundae with Xanax and Valium, and/or something harmless like more stout, Ambien, or Benadryl, depending on what was conveniently on-hand at the time. I guess this time it was different.

"I don't know if he ever told you, but he was in and out of state hospitals from age ten to fifteen," he says. "The only thing that got him out of those shit holes was moving across the country. My biggest fear is thinking he was drugged and fudgepacked every day without knowing it. We knew nothing about Aunt Zee, except that she never had anything more than twenty cats and bingo at the community center, but she took us in even though that cocksucking state worker did everything to try and change her mind. 'An order of lunatic with a side of smart-ass,' that's what he said. But fuck, she adored us the second we met her."

I don't know who I am. Maybe I never knew. This person here with you, Landon, this person next to you, who is she? I know I'm me in the flesh, that I've grown up to be this thirty-one-year-old thing in physical form, but what is all of this and what am I supposed to want?

"I was thinking about the denial over perdition that you mentioned in your book. I get it now. Fuck existence of heaven and hell. Any place I don't end up with Evie is bullshit. So heaven can fuck itself, and I assume I wouldn't get to see her in hell, either, so that place can fuck itself too. I want to be what I am right now, with Evie and Otis and Aunt Zee and music. All the rest can fuck itself. You know, I was only eleven, but I knew when I met Evie that I was going to marry her."

I knew when I met Otis that everything associated with him would break me.

"She was only nine, but she was everything, even as a little girl, you know?"

I knew when I got into his El Camino that I chose wrong.

"The most romantic thing in the world is knowing you're going to fuck the same person for the rest of your life," he says. "I get hard just thinking about it."

I didn't know specifics, but I knew.

"My favorite thing to do with her is fill a huge-ass ice chest with ice, then throw in a bunch of forties, ice cream, cookie dough, and snag enough takeout from Long John Silver's to feed a Mormon family. Best time to do it is summer, 'cause it's hot as fuck and the house heats up to over a hundred. I take Aunt Zee to the community center for bingo so Evie and I spend the day ass-naked listening to records, eating, getting wasted. We try to fuck with every album change, but sometimes we're both too spent to do it, but it's being there that matters, you know? By the end of the day we're usually passed out in a booze-food-fuck coma."

I wish he'd just let me slink back to shitty suburbia and fail judgment-free. That's easy and expected; that's the life that I've been set up to lead, but when he constantly shows up unexpectedly like this, it reminds me just how shitty it is, how shitty and yet amazing it was to be on the road with them.

"Couple of summers ago, we saved up enough to do that every weekend," Landon says. "Then she got a hush puppy stuck in her cooch, so that kind of killed it for a while. But the romance was there. And fuck, is she classy. Most people don't think so, with all her tats and piercings. This kid down the street's been obsessed with her since she was a little kid, and he came over one time in high school and said to her, 'I still want you even with all the piercings and tattoos.' Fuck that shit. You know what lingerie is to me? Ink and metal. People always go on about accepting people despite all the shit wrong with them, but I want Evie because of what she is."

Someone decide for me so I can enjoy the drugs, the free will, and Functional Otis, and blame all the shit—Landon, tour life, and Puking Otis—on them. Someone yank me out of this car and drag me to work so I can make them the oppressor, but still quietly enjoy my warm bed, hot showers, affordable group medicine.

"That's what it's about," he says. "You want someone like crazy because of *what* they are, not *despite*."

I sink into the seat of the car, and let my eyes droop into crescent slits that close only occasionally. It's quiet for a while. I press my lips together, close my eyes, and exhale.

"'She's my Evie.' That's what Otis says to me. Are you just going to turn your back on that?"

Ignition

I make Landon drive me home. When he pulls up to my building, I see Mom's car parked in a visitor spot, and it really makes me wonder how I managed to become the meat in this fuck sandwich of a fiasco.

"I only have one arm left," he says, "so if you're not coming home with me, you better learn how to drive your own ass to the ER next time." I climb out of the car and slam the door before he has a chance to start a new thought.

Up in the apartment, I hear Mom crawling on the floor, scrubbing muck off the cheap linoleum in the kitchen. "This place is filthy," she says from behind the counter. "I don't know why it's so hard for you to keep this place clean. This is urban blight, if you ask me. You get this lazy mentality from Dad's side. And what were you trying to prove with a stunt like that? It was that boy who put you up to it, wasn't it?"

She changes subjects so fast that I don't have a time to defend myself against the first, much less think about the second.

"You're going to let a gay, fat man ruin your life?" she asks. "You always pick the losers. If that was your definition of a man, then you need to be medicated under the supervision of a professional. What did you see in him?"

"I guess I jack off to guys like him," I say.

She hisses in response.

I round the counter to see her on her hands and knees, red in the face from either the intense scrubbing or her opinions. The pathetic thing is that if it weren't her doing this right now, it would be me, as if the infatuation with bleach manifested itself in our family genes like some inherited chromosomal abnormality. It has to stop with me.

I lie face-down on the couch, let one arm dangle against the carpet.

She gets off the floor. "The only thing in your cupboards is candy."

"Oh, stop acting so surprised," I say.

"You don't have a single fresh fruit or vegetable. You'll regret that when you get colon cancer. You'll have to walk around pooing in a bag for the remainder of your life."

"You want to talk cancer, go ask the EPA about the debilitating mutations and cellular damage that neurotoxic pesticides cause."

"All that is regulated."

"Last I heard, American farmers were growing their crops overseas, then importing them back into the US with a stamped seal of regulatory approval. I'm sure the feds have no trouble turning a blind eye when it comes to sparing the agricultural industry from economic blunder."

"Then go organic."

"So I can pay an arm and a leg for a mouthful of aphids, caterpillar larvae, and fly eggs? And organic doesn't prevent the farmers from taking a dump in the harvest. Why do you think I was always dealing with E. coli recalls at Safeway?"

She grumbles and heads for the other room. Holy fuck. I think I won my first argument with her.

***

Later, Mom drags me to the mall, and I come only because she threatened to find a psychiatrist who makes house calls. According to her, my hermitlike existence is the first step toward committing some newsworthy crime. We're in a coffee shop now, waiting for our breakfast, while she reads aloud an informational pamphlet on common mental disorders.

"Lately," Mom says, reading verbatim, "have you experienced a strain on your personal relationships, bleak outlook, difficulty concentrating, weight gain or loss, problems sleeping, feelings of guilt, and psychosomatic ailments?" What does she mean by *lately*?

"Did you hear on the news about that woman who set her three kids on fire because she heard voices telling her to do it?" she asks. "It's going to be impossible for you to qualify for health insurance now. And if you do, it'll cost an arm and a leg. Hey, do suicide attempts have to be disclosed to employers? Mental illness is hereditary. Couple of my cousins had it, and so did my uncle."

"Then I guess it all comes from your side," I say.

"You better have that rape whistle ready when you're running to your car after work. A girl was just abducted in Elk Grove and had her kidneys cut out. And a university student was raped, murdered, and dumped in the river the other day."

"Why don't we ever hear about people luring door-to-door salespeople into their homes and slaughtering them in their garage?" I ask. "It's always some female college student or secretary from suburbia who ends up dismembered and decomposing in a body of water."

"Oh, stop being so negative all the darn time."

I wonder if I'm dead and don't know it yet. Maybe this isn't so much the trials of life or fires of hell as it is limbo.

"Hazel?" She nudges my shoulder and I bob back in my chair and sulk into a slouch. "Hazel."

"What?" I ask.

"You need to get your eyebrows waxed."

The band was without its heart this weekend so that he could stay in town at Aunt Zee's and wait for the hospital to release me. They'll be without him for another six weeks so the bones in his arm can heal, and probably another few so he can practice again. Landon never mentioned it on the ride home, but I know.

"Hazel!"

"What?" My vision clouds over and I can't see the intensity of her expression.

"Do you want to get your eyebrows waxed or not?"

"I don't know."

"How can you not know? Are you feeling okay?"

"I...maybe."

"What's that supposed to mean?"

"I don't know."

"Well, what do you want me to do?"

I want her to explain why, even when all that I've ever wanted was her acceptance, she's never tried bringing herself down to my level. The day after I landed the job with Safeway, she walked through my apartment door and the first thing that flew out of her mouth was, "A boyfriend, a Toyota, and a renovated two-bedroom apartment in Northern California. Take a mental picture. This is as good as it'll ever get for you."

"What do you want me to say?" she asks now.

"I don't care." I don't. I could be sitting in the pits of hell replaying the memories of all her Jabba-the-Hutt jokes, and I wouldn't feel any different. I don't have the energy to care.

"Quit acting like I'm the bad guy," she says. "I'm being realistic. You need to befriend reality. Bad."

***

I deteriorate in front of the TV, warmed under a blanket of candy wrappers and cookie packaging, intermittently waking up with the panicked belief that my skin fused to the couch during one of my fourteen-hour comas.

Some morning, who knows when, Sarah shows up at my door. "Since you obsess over smells, I decided against flowers," she says and hands over a two-pound box of See's Candy. "And they didn't have any balloons for the occasion so..." She tapers off and lets go of a "get well" Mylar balloon with a cartoon Band-Aid on it. "So..."

"Don't."

"Yeah."

I let her in and we sit on the couch exchanging fragmented dialogue.

"Book signing's today," she says.

"Yeah."

"LA."

"Hmm."

"You going?"

"What time?"

"Four."

"Okay."

"Really?"

"Yeah." Because I have no excuse not to go: I was probably fired for job abandonment last week, and the only thing I'd end up doing instead would be eating my way through the two pounds of See's and passing out in diabetic shock.

***

The signing's at an indie used book and music store, kind of like Sacramento's Dimple Records, only cleaner and more LA-superficial: even the punks here don't exempt themselves from chest implants and orange tans. But it's quaint and eco-friendly, sustained by solar rays and compost piles on the roof, and there's a small in-house café that only serves coffee in reusable mugs stamped with logos for fair-trade coffee. The place bustles with collectors searching for old records and first editions, and some even have *Winter's Persimmon* in hand.

I sit down at a small table, glassy-eyed and choking on anxiety in front of a store filled with Riot Venom fans flipping through the book. I know I shouldn't be here; in fact, everyone probably knows. The whole production feels fraudulent because the buzzing interest has everything to do with a breakout opportunity purchased with Landon's credibility. There are probably only thirty eyes on me but it feels like hundreds, and if I thought too much about it, I might scream.

"What was all this supposed to mean?" someone asks over the silence.

I don't have to look up or hear the scuffle of his voice to know that it's Kree's question. He's probably worn the enamel off his teeth asking it. I watch him squirm uncomfortably amidst the punks (more specifically, SoCal punks), and I realize he's sacrificed his comfort zone as well as an afternoon in front of the TV with Tom Green to be here, and right now, it's enough.

I meet him after the signing in the corner of the small café so he can congratulate me on the book. Our table's wedged so close to the counter that we have to yell over the foam machine and blenders. "No wonder you were so miserable before," he says. "You weren't doing what you knew you were meant to do. I mean, for God's sake, Hazel, you were hella depressed." I think that's his way of congratulating me.

"Did you read it?" I ask.

"It was riveting."

"Is that a word you saw on the front of *Entertainment Weekly*?"

"I didn't understand it, but that means it's good." This is bullshit, but it tastes good. "Man, it's a freak orgy in here," he says through the side of his mouth. It wouldn't be Kree, I suppose, if he didn't instantly shit on his credibility. "My mom said that your mom said that Patrick didn't work out." He rubs his hairless chin in phony disbelief. "I was happy when I heard. You looked so miserable. He seemed so controlling."

"Shut up."

"Okie dokie, artichokie," he says. "How's Avaline?"

Every day, I hope she and Joey will go through the graphic breakup of the century, resulting in her committing some indecent crime against herself, eventually landing her right back on my porch, begging to be taken in. But she hasn't. Fucking whore.

"So what drugs are you on now?" he asks.

"None."

"You can tell me," he says, as if we're sixth graders exchanging secrets. "I'm on Zoloft." The turntable does a double screech: I don't think we're on the right sides of the table. "I had to do something. It was one thing to be sad all the time, but I was always tired and didn't want to do stuff I used to like doing," he says.

This tops Avaline putting her dog on puppy Prozac. We might as well be filming a fucking Prozac testimonial right here.

"I was sleeping a lot, eating a lot, lying around the house a lot." I always assumed he was just a lazy ass. "I think the depression thing is labeled badly 'cause everyone thinks it's something to be embarrassed about, but it's not. And my last girlfriend didn't get that. Anyway, this is for you." He slides over a burned DVD in a scratched plastic case, then proceeds to summarize the "movie" he wrote and codirected. "It's about these kids who go through a hard time after one of them commits suicide."

One, I can't believe he just got done explaining the benefits of Zoloft, then followed it with the word "suicide." That's a word that has never existed in his everyday conceptualization of life. And two, it sickens me to know that he could skate through the first thirty years of his life doing jack shit, then move to LA, lose all his baby fat, and suddenly experience (and seemingly support himself on) his deepest aspirations. Fucking shit.

"What's the matter?" he asks.

"I'm going to be a forty-year-old whore so desperate that I hump everyone and everything," I say.

"You're not going to be a forty-year-old whore. You'd be a slut. Whores charge people, sluts give it away for free."

"I'm going to kick the can as an 800-pound, maggot-filled recluse, with gallons upon gallons of shit backed up in my intestines. Just wait," I say. "You'll find me on the crapper, covered in roaches and maggots, ice cream and Red Vine containers littered around my carcass, decomposing inside an enclave of toilet paper and Post-Its." The last few words scrape out in a high-pitched squeal.

"Why are you so obsessed about becoming 800 pounds? At five foot two, you could never weigh that much. You'd max out around 180, maybe 200. After that you wouldn't be able to get out of bed."

I guzzle my coffee like it's hard liquor. It scalds the roof of my mouth.

Fueled by roach and fat fears, I go home with Kree to his studio apartment, and he returns a tattered box of my college journals that he accidentally took during our breakup. "I used a lot of your dark humor in my script," he says. "But I made the moral up myself."

"What? Don't kill yourself?"

"No, that people should do what they were meant to do."

Oh, brother. "I kept telling you to get out of your room and do something with your life, and look how far you got." My last memory of him was of butter, jam, crumbs, and a bad British accent, so it's impossible for me to get over how a clueless sloth, a bumbling idiot who couldn't act, who didn't do anything with his life during college or in the years after, could compose his life and come back and kick me in the ass with his newfound revelations.

"When'd you guys break up?" He points to my bag, the new Riot Venom album poking from the top. "Did he get too famous or something?" he asks, unloading a shotgun round into my left lung. "Turn into a man-whore?" And there's another in my right. "Whatcha thinking?"

"Just hit me when I zone out."

"No, come here." I fall against the dresser to escape his trademark gun-in-front-pocket, but he pulls me in for a rough embrace. "That's what I miss about you. You think hard before saying anything. God, I missed you, hazelnut. It feels like I'm home when I hold you. I missed your hair, your smell, you taste. Where are you? I know you're in there somewhere."

"What's that mean?"

"You're so thin and spacey. It's like there's nothing left inside of you. I want get you feeling again."

I'm offended, yet somehow flattered, and I cave because he grips onto me like I'm the only one he wants, like he knows a decade of my hang-ups but still accepts me in spite of them. I don't know why no one told me that sex was the ultimate way to self-medicate. Had I known, I would have used him from the start.

***

"Do I feel different?" I ask as I ride him rough in bed, keen on accomplishing the inconceivable: making it to the finish line before him. And as I stretch my hands into the air with the finish-line tape just yards away, he grabs my tits and hurls me off the racetrack.

He's a spent pile of jelly between my legs, selfishly getting to absorb endorphins by himself. "What the hell?" I ask. "You're thirty-one and you still don't know how to hold off?"

"You're lucky I got that far." He pulls me in for a kiss, but I smack him and dig my knee into his chest.

"You know," I say, "the female praying mantis—post-fucking—bites off the male's head and dick in a fit of hunger. That means the guy only gets to fuck once and doesn't even get to enjoy the endorphins because he gets his head and dick chomped off. And it might not even be in that order. Maybe it's *dick* first, then head." I slap him on the forehead to emphasize the point.

"When'd you get such a bad mouth? That isn't you at all."

I wobble off him and shudder when my bare feet slap against the carpet probably plaguing me with nests of plantar warts. In the bathroom, I step into his water-stained tub and kneel at the spout. Through the slab of wooden door, he sheepishly tries to reason with me, and it already seems like we're back to our old routines.

"I can try again in an hour, but let's eat first," he says. "I know you said fish sticks were the hot dogs of the sea, but I got a giant Costco box in the freezer."

"Fucker," I say, kneeling near the bath spout to wash him out of me. I plunge a finger inside of me and mid-excavation, I pull it out to find it blanketed in a slime casing of his sticky, boring, plain, ordinary, clueless ejaculate.

***

When I board the plane back to Sacramento, Kree is still tagging along with me for whatever reason, but I don't object because I don't know how. I'm hovering between Mom's "this is as good as it'll ever get for you," and my own maggot destiny.

"If you had to choose between eating shit or drinking pus, what would you pick?" I ask him. "Let's say the person had hepatitis or something."

"What kind of question is that?" he asks.

The plane hasn't even leveled off at a comfortable altitude when he asks if I want to move to LA and live with him, or if we should get a place in Newark to be near our parents. I wish we weren't sitting elbow to elbow, because he's sandwiched me against the window. He gnaws on carcinogen-laced beef jerky as he speaks, but all I can really picture is the sight of him coming without me.

"I don't think so." I hope the vague response will help him understand that a minute of sex does not mean anybody's back together.

"Think how awesome it'd be if we had our own house." He weaves his jerky residue fingers through mine and squeezes.

"That's ridiculous."

"We could get a dog."

"And some cats and toilet paper?"

"And we could have Fourth of July at our house, and both our families could come over."

I toss his hand off and attempt to move away from him, but I'm already smashed against the wall of the plane. "I hate your family," I say.

"And they hate you, but isn't that a given? Your mom hates her in-laws, so does my mom. That's normal. That's everybody." He moves closer till his face is inches from mine. I put my palm against his chest and shove him back into his seat to maintain enough breathing room. "This is what we're supposed to do at our age."

The plane levels, the captain announces it's safe to get up and use the bathroom, lower our tray tables for beverage service, or in the case of the person in front of me, recline his chair to give me three inches less room to breathe.

"It doesn't work that way," I say, taking shallow breaths.

"How's it supposed to work?"

I need those three inches back.

"I don't know, it just...doesn't."

"I think you're just being argumentative." He must have learned that one in his last relationship; he's never said that to me before. "No relationship is perfect," he says.

"Like your body hair in my kitchen?"

"Huh?"

"If it's not a pube on my kitchen counter, it's a chest hair." Fuck, just give me back those three inches. I need them more than the air I'm breathing. "Next, it'll be nose and ear hair, and it'll all end up in my food and I'll die with a stomach filled with your hair."

"What do you want me to do? Wax?"

"I don't want to be with a guy who has to wax just so I won't end up eating his hair."

"I'm sure I've eaten your hair a ton of times."

Three motherfucking inches.

"Hey, we didn't use a condom," he says so loud that everyone, including the pilots locked behind the cockpit door, probably heard. "What if you're pregnant? That'd hella kick ass if we had a baby. Together."

The commitment-phobe in me just jumped two rows of seats and tore open the emergency exit to do a freefalling dive for Earth, sans parachute. "Please stop talking," I say. I want to put my elbow through a window, but I doubt my huge ass would make it through the small hole even with the pressurized suction.

"We could get married and take our kids to the beach. This is perfect, 'cause your mom was always saying how after thirty-three your eggs go sour." My glare doesn't seem to faze him at all. "Come on, we knew we were going to end up together. We broke up because of money. That's stupid stuff people break up over."

Between the words "baby" and "money" my skin spackled itself in sweat, and my pulse surged into the triple-digit range at the thought of having to spend the rest of my days with his sticky, boring, plain, ordinary, clueless ejaculate. I'm suffocating. I'm right back where I started. I have to get out of here.

"What's the matter? You need some water?" he asks.

"Does it look like that's all I need?" If I don't get out of this seat, I'm going to smash in his face.

"I want to take care of you and you could take care of me and we'll be so happy, 'cause we're both doing what we were meant to do. You're my hazelnut."

"I am no one's nut," I say and rip off my seat belt and attempt to worm under his tray table for freedom, but he blocks me. "You can't even take care of yourself!"

"I'm different," he says. "Everything happens for a reason. If we hadn't broken up, I wouldn't have gotten my life together and you wouldn't have gotten over that midlife crisis."

"Hey! It was a quarter-life crisis." I shut my eyes, hoping to trick my mind into thinking that I'm not crammed in what feels like a rabbit cage, thousands of feet from Earth. "This shouldn't be as good as it gets."

"It's not like that. You had to know we'd find our way back to each other. We've been together for so long, we can't just throw that away. Understand, rubber band? You don't have to be tormented to be a writer. You can still get married and be happy and take care of a family."

"Who the fuck are you to tell me how to write?" I ask. My throat closes up. I want to be anywhere else but doing this with him.

"You got a book published. You didn't need some emo fag in drag telling you what to do."

"Don't call him that." But apparently, I did.

"We can live wherever you want," he says. "And if you don't want to work, then don't. I just don't want you to be miserable anymore."

I'm ill enough to blow chunks all over his face; all I see are the two biggest fuckups from two different families never outliving the whispers and gossip about their mental health. We'll drop our kids, or accidentally leave them to roast all day in our car, and we'll never be able to hold down normal jobs. "Why won't you kiss me after I go down on you?" I ask.

"What? I don't know. That's where I pee and... I don't want to drink my own pee."

"This is why we don't work. If we did, you'd want to kiss me afterwards and I wouldn't care about your pubes."

"Aren't girls supposed to like going down on guys?"

"I'd rather have a root canal every night than dive headfirst into your cock and balls."

"Is it 'cause it's too big for you?"

I clamp my lips together to prevent the soft laughter in my throat from gaining momentum, but I can't help it: his expression is so solemn—as if his question were truly meant to be taken seriously. My mouth opens to release a girlish chuckle and it grows to the point of being obnoxious; people are turning to stare.

"That's pretty messed up," he says.

"No, what's messed up is you refusing to sleep with me."

"You kick me in your sleep."

"Can't you just take it?"

"If I kicked you in something equal to my balls, would you be able to take it?"

"That was the wrong answer." I hush up when I realize what a psycho I've become over the last year; so much screaming at my exes in public.

"There are no right answers, 'cause no matter what a guy says, you girls gets mad. You're fat, you're skinny, bigger is better. Anything other than perfect, you blow up. You don't want us to call all the time 'cause then we're too clingy and overbearing, but we're clueless jerks if we don't call the specific amount of times we're supposed to. And how do we know how much to call? We got to mind read, of course. Fine, we'll call you three times a day. What? Now you're saying we're stalking you? Then you give the green flag, 'Go ahead, watch porn, I don't mind.' Twenty seconds later it's, 'You sicko!' No, Avaline is not hot. Fine, I lied; she's hotter than everyone I know. See, I told you you'd get mad if I told the truth. You're hot too. Yeah, hotter than her. No, I'm not lying. Fine, I was lying but you're still really hot. No, not sex-object hot. See, that's the reason I didn't say you were hot in the first place, 'cause you'd get defensive about being objectified. Fine, you're beautiful and classy. No, I didn't mean in a boring librarian way. You're everything, okay; you're whatever the hell you want us to think. What the hell is wrong with you people?"

I sit back feeling somewhat sadistic, responsible for this rare side of Kree surfacing in the middle of an airplane.

We separate at the baggage claim. He doesn't realize it, but I'm redefining humanitarianism by refusing a future with him.

***

A few weeks pass after the "hospital incident" and I only attend one session of "therapy." For one thing, it represents everything I've ever been against, and for another, the asshole won't quit saying "suicide." It's like a big, red button on his clipboard that he keeps slamming his fist against and tickling between blows. I end up walking out on him because of his bullshit opinion about why Otis fucked me up so bad.

"It was a raw affection," I say.

"Because you thought his condition was similar to yours?"

"If that were the case, I'd be scissor-fighting Avaline." And I fall quiet. That skank hasn't called once to check up on me.

Easter rolls around, and without an excuse to forego the family festivities, I find myself stationed at the kid's table, mindlessly organizing the food on my plate in neat piles. No one really talks to me anymore. I've become the unemployed senior citizen of the family, sitting mute, bitter, and thankless in the corner while everyone gallivants around, chatting and gorging themselves with holiday crap. They do, however, come up every so often to ask questions they've probably drawn straws for.

"Did you make any friends on the psych ward?"

"Are you living in a halfway house now?"

"Are you mooching off disability?"

"Do you have a parole officer?"

"I see you're not morbidly obese anymore."

The good news is that no one's trying to set me up anymore. The psycho of the family officially proved herself to be a genuine psycho, no longer of the quality necessary to hook up with their acquaintances.

"You have lint all over you," Mom says, forcing me to follow her to the bedroom so she can remove it. She bats me with a brush in violent strokes as if intentionally trying to hurt me. After the beating, I head for busywork in the kitchen, hoping it will keep the sharks at bay.

"Which kind of pie do you want to ruin your diet with?" Auntie asks.

"The poison one," I say.

"What?"

"The frozen one."

"You don't need pie," Mom says. "You finally have a Kate Moss collarbone."

I load dishes into the sink and turn on the faucet. Mom startles me by dumping a stack of dinner plates into the sink, and a wave of ham grease and sweet potato mash splashes onto my white sweater. "Did you hear," she says, "that another postal worker went psycho and shot five people before turning the gun on himself?"

Ten years ago, I was in my first adult relationship: it included the adult attributes of domestic partnership and money disputes. I'd give anything to be there again, early twenties, still in school, because we were both young and had potential, and it was back when our families exchanged plates of holiday baked goods instead of insults, before he and I said things we couldn't take back, before we worried about pubes and Prozac, before we learned to resent one another. Before every mental image of my future somehow involved Otis.

It's done now, I know. Kree is done. Otis is done. And I've got to go back somehow, back to ten years ago, before pill-popping overdoses and purchased artistic opportunities and life on tour and Otis and Landon and Kree and Safeway, before all of life seemed as if it was only worth living if I had the world figured out.

Diaspora

The heat's arrived. So has the state fair. I know this because I hear the fireworks at CalExpo going off every night around 10 p.m. I don't remember the last time I left the apartment. I have a half-dozen Costco toilet paper blocks crammed into the closet, and I've stocked up on enough supplies to sustain myself through another World War. I stay in bed for weeks at a time, maybe longer, all my thoughts and nightmares merging in random flurries, forming then scattering without the slightest significance.

The months of living a slothlike existence have dried the surface of my lips so that they feel like the rind of overbaked ham, and when I readjust my head against the pillow, my lower lip splits like the ground above the San Andreas fault: needle pricks of pain; blood draining over my tongue and down my throat.

It's been days since I've lifted my body from the bed, so it takes a few attempts to pull my torso off the face of the mattress. When I sit up, I can't even slump into a slouch. My back is so inflexible that it feels like I've been nailed to a slab of plywood. It takes a concentrated effort to walk to the bathroom. I don't have the muscle mass I used to and I'm teetering for support on my joints alone.

Flicking on the light is a physical feat. The sputtering vanity bulbs highlight the bends of my emaciated limbs. My chest has dissolved, nipples wasted into zitlike protrusions. When I wiggle my mouth, the slice in my lip seethes and my face flushes a vibrant pink. I look like a brittle cadaver with a mild sunburn.

***

I head to Safeway, worried that gangrene will rot what's left of my face off; they have the medicated Blistex that I like, and even though it's my former store, I go in anyway and hope no one will recognize me in sweats, a robe, and hair that hasn't been trimmed in months. I probably have crust in every orifice of my mug, but gangrene is always worse than crust.

I push a cart down the aisles, winded by the chore of walking, using the cart for balance and support. They've changed the aisle setup since I've worked here. Detergent is where the rubbing alcohol was, rubbing alcohol is where the Blistex was, and the Blistex is where my ex-boss is currently feeling up the side of Avaline's temple as he masks his intentions by helping her find some herpes cream.

Maybe it's the resentment I have toward him for being promoted into a position that I also applied for, or maybe it's the way Avaline laughs and grabs onto his wrist as if she was classically trained in the formal art of whoring, or maybe it's everything from my ex-boss' boner, to Mom's blazing emotional scars, to every one of Kree's pubes, to Landon's wit, to Otis' puke, to social superficiality, to environmental degradation, to punk hypocrisy, collecting to make me kick off my terrycloth slippers and hurl myself at Avaline's 102-pound frame.

"A hundred and two pounds, you motherfucking whore," I say and launch myself toward her like a flying squirrel across branches. She falls backward against the linoleum, kicking and shielding her face. And even though my muscle atrophy allows me to do nothing more than slap and scratch at her arms and face, I feel kind of bad. Unlike the whore who kicked my ass in New York and subsequently Santa Cruz, this whore was at one point a somewhat-friend, and she is screaming on the ground in aisle seven of my former Safeway as if she's never been in a fight before.

A pair of arms clamp around my waist and pull me off her like an arcade crane. "Jesus, Hazel," my ex-boss says. He examines my face in detail. I worry about facial crust, but he mentions something about Skeletor.

✱✱✱

Security escorts Avaline and me out of the store, telling me to walk one direction down the strip mall, and her to walk the other. Even though my joints took a beating from the physical exertion of the fight, I feel energized.

I round the side of the building and figure I'll sit for a while on the docks before heading out front to my car where Avaline might be waiting with a tire iron or 500-something Mercedes horsepower. As I round the dumpsters and climb up onto the docks, though, I see her coming around the opposite corner. She gives me the finger, and it's so awkward that it looks like she's never done it before in her life; it wobbles, and she has to manually fold a few knuckles back to keep the other fingers from snapping up. It makes me smirk.

Though there's delivery gunk and garbage water streaked over the docks, I sit down on the edge and let my legs dangle against the cement. My muscles burn for sustenance, and when I slouch down, the weight of my head almost pulls my body over the edge. I tongue the split in my lower lip. It's still burning.

"Why'd you kick my ass?" she asks, sitting down beside me.

"It should have happened eons ago," I say. "Couldn't hack it with a drummer?" There's an edge in my voice. She slides away from me a few inches.

"It sucked to travel like that," she says. "I don't know how you did it."

"I didn't. I don't."

"And everyone was a dick, especially that one asshole with all the tattoos and piercings." I can only imagine the field day Landon had with her. "That concert scene is exhausting. Every night you listen to the same goddamn racket and drink the same disgusting beer and eat the same greasy fast food and you're always waking up hung-over, and I got my purse stolen like three times." It's hard to picture a prissy pussy like her roughing it on the road. "And it was always all about him, his concerts, going where he needed to be. There was nothing for me to do, no ballet, nowhere to get a good manicure." It's truly a statement when a needy, codependent, chemically imbalanced spoiled brat can come to conclusions like these on her own. I couldn't have been too far off. "It was always about him and never about me. I need a boyfriend to make the relationship all about me. Plus, Otis is a retarded psycho. All he did was wig out."

"Otis," I say.

"Hey, do you eat steak now? You want go to Bob's in SF tonight?"

"He's okay though, right?"

"They have this three-pound porterhouse that'll make you want to put cow in your mouth a lot more."

"Are they still touring, or what?"

"Who?"

"Landon...and Otis."

"Them? No. He needed a liver or something, so he got a piece from that asshole and then I think they put him in a nut house or something. Hey, if I get the lobster tails, are you going to nag me about how they're the cockroaches of the sea?"

"What do you mean 'liver and nut house'?"

"Lobster wouldn't cost so much if they were really the roaches of the sea."

"Can you get over yourself for one fucking minute? Take yourself off the fucking stove for one fucking second." I want to shove her off the docks, but fear it'll lead to another scratching match.

"Last I heard, he was in some place, some institution or something, that cooked and cleaned for him and made sure he didn't kill himself all the time."

"Shit." I'm mildly concerned, mildly apathetic, but mostly relieved to be removed from the chaos. Even if it's a rumor, even if she's manufactured all of this in the midst of her psychosis, it's nice to be at a distance. It sort of feels like I'm hearing a radio advertisement for disaster relief, and even if I wanted to do something, there isn't anything that could fix a tragedy of such magnitude.

I guess it's better that they've (as cliché as it may sound) crashed and burned before the scene could burn them out. If there's anything I've noticed about typical punk bands, they are not fine wines whose flavor and substance matures over time; most ferment into rancid sugar that leaves behind a bitter aftertaste, and in my mind, it'd be more of an embarrassment to go down because of a shitty album than a shitty liver.

"I heard it was a nice nut house. Not the ones where you live in cages or anything," she says.

I think about halfway houses and private institutions that could possibly be, in her opinion, nice. I wonder if he hates it and screams until they drug him to sleep. I wonder if he likes it and will end up getting that social disease where he'll never be able to fit in with normal society again (not that he was that great at it in the first place...not that I'm any better). And I wonder what additional strain it's put on Landon.

"You miss them?" she asks.

I visualize what it'd be like to hit the road with them again. Yeah, it'd be bohemian and come with a spark of self-actualization, but my savings would run out, the music would dissolve, and I'd probably end up behind Safeway under a different set of circumstances: dumpster diving for food while Otis throws a tantrum on the docks.

"What's today?" I ask.

"Wednesday," she says.

"Yeah, but when? Is it July?"

"July 28th."

According to my doctor, I have a life expectancy of eighty-eight. I don't know how I feel about so many more years. I know that it isn't punk to entertain old age (hell, it isn't punk to make it past twenty-seven) but there has to be more out there than these extreme ends of the spectrum, bohemian and bourgeois, the only two lifestyles that I've known.

I could find a new job. I hear social work is rewarding. I could go back to school. Mom's always wanted a lawyer. I could pick up a hobby like knitting. Or drinking. I could get pregnant. Marry rich. Marry Kree. Do porn.

"You know, I really thought it was gutsy that you just up and quit your job to live like that," Avaline says. "You come off so anal banal, but there's an inner beatnik in you somewhere. Come on, let's get steak. And if you don't want to eat anything, just bring a box of Twinkies like you did last time."

There's so much I need to do to in order to get my shit together, but right now, I'm going to sit with my back to Safeway next to Avaline, who's holding tissues to her battle wounds and moaning about the patches of hair missing from her bangs.

To the left of the docks I see my ex-boss' scarlet BMW buffed to a slick gemlike shine. He personalized his plates to have "SS" on them, which he said stood for Safeway's generic product line, Safeway Select. He bought that car after getting his promotion and the day he drove it home, he came into the store, tossing the keys back and forth, asking if any of the cashiers or stock boys wanted to drive it around the parking lot. A few of them took him up on the offer. Landon, on the other hand, blanketed the driver's side door with snot rockets. At least I assume it was Landon.

"You see that red Beemer over there with 'SS' on the plate?" I ask Avaline.

"Yeah, why?"
"I'll do steak with you," I say.
"Yeah?"
"If you do something with me," I say.
"Okay."
"Let's key that douche bag's car."

Acknowledgments

Thanks: To Lily for her hard work and faith. To Nathan who was more than an editor and a fellow diet soda addict. He was the guide, cheerleader, and comic relief which carved this into what it is today. To everyone else working behind the scenes at Casperian Books, even the puppy. And to Jeannette, Michael, and Joey Joe-Joe for your friendship, support, and the unparalleled good times.

CPSIA information can be obtained at www.ICGtesting.com
228016LV00008B/20/P